Happy Like This

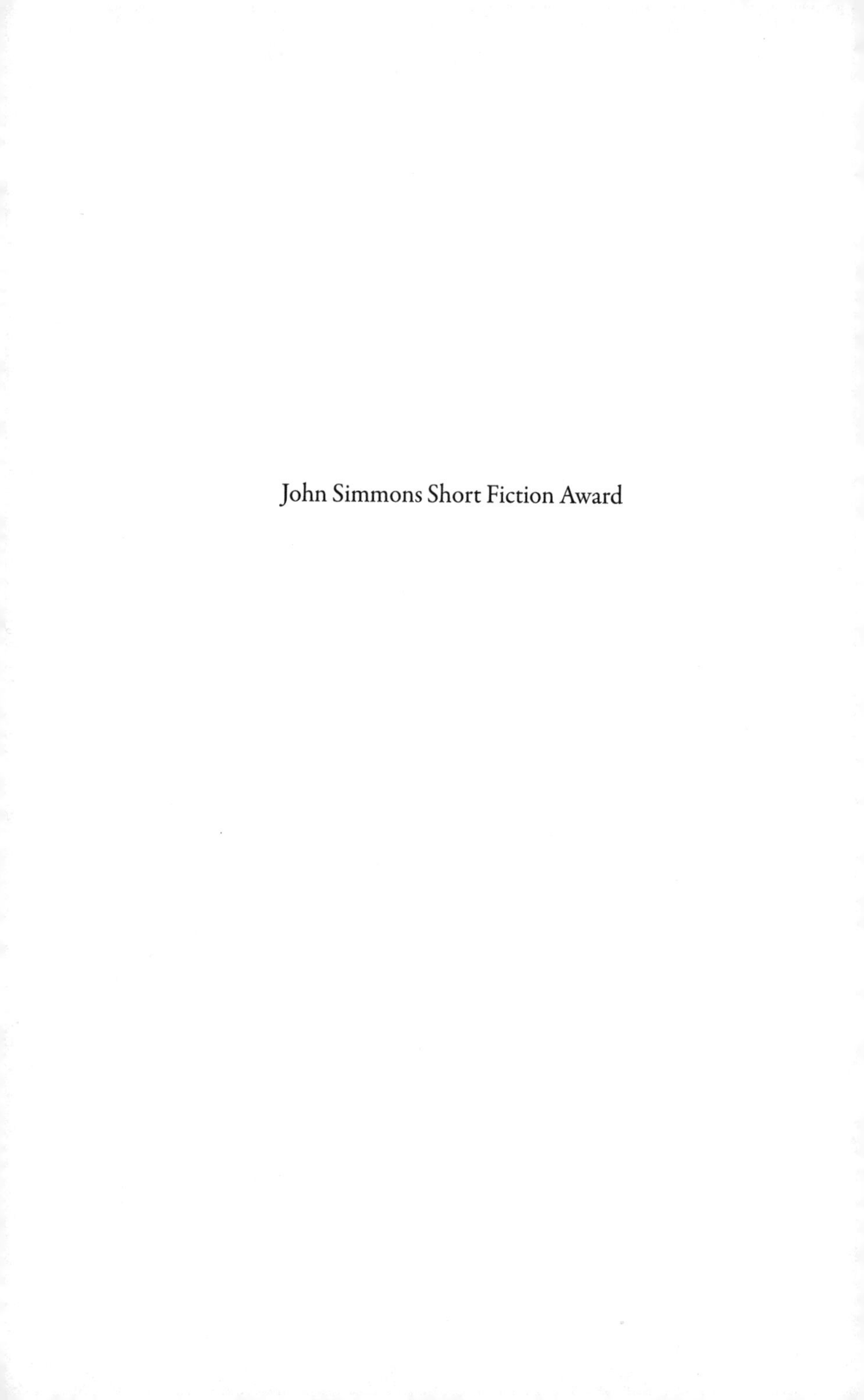

John Simmons Short Fiction Award

Happy Like This

Ashley Wurzbacher

University of Iowa Press · Iowa City

University of Iowa Press, Iowa City 52242

www.uipress.uiowa.edu
Printed in the United States of America
Text design by Sara T. Sauers
Printed on acid-free paper

Library of Congress Cataloging-in-Publication Data
Names: Wurzbacher, Ashley, 1985– author.
Title: Happy like this / Ashley Wurzbacher.
Description: Iowa City : University of Iowa Press, [2019] | Series: John Simmons Short Fiction Award | Identifiers: LCCN 2019011977 (print) | LCCN 2019017522 (ebook) | ISBN 9781609386849 | ISBN 9781609386832 (pbk. : alk. paper)
Classification: LCC PS3623.U79 (ebook) | LCC PS3623.U79 A6 2019 (print) | DCC 813/.6—dc23
LC record available at https://lccn.loc.gov/2019011977

For my grandmothers,
Marta and Alice

When perhaps all along what I have really wanted
most is the friendship, the love of women.

—CAROLE MASO, *Ava*

They're happy like that; I'm happy like this.

—VIRGINIA WOOLF, *To the Lighthouse*

Contents

·I·

Like That

Sickness and Health

INTRODUCTION

Some leave trails of evidence: needles, syringes, thermometers, clumps of hair in the shower drains, the sounds of retching from a bathroom stall, mittens on a bedside stand waiting to be worn at night, on doctors' orders, to prevent self-mutilation. Others leave no trace of their afflictions, which still follow them, shadowy, reminding them constantly and obnoxiously of themselves, like responsibilities. Still others seem already better, their ailments having vanished quickly in this new place, with this new opportunity to start over, be normal. Change, for some, the surest salve.

There is the one with the seizures, presumably fake; the one who draws her own blood; the one who injects herself with saline; the one whose "bulimia," fully under her control, can be shut off as if by a switch; the one who rambles nonsensically; the one poisoned by her own mother; the one whose back pain seems to have no source and no solution; the one who's faked cancer; the one with the headaches; the one who stirred rodenticides into her breakfast cereal; the one caught pricking her finger and letting her blood drop into her own urine samples.

There is Mia in the middle of all this, taking notes.

Her paper is titled, tentatively, "A Qualitative Study of the Effects of Factitious Disorders on the Social Lives of College-Attending Females." It is the most complex study of her career, which isn't saying much, given that her career is only just beginning. Still, Mia is beginning to suspect that it *will* be the most complex study of her career. It is sociology, ethnography, epidemiology, documentary, creativity. It is, it turns out, the intersection of a few too many things. Mia had thought she'd be able to take these things and braid and bend them like switches into shape (Ambitious, her dissertation director had said of the project, but Mia had wanted a challenge, wanted to push herself), but more and more, she is finding that they're intent on crashing violently against each other, that they are simultaneously unable to harmonize and unable to be separated, like some lovers.

Hers is a methodology limited by its intimacy. She was warned about this limitation at the beginning, when it was decided—by her dissertation director, not by her—that in order to best gather around-the-clock results, Mia should reside, full time, in the same dormitory as the subjects of her study, serving as a kind of resident advisor. She had resisted at first, but as it turned out, the move coincided neatly with her breakup with Ben, with whom she'd spent five years and with whom it had been decided—by her friends, by her family, by Ben, not so much by her—that she was supposed to spend the rest of her life.

The rest of her life: looming, open-mouthed. She was heading straight for it on autopilot but couldn't recall having chosen or engineered it. So she took control; she fled. Which is to say, two months ago she put her things in a storage unit by the freeway and moved into a 180-square-foot room in a university residence hall in a corridor that would eventually become known, due to the eccentricity of its inhabitants, as the Waif Wing and in which she still lives.

OVERVIEW OF FACTITIOUS DISORDERS

> Persons with factitious disorders behave as if they are ill or in pain by self-inflicting, faking, or exaggerating symptoms. Persons afflicted with factitious disorders may mimic or lie about symptoms, use drugs, alter diagnostic tests (for example, by contaminating urine samples), induce vomiting, or inject themselves with bacteria in order to induce symptoms and thereby draw attention or solicit the nurturance, sympathy, and/or leniency that they associate with the sick role. Generally, individuals perpetrate factitious disorders because they believe that these benefits and special treatments are not obtainable in any other more practical way. Factitious disorders are diagnoses of exclusion (per exclusionem), meaning they are diagnosed by a process of elimination when no other known diagnoses can be reached with complete confidence from testing or examination. They often come hand in hand with other mental or personality disorders.

Her sample: twelve college-attending females (n = 12) at a large, metropolitan, four-year research university, aged eighteen to twenty-two and consolidated into a common section of campus housing. All of the subjects have been repeatedly hospitalized for symptoms that have been determined to be the result of factitious disorders—that is, fabrications. Aside from their common lack of a biomedical diagnosis, their closeness in age, and their gender, the girls have few universally shared attributes, representing as they do a variety of diverse geographical regions of origin, socioeconomic statuses, educational backgrounds, ethnicities. They know they're being studied but don't know precisely what for; they've given their consent. They make no efforts, as far as Mia can tell, to censor their speech or actions in her presence, as she helps them dress for parties, watches movies in their rooms, attends social events with them, brings them cups of tea when they're too "ill" to leave the building. While they sleep or attend class, she types frantic notes about them into the document that will become her dissertation.

> Research has demonstrated that adults with factitious disorders often suffer from personality disorders and have poor coping skills and difficulty forming healthy interpersonal relationships (Monroe and Serrano, 1999; O'Flaherty, 2004; Vanzetti, 2010). It has also been demonstrated that in cases of factitious disorders by proxy, the child or "patient" involved may experience social anxiety, depression, and difficulty relating to or communicating with peers (Becker, Bell, and O'Flaherty, 2007; Smart and Taylor, 2008; Huang, 2011). Existing literature has examined the role of school psychologists in detecting and addressing factitious disorders by proxy in schoolchildren (Roth and Van Rosenthal, 2005). However, no existing studies have addressed the impacts of factitious disorders on the social lives of young adults—specifically young women—old enough to live away from home but young enough to still feel bound to their parents or caregivers, despite physical separation from them. Such a demographic is a fertile one for study, hovering as it does in the liminal space between childhood and adulthood, restriction and freedom, dependence and independence.

Each girl has been assigned a number by which she is to be referred to in Mia's dissertation. Mia memorized their numbers before their names. But she has caught herself, several times in the past month or so, referring to the subjects as "her girls." As if, when the study was over, the article published, she could keep them always with her. As if we can ever belong to each other.

SUBJECT NO. 7: SYNDROME BY PROXY AND CHRONIC PAIN

In the case of factitious disorders by proxy, the perpetrator of the symptoms is someone other than the victim herself. Most often, this takes the form of a parent—usually a mother—inducing or fabricating illness in a child. In such cases, the caregiver derives vicarious attention and sympathy, which gratify his or her own emotional needs, from the medical attention paid to the child (Becker, Bell, and O'Flaherty, 2007; Francis and Ngo, 2012). With age, the child may break free of the fabrication; alternatively, the child may become an agent colluding in the process and, eventually, actively harming herself (Torres, 2003). One subject of this study (n = 1) experienced factitious disorders by proxy as a child under the care of her mother. Born in West Virginia to a coal miner and a housewife who had worked, prior to the subject's birth, as a licensed practical nurse, Subject 7 suffered from strange fevers, vomiting, and hypernatremia (abnormally high sodium concentrations in the blood) induced by her mother through the (ab)use of over-the-counter and prescription medications and injections between the ages of two and nine. Following the discovery of her mother's role in her afflictions, the subject was removed from the care of her parents for several years before she was returned to them at thirteen, all of them having undergone therapy and psychiatric testing.

Lauren, a child like a canary, lowered into dark places where no child and no canary should be. Mia imagines Lauren's childhood: her father with lungs like two slabs of charred meat abandoned on a grill and her mother, for some reason, making problems in the few places in her life where there weren't problems already—adding to coal dust and cave-ins and worry and never enough on the EBT card an endless barrage of office visits, diagnostic tests, and hospitalizations. *Don't try to understand,* Mia's director had told her when she'd wondered aloud how a parent could do such a thing to a child, to Lauren, *because you never will.*

But Mia does try. She thinks of how Lauren's family's church raised money to help pay the medical bills they didn't realize were unnecessary, preventable. How Lauren's classmates, led by the teacher from whose class she was almost perpetually absent, raised the money to grant what Lauren's mother had indicated was eight-year-old Lauren's dying wish: a ride in a hot air balloon. Mia pictures Lauren and her mother floating above the Appalachians, as high in the sky as Lauren's father was deep down in the mine. She pictures Lauren's father, unaware of his wife's ruse, never home and often drunk, carbon-streaked and grateful for the darkness and privacy his subterranean workplace afforded him, in which he could hang his hard-hatted head and cry in silence, humbled by the support he'd received from his fellow men though he'd refused, out of pride, to ask for their help, and later, shamed by his wife and disgusted by the child she'd used as her pawn.

But weren't we at our closest there in the hospital waiting room? his wife—Lauren's mother—asks him, in Mia's fantasy. Clinging to each other, remembering their probably forgotten, coal-smudged love, praying for their daughter, the one thing that still bound them to each other. *At the very least,* she may have told him, desperate to justify herself, *it kept you above ground. It bought you days in the sun you wouldn't have had; it bought you time up here with me, with our girl.* A sick woman, certainly, hovering over Lauren in hospitals, explaining her "pain," refusing to leave her side (seemingly out of devotion, truly out of the knowledge that the girl's symptoms would subside in her absence), wearing heels and her best JCPenney dress, awash in attention and sympathy for her broken daughter. Maybe she needed this, did this, because she couldn't admit that it was she—exhausted, bored, tired of the little black flecks of carbon in her hair and in her lungs, tired of her marriage, tired of herself—that was broken.

After she was removed from her parents' home, in the care of her aunt, Lauren began experiencing chronic pain—her back, her neck, her abdomen. Back into the hospital she went, her aunt by her side, dumfounded. No explanation, no diagnosis. "Seizures" from which Lauren could be roused suspiciously easily by the mention of a favorite food or the presence of a longed-for friend or family member followed a few years later. Her doctors concluded, when no other explanation offered itself, that this pain and these seizures, unlike Lauren's childhood ailments (to which they seemed to be unrelated), were her own fabrications.

In the Waif Wing, Lauren can often be found lying on the mock granite hallway floor, staring at the ceiling. The other girls have adjusted to her habit, stepping over or around her as the need arises; it was Mia's initial hypothesis that this dearth of attention, this proceeding-as-normal, would deter Lauren's behavior. Indeed, her seizures seem to have stopped, quite abruptly, following her move into the Waif Wing, but the pain persists, and she claims an inability to sleep in a bed, insisting that mattresses hurt her back. Cold stone, on the other hand, has healing powers, straightens and soothes her spine. So she says. She is, after all, a child of mountains and mines, a child with a mother hard as rock.

When asked by Mia, one day, to sketch her pain, Lauren drew a rose. Her spine, she narrated as she drew, was the long and gently curving stem, full of thorns that sprouted from each fertile nerve and patch of flesh, and the blossom was her head, registering her pain in bursts that were red and furious but that opened slowly like petals, taking their time.

What afflicts Subject 7? What does a physician, a surgeon, a student, do with an odd horizontal habit and a drawing of a rose? Though all of Lauren's doctors have concluded *per exclusionem* that her pain must be no pain at all, Mia isn't sure. She pictures Lauren much younger, not understanding, only knowing that when she's hurting, hospitalized, her parents and doctors and friends hold her more closely than before. As a child, she was likely unable to make the connection between her chronic illness and her mother's care, so profound was her trust of her mother. Alternatively, she may have feared abandonment if she'd stopped being sick, feared losing her mother if she confided the truth in a doctor, an outsider. Perhaps she still fears these things now. Perhaps, Mia thinks, she is simply skilled in the cold economy of purchasing love with suffering. But isn't this a transaction motivated by pain? Genuine, inexpressible pain?

Maybe Lauren's pain, this time, is true and sincere and truly and sincerely beyond science or scholarship. Maybe a just-so cocktail of psychology and routine can put pain where it wouldn't otherwise be, in a place that's hidden from radiology and reason. Is it possible? Mia wonders. Who's to say that real pain couldn't bloom from a hole dug out where there once was none?

Mia imagines Lauren and her mother up in that hot air balloon, the world below them looking like an outspread board game, something whose rules don't matter, something that might be folded up and put away. The wind in their hair. Mia hates this woman and what she did to Lauren, but whatever they saw that day from the sky must have stayed with the girl, must stay with her still. Strange as it may seem, Lauren speaks often of missing her mother, her home, the place where she was a phony patient in a room full of flowers, back where the Appalachian range bends northward like a great scoliotic spine.

DATE: TWO CASE STUDIES

There are scores of case studies in Mia's notes, dates and dances and parties. Take, as a sample, this one: they are driving to a bowling alley, Kat (Subject No. 1: seizures) in the front seat, her date at the wheel, Lauren and her date in the back, Mia squished against the back door on the other side of Lauren's date, whose knee knocks against hers when the car hits a bump. At the bowling alley, they slip their feet into unsanitary shoes. Kat (no seizures today) and her date spend the evening draped across each other, limbs dripping over shoulders like fondue, engaged in giddy I-don't-know-you-but-I-like-you conversations that make Mia feel embarrassed on both of their behalves. Their interactions are sickening in an entirely mundane way. She watches, records notes.

Mia barely participates in the game, slinging the ball with apathy down the lane when it's her turn. Lauren's date misspells her name—M-E-A—when he enters it into the scoring system, praises Mia, and offers to help her improve her technique. He's a junior, a few years older than Lauren, whom he pointedly ignores. He watches Mia, who watches Lauren watching her date watching Mia. Lauren laughs too loud and at the wrong things. Mia excuses herself and retires to the restroom to write and to hide somewhere away from his eyes. When she returns, she finds Lauren guiding her date's hands onto her shoulders, where they squeeze, massage, work their way down her spine. Notes are scribbled, observations are made: how pain, or its pretense, is used to build bridges. That feels *great*, Lauren says. I really needed this.

When her date locates Mia, crouched behind rows of multicolored bowling balls like giant petrified scoops of ice cream, he lets his grip on Lauren's shoulders loosen, and Lauren grabs his hands, restoring them to their place on her body.

It's just, Lauren is saying to her date as Mia approaches, my grandmother just died. I'm still kind of getting over it. We were really close.

Lauren makes her eyes big, tries to sink those eyes into him, brand him with their heat.

Mia hasn't heard anything about a grandmother's death and is quite certain that Lauren is lying. Lauren's behavior is consistent with existing research that indicates that, when attention or sympathy begins to wane, factitial patients often fabricate secondary crises in hope of engendering renewed concern and soliciting additional nurturance (Bell, 2008; Fordham and Fulton, 1995). She scribbles all the way home, in her spot in the back seat of the car, Lauren in the middle this time, laying a hopeful head on her date's cold shoulder.

This was before Mia began referring to the girls as hers. Later that night, she held Lauren as she cried, as she said, over and over again, What's wrong with me? Mia, it hurts, it hurts.

Or take this one: just the other night, Chiara (Subject No. 6: bloodletting) and Skye (Subject No. 11: headaches) and their dates all in a row at the movies passing popcorn, faces lit by the screen, Mia one row behind them, open-notebooked. Chiara and her date kissing ravenously. Skye's date keeps checking his phone, during the film and after. As they're leaving the theater, Skye sinks to the floor, swoons, conveniently in her date's direction, like a Victorian maiden. Oh, God, these headaches, she says, as her date wraps a muscled arm about her. Everything went black for a moment. I'm fine, it's nothing, I'll be fine. He keeps his arm around her for the rest of the night, quite clearly pleased with himself, having swept to his lady's aid, and Mia looks on trying to count the times she's seen this sort of thing before—in bad movies, in real life—and thinking, if this is the start of something, it isn't something good.

So sometimes they play their weaknesses like cards. Other times they ignore them, stay strong, downplay their pain, if it exists. Their tactics are varied and inconsistent and very much like the tactics of anyone setting out across the thin ice that is maybe-this-could-turn-out-to-be-love. It's been months since Mia herself went on a date—without the girls and without her notebook. But when she does, she will do so with a renewed sense of what she does *not* want it to look like, how she does not want it to go.

It seems to Mia that anyone who would draw conclusions about the girls' conditions from either of these scenes or the dozens of others like them—who would suppose that the girls' actions and reactions were linked to their disorders, results of their abnormalities—must surely have never been eighteen, or twenty-eight, for that matter, or lonely, or in love, or freshly out of it. The case studies sit among her files, her stacks of papers, but she regards them with hesitance and bafflement as things too strange to comprehend and yet too familiar, too fundamentally human, to imbue with any special, pathological significance.

HYPOTHESES

It was hypothesized that removal from the care (or abuse) of parents, the increased independence brought about by the college environment, and the social pressures caused by the around-the-clock presence of peers would lead to the gradual amelioration of the subjects' symptoms. It was hypothesized that the dormitory in which the girls were housed would provide the kind of safe, supportive, communal environment that many of them had previously sought through hospital care. It was also hypothesized that until amelioration of symptoms had taken place, the subjects' disorders would negatively affect their social, sexual, and academic lives, as well as their relationships with each other, as they might view each other as competitors in their quests for attention and nurturance. Finally, it was hypothesized that the stigma attached to these disorders would act as a motivating force in pushing the girls to overcome them.

The world is lonely in the passive voice—hands-off, germ-free, the scholar carved out and replaced by a vacant space that insists (rather lamely, Mia thinks) on its own authority. In this voice, Mia's words and actions are orphaned, they float; her hypotheses and evaluations are hidden behind a sheer authoritative cloud, like the one behind which believers place God.

The truth is, she grows more skeptical every day, not only of her hypotheses, which are consistent with existing research (O'Flaherty, 2004; Torres, 2003; Van Rosenthal and Roth, 2005; Vanzetti, 2010), but of the girls' diagnoses—the designation of their pain as artifice—and of her own ability to objectively analyze them. Her dissertation director reminds her each time they meet that she is not responsible for questioning the designation of the girls' disorders as factitious, nor is she responsible for providing care for their symptoms. Numerous professionals more qualified than she have made that call as decisively as possible, and she, a doctoral student in sociology, is in no position to challenge it.

MEETING

Mia sits in a pea-green plush chair in her dissertation director's office, picking at the upholstery, her notes spread on her director's desk. She thinks of the night before, when she found Jinny (Subject No. 9: faking bulimia) vomiting in the bathroom, the stall door swinging open. Mia had stroked her hair, rubbed her back. The doctors say you could stop this at any time, she'd said softly to Jinny. This is not a real eating disorder. You're not sick, Jin. You don't have to be sick. But as she watched the tears stream down Jinny's face, she thought: No—this is pain. This is a frantic attempt to alleviate genuine pain. This is a sick girl.

You know, Mia, her dissertation director is saying, you're not responsible for questioning the designation of these girls' disorders as factitious, nor are you responsible for providing care for their symptoms. Numerous professionals more qualified than you have made that call as decisively as possible, and you, a doctoral student in sociology, are in no position to challenge it.

Yes, Mia says. She picks, picks at the pea-green upholstery. I know.

BOY: PART I

Their periods sync up, and there is a great sharing of paper products and small white pills. There is the seemingly constant sound of flushing toilets, water in pipes. It's around this time, many hands pressed to abdomens, that the boy passes through the Waif Wing for the first time.

They'll begin to see him often, passing by on his way to the boys' side (the healthy side) of the dorm, and sometimes he'll pause almost imperceptibly in Mia's doorway. Their eyes meet. He seems at once older than his age, experienced, and radiantly innocent. He carries a Rubik's Cube, the colors jumbled, wanders by absorbed in his puzzle, the squares of the cube clicking, and pushes through the double doors at the end of the hall. Then, like a ghost, he's gone.

Each time he comes and goes, Mia watches the doors swing where the boy used to be, remembering the intensity in his expression, his concentration, his hands moving so smoothly, and his ridiculousness—cubing as he passes through a hallway full of girls. She finds it all, somehow, irresistible.

Christ, she thinks, what is wrong with me? Her social scientist's brain tells her it's his health that attracts her, surrounded as she is by the sick and the weak; she's making him into everything she's missing. Still, if she had the means, the funds, the stamina, she would very much like to study this: why attractions and infatuations strike us the way they do, fast and blunt and absurd, and what makes us run headlong and stupid after them, the implausible joy they propose.

SUBJECT NO. 6: BLOODLETTING

Two of the subjects in this study (n = 2) have been repeatedly
hospitalized and are currently participating in ongoing therapy
after years of self-inducing anemia by drawing their own
blood and disposing of it by flushing it down the toilet. One

> subject went so far as to consume rat poison, which contains anticoagulants. The other, Subject 6, was discovered to have swallowed her blood, so that, vomiting it, she would give the appearance of gastrointestinal bleeding. Due to the subject's repeated hospitalizations and perpetual dizziness and weakness, her mother left her position in politics to be by her side, as the "mystery" of the subject's low blood count—frequently so low she should, by all calculations, have been dead—remained unsolved.

Mia deletes every instance of "Subject 6" in her document and replaces them with the subject's name—Chiara—though she knows her adviser will admonish her, remind her of the importance of confidentiality. She leafs through Chiara's records. Hard to reconcile the vampiric image those records evoke—wraithlike, grotesque, easily bruised, consuming herself—with the girl she's come to know here in the dorm. The girl who has sat on Mia's bed watching chick flicks and dipping chips in chunky salsa, whose dress Mia has zipped in that hard-to-reach place in back, standing behind her, as she prepared for a dance. Whom Mia has lent lipstick, dazzling red.

Yes, hard to reconcile all this with blood transfusions, needles, emaciation.

Born to an old-money couple in an affluent East Coast city suburb, Chiara was the picture-perfect daughter: straight-A student at a private Catholic school, volleyball star, student council president, Daughter of the American Revolution, Ivy League–bound. Father a lawyer, mother a state senator, both parents devout Catholics, taking the body and blood of Christ into their open mouths each week. An only child following the death of her younger brother, who was hit by a car while crossing the street in front of his elementary school. Chiara hadn't been there to hold his hand and guide him across in her navy slacks and starched blouse; she'd been home sick that day, in the care of her nanny. Mia circles this fact in her pages of notes on Chiara, circles it and circles it again, thinking of how it was in that bed, ill, that Chiara last experienced her family as a whole and intact thing. She had fallen asleep febrile, still a sister, and woken up well and alone.

It isn't the job of the sociologist to explain the unexplainable—that is, in this case, to make sense of what these girls have done to themselves, their bodies, their families. Still, Mia imagines Chiara's brother's funeral, her mother's too-articulate, well-groomed public grief, the airbrushed dignity of it, how frustrating it must have been for Chiara, who surely looked at her and wondered: What if you lost me too? Then Mia thinks of this same mother abandoning her career, declining to run for another term as her daughter wasted away, kneeling by her one remaining child's bedside. Perhaps Chiara felt vindicated, her blood in her mouth and her mother on her knees. Perhaps this was all she'd ever really wanted, parents by her bedside, a chance to sleep saintlike in peace, relieved from all expectations and all duties but to live, however tentatively. Mia can't know for sure; these are only theories, and correlation does not imply causation, but she knows that it's hard to say *I want you to take care of me*, which is why, for the most part, we don't. Why we turn to other methods by which to make our point.

Chiara had been a high school student, shadowing a physician at a hospital, another sparkling line for her college application letters, when she'd become schooled in blood—others', her own, how to draw it. Her brother had been dead for a year. She stole equipment, stashed it in her room, and kept up the ruse for two years: transfusions, injections of iron, platelet counts, prayer. It was while praying by her bed one night, clutching the dust ruffle where it met the carpet, that Chiara's mother, having cast off her power suit for sweats and a hoodie and unkempt hair and tears, a modern Madonna, discovered the needle case and transfusion tubing tucked between bars in the frame of her daughter's bed.

It was just such a relief not to have to be perfect for once, Chiara told her mother, told her therapist, and, recently, told Mia. That Catholic need to confess, confess, confess again, confess better. It was a relief not to have to be the best, on top of everything all the time. To take a *break*. There were people praying for me, people holding my hand, people offering me their blood. I slept better at night knowing they were worried about me. I realize this must make me a terrible person, but. There it is.

She's full now, of blood and life, pink-cheeked; she seems to be better, at least for the time being. Full of other people's blood, donated like change into a collection plate at Mass, that money smell. Mia wonders if it's changed Chiara, the presence of this gift-blood, intimate souvenirs beneath her skin. Does it make her feel loved, valued? Does she feel connected, as if by capillaries, to whatever strangers rolled up their sleeves and offered up their exposed arms, Christlike, for her sake?

No, you wouldn't guess it to look at her—that she'd swallowed her own blood. She's a nice girl, respectful, clever. Beautiful. Boys love her, her lingering Ophelian frailty, her long hair. But Mia can't help but feel a little afraid of Chiara, knowing what she knows. The primitiveness of the approach is what disturbs her most. It reminds Mia of leeches, humors, patients of the past bleeding into dirty basins, thinking it would save them.

DINNER: A CASE STUDY

Because she's beginning to forget what it's like to be around healthy adults, Mia leaves the dorm one Friday night for dinner with her control group: her friends.

Her friends parade in with husbands fastened to their arms like handbags and babies fastened to their chests like—babies. Mia recognizes her friend Elise's son. She received a photo card from Elise in the mail just a week ago that read, Happy fall, from our nest to yours! and included the boy's name, Jack, and his age in months (which Mia has forgotten) in the bottom corner of the photograph depicting the baby nestled among autumn leaves, wearing a puffy coat with the hood drawn up and tied beneath his chin. Is that a baby, Mia had wondered when she first removed the photo from its envelope, or is that a midget chimp in a spacesuit, ready to be launched to the stars?

Somehow Mia ends up at the end of the table by the husbands, who talk about tennis, tennis rackets, tennis balls, golf, golf clubs, golf balls, and babies. They wear subtle-hued sweaters over collared shirts. One of them, ambitious, wears a fedora, which his wife asks him to please remove when the appetizers arrive. Mia remembers their weddings, the perfect white cakes in tiers, the vows: As long as we both shall live.

Jack threw up on my shirt just as we were walking out the door, says Husband 1, Elise's. See this, here? He points to a stain on the cuff of his sleeve. Didn't even have time to change!

Ha ha? Mia says, just guessing. She is suddenly overcome by a desire to speak of the boy who continues to pass through the Waif Wing and who stopped to introduce himself just the other day, holding out his hand when she encountered him in the hallway. She wishes she could describe him, conjure him perfect before her friends, but she knows this is neither the time nor the place nor the audience (indeed, she realizes, there may be no right time, no right place, no right audience for such a disclosure). She keeps her mouth shut.

Elise hands her the baby. Just look at that smile, she says. Jack, can you smile for Aunt Mia? Can you show her your big beautiful smile?

Jack begins to cry.

So, her friend Paige says, securing her two-year-old daughter Penny's orange juice–filled sippy cup with one hand and spearing a crab cake with the other. Have you talked to Ben?

Here it comes. Mia shakes her head, little Jack screaming in her ear. No, she says. Because, you know, we're broken up.

Paige continues, I saw him at the movies last weekend.

Oh, Mia says. Please pass the crab cakes.

Penny and I were coming out of the five-thirty showing of *Mr. Bubbles's Big Race*. On our way out of the theater, we saw Ben standing in the ticket line. Not for *Mr. Bubbles*, of course! Ha ha. Paige pauses before adding, He was with a woman.

Well, Mia says, being that, you know, we've broken up, I can't say I'm that surprised.

Oh, Mia, another friend calls from the opposite end of the table. So many lost years! And you're almost thirty and not getting any younger.

And you were so good together! Paige says. Doesn't it hurt?

Of course it hurts, Mia snaps. That doesn't mean it wasn't the right thing to do.

He's a good man, Mia, says Elise.

Impossible, Mia thinks, to make them understand. How she wasn't—isn't—ready for this: sippy cups and chimpish astronaut babies and *Mr. Bubbles's Big Race*. Ben's consistent, unwavering optimism, the drudgery of it, the simplicity. How he sapped the complex from complexity. His favorite truism: It all comes out in the wash. Meaning that you shouldn't worry, shouldn't care too much; meaning conflict was useless, and action, and passion; meaning don't mind the baby's vomit on your sleeve; meaning we all ought to just float through our lives and toward our deaths like people in inner tubes on rivers. He was a good man (*is* a good man, she corrects herself—here she is thinking about him like he's dead, like she's murdered him); he was so good and patient and kind and not jealous and all the things the faithful say love is, that she couldn't believe him, didn't believe *in* him. *Yes, it hurts.* That doesn't mean it wasn't the right thing to do.

Mia hands still-screaming Jack back to Elise with apologies. He stops crying as soon as he's in her arms. This is a family, Mia thinks, observing them together, Jack and Elise and her husband with his collared-shirt-and-sweater ensemble. A family like Lauren's, like Chiara's. She studies them with a gallery gaze, as if they are a portrait in oils. She thinks of her friends, their prefamily days now archived. Once, Elise and Mia had sucked Jell-O shots off of each other's bare stomachs.

Shots were sucked, laughter was shared, fidelity was sworn, good times were had. She supposes these are days confined now, at least for her friends, to a memorial purgatory—neither here nor there, not quite belonging to them anymore, fit for the passive voice.

NO MEETING

The morning after dinner with the friends, Mia hits the snooze button on her alarm clock. She calls her dissertation director.

I'm sick, she says. I'm sorry. It must have been the crab cakes.

Her dissertation is full of names rather than numbers, her notes full of doodles rather than words. She waits for her director's reproof, but hears only silence on the line. Hello? she says.

Then, as if she sees right through Mia, over wavelengths and frequencies and through facades and walls, her director says, We've known from the start that your close proximity to the subjects would be your study's greatest limitation. But keep in mind, as a model, the work of Roth and Van Rosenthal; or consider the way in which Smart and Taylor negotiate—

Of course, Mia says. I will. It's a challenge, but I'm bearing it. It's just, my stomach, those crab cakes! Can we reschedule for next week?

After she hangs up the phone, Mia hears a noise outside her door. When she opens it, she nearly steps on Lauren, a breathing plank on the hallway floor. From her feet, Lauren, just awake, reaches for her hand. Mia takes it and pulls. Lauren keeps her eyes closed for a short, vertiginous moment, adjusting to verticality, then trudges down the hall to her room.

BOY: PART 2

A cold, wet day, Mia sipping tea. He comes in from the rain, pauses in her doorframe at his usual time in his usual way, Rubik's Cube in hand, water droplets perched in his hair like tiny crystal balls poised to forecast the future. Hey, he says.

Mia says, Look at you. You're soaked. You shouldn't be out in the rain without a . . . A what? Words evade her. She reaches into her closet for a towel and hands it to him. The perks of living in a dorm room: nothing's ever too far out of reach.

He wipes the crystal-ball drops from his hair. The future is here, now.

She says, Would you like some tea?

He shakes his head, laughing gently at her swift change of subject, her mishandling of her words. This boy, Mia senses, is patient and kind, the type that wouldn't be ashamed to run to the store to buy you maxi pads. That at home with himself, secure in his masculinity, respectful of you and your body.

God, she thinks, is this just Ben all over again, except young and off-limits? Is it possible that the only difference between them is this boy's unattainability, the challenge it poses, the hot little match it holds to her heart? Then she corrects herself: no. No, this boy, with his respect for a good puzzle—he's different. He has to be.

He tosses her the cube, each side a solid color. Here, he says. Mess this up for me.

Mia scrambles the cube ten, twelve times. More, he says. Try twenty-five, thirty moves.

She scrambles, hands it back to him. He studies it for a few seconds, then goes to work.

What's your best time? she asks.

Twenty-nine seconds, he says, but I'm still learning all the algorithms.

He shuffles, paces the hallway. Kat stops to watch. A short moment later the boy hands the cube back to Mia, solved.

She scrambles, scrambles, muddles those perfect sides. She hands it back to him in chaos, and when she does, he thanks her.

She says, You sure you don't want a cup of tea? You look a little pale.

He doesn't, actually, but things keep diving out of her mouth, splashing clumsily.

Oh, no, he says. I feel fine, thanks, Mia. He looks around, at the girls' cracked doors, at Lauren lying on the floor at the end of the hall like an art installation that doesn't please, only confounds. There's nothing wrong with me, he says, and smiles, and says, See you around.

After he's gone, in a state of preposterous near-panic, Mia tries to remember how he spoke the words: There's *nothing* wrong with me.

There's nothing *wrong* with me. Or, most likely: There's nothing wrong with *me*.

As opposed to you, all of you.

HELP

That night Mia calls Elise and asks her to come over. When Elise arrives, bearing an iced Bundt cake on a platter, Mia begins to cry. She can't help herself.

Oh, sweetie, Elise says. Oh, honey.

Mia thinks of the cup of coffee Elise surely abandoned to come here, gone cold on the kitchen table. She thinks of Elise's baby crying, her husband hushing him. She thinks of Elise half-thinking of these things, obligations, priorities, while she holds Mia close, a colossal inconvenience, a child.

What went wrong, Mia? asks Elise. She's talking about Ben, of course, but this isn't about him. Is it? It seems to her that there are so many things to cry about, both known and unknown, and she hardly knows where to begin—people poisoning each other, people poisoning themselves. People, just people, their broken hearts.

She mutters between sobs, her face pressed to Elise's shoulder, It just got to be too hard.

But this is a lie, and she knows it. The truth was, with Ben, it was always too easy—easy to be with him, easy to be without him. She didn't trust that ease. Couldn't bear it. His middle school principal shirts all in a neat row in his closet, evenly spaced, not touching. Once upon a time she'd told herself this was quirky, but now she reflects that it was just the opposite: the absence of quirk. She pictures the students at the middle school all in a row like those shirts, evenly spaced, not touching—was that how Ben kept order? Everyone with their hands to themselves? Could you live that way, be happy like that? He could. She couldn't.

Ben. He's become a reminder of the reason—or one of the reasons—she's begun to suspect that she's not cut out for this field, sociology.

She would so love to understand society, but she'd love even more to understand herself. Why couldn't she stay put with him, be content? Iron the shirts, hang them in the closet, love them as they were?

Because his love had been membranous, like skin. Once she had punctured it, come out of it, she felt the cold colder and the heat hotter and the wind sharper. Everything bit and burned with no protective layer to shield her. For better or for worse, this was what she had wanted: exposure. The only time she and Ben had spoken on the phone after the breakup, he'd told her that after she left, he had gotten a cat. He'd gotten a cat, and she'd gotten twelve very disturbed subjects in a university residence hall, and that was messed up, surely, and yet right after he told her about the cat, she had thought, Yes, that makes sense, this all makes sense, a replacement cat.

Oh, honey, says Elise. Oh, sweetie.

Here's the thing: during their relationship—and even now that it's over—she'd sometimes catch herself thinking about what he might do if she were dying. If she had cancer, say. If she'd been in a terrible accident. How he'd rush to her bedside, fully awake and present and desperate. How would that change things between them? They'd appreciate each other more, maybe. He'd have more passion for her, maybe. Their story would become more interesting—the introduction of conflict would raise the stakes, bind them together, maybe. How sick is that, to think that way? This she can't tell Elise. This she won't tell anyone.

SUBJECT NO. 10: NONSENSE

Mia: [Subject 10], today is Monday. What day will it be tomorrow?

Subject 10: July.

Mia: [Subject 10], how many legs are on a cat?

Subject 10: Three.

Afflicted with a variation of the extremely rare and assumably factitious Ganser Syndrome since the age of fourteen, Subject 10 slips periodically and randomly from coherence into nonsense, upon which slips she begins to provide absurd answers to simple questions. Despite these semifrequent lapses in sense, during which the subject exhibits behavior similar to that associated with serious mental illnesses like schizophrenia, the subject is, for the most part, socially adept, with many friends, a fact that suggests that she exercises control over the timing and context of her descents into incoherence, employing them only in times of emotional need.

Crystal is a battlefield, loud and chaotic and hard for Mia, a civilian, to comprehend. Raised in Nebraska in a house since reduced to rubble by a chain of furious tornadoes—or so she claims—by parents about whom she refuses to speak (and about whom little can be gleaned from her records), Crystal left home after high school and joined the military, headed on the morning of her nineteenth birthday to Fort Jackson, South Carolina, for basic training.

Crystal, whose symptoms seemed to have slipped into remission at the time of her enlistment, began experiencing symptoms again shortly after the start of basic training. She was punted from doctor to doctor, and when no decisive diagnosis could be reached, she was accused of malingering, faking physical problems in order to evade her duties to the military. You know, they said, you signed up for this, girl. You gave your consent. But nothing could be proven, and evidence suggested that Crystal was motivated less by material gains or the evasion of her duties to her country than by emotional needs for companionship and attention. After some time and much ado, she was granted an administrative discharge and came here, to the Waif Wing, to start over. Sometimes Mia fears windows broken and doors kicked in by outraged troops, the troops she rejected, coming to hunt Crystal down.

Crystal recalls basic training the way some soldiers—actual soldiers—recall combat. See, in the army, she says as if she spent her whole life there, you want to be just average. Not too quick, or they'll give you special responsibilities. Not too slow, or they'll rip you a new one. She says, I'll never forget my final road march, ten miles with a forty-pound rucksack. I was limping so bad that people from other platoons were lifting up my rucksack, pushing and dragging me along next to them. I never thought I'd make it, blisters on my feet the size of quarters, but my battle buddies, they saw me through; I did it. I thought my feet would fall off!

And what of your disorder? asks Mia. Your illness?

What about it?

The lapses, Mia says. Your records indicate they'd resumed by then.

In fact, the records are quite specific on the subject of Crystal's lapses of sense during her time in Fort Jackson. They speak of her surrounded by her peers, her battle buddies, one of them rubbing her feet and attempting to quiet her while she writhed on the ground, blathering. They also indicate that she never actually finished the road march of which she often speaks so nostalgically. They suspect that a brain dysfunction predisposes Crystal for pathological lying.

Spaghetti? says Crystal.

It can't be PTSD, her doctors had said. She hasn't experienced trauma. This girl's never been to war.

Mia thinks of Crystal's radio silence on the subject of her parents, her blown-down home. She thinks of some of the literature she read while preparing for this study, of the story of a girl who drove needles into her own eyes in order to be hospitalized and thereby escape her father's abuse. Mia thinks and thinks. She thinks Crystal is full of it, but then again, who knows? Pins in the eyes! Mia touches her own eyes, intact and glorious.

Who knows?

Anyway, some cats really do have only three legs. There could be any number of reasons why. And what is most conversation, anyway, but rambling about nothing? Isn't all talk just the weather and clumsy innuendos and what-the-baby-did with a few kernels of truth slipped in among them almost by accident?

You're excusing her, Mia. Again she channels her dissertation director: *Not your job.*

She remembers a time, right after graduation, she and Elise and Paige and a few other friends and Ben, all sitting around high in her first apartment. The only furniture was a single futon that, for some reason, none of them occupied. Her head resting on Paige's shoulder, all the windows open. Someone kept saying the word "cumquat" over and over again, and it was both paralyzingly hilarious and devastatingly profound at the same time. A stupid moment in the grand scheme of things, entirely erasable, and yet here it is, alive again inside her like a virus.

Oh, Crystal. Spaghetti. Cumquat.

MEETING AGAIN

Four months in comes the dreaded question: What are your conclusions?

Mia gestures to the stack of papers that is her article in its current form—the case studies, subject profiles, observations, names, and numbers. Well, she says, well—I'm still working.

Her director looks her straight in the eye. She says, Remember, you signed up for this.

Yes, Mia says.

It isn't your job to fix these girls, her director says. It isn't your job to love them. It's not even your job to study them. It's your job to study their *interactions*, the effects of their conditions on their social lives. The effects on society, on others.

Yes, says Mia. Yes.

BOY: PART 3

He's sitting on her bed, hands working the cube, which clicks like a clock in double time. She feels old, silly, hypnotized.

How many ways are there to solve that puzzle, anyway? she asks. She could do the math herself; why is she acting like she couldn't?

He takes her notebook from her hand. His fingers brush hers. They've been inching closer together for months; here's another inch. He opens the book to a clean page and slips her pen from the spiral binding. Watch, he says. Eight corners, twelve edges. 8! possible arrangements of the corner cubes. He explains the factorial, walks her through the formula she could have reached on her own:

$$8! \times 3^7 \times \left(\frac{12!}{2}\right) \times 2^{11} =$$

You have a calculator? he asks.

She does. He punches away. 43,252,003,274,489,856,000.

Forty-three quintillion, he says. See? 43.25 quintillion possibilities.

Then she says, What are you doing tonight?

Later, after he's gone (coming back in a few hours to watch a movie; she'll keep her door cracked, invite the girls), she will ponder the figure on his calculator. She'll do calculations of her own. She'll calculate that if you had as many Rubik's Cubes as there are permutations of its results, you could cover the earth with those cubes nearly three hundred times. She'll calculate—or try—how much longer she can go on like this. The speed of her heart, the size of her bed. The years between them, her and this boy—the months, the hours, the minutes. Her ears ring.

Oh, and what are you gonna do, she thinks to herself, have him spend the night in your dorm room? Join him in the dining hall over—she glances at the daily menu—chef's choice?

Colors clicking in her brain, a mess. More than one cannot fit on this dormitory mattress, and besides, what kind of message would that send? She's the adult here; she ought to be a role model, chaste and nunnish. But.

More calculations: odds and consequences, codes, possibilities, fractions and infractions. Then a knock on her door. It's Chiara. She holds out Mia's tube of lipstick, long lost, half used. Thanks, Mia, she says through blood-red lips. A few of us are going out tonight. Come with?

PARTY: A CASE STUDY

Five minutes after the girls have left the dorm—nearly all of them gone, just a few here and there remaining in their closed-up rooms—Mia knows she should have gone with them. She's in no position to pass up opportunities for observation. This is bad scholarship: she's enslaved to something impractical, something sexual, and it embarrasses her, though there's no one observing or judging her but herself.

In the bathroom, she splashes water on her face. The trash can is full of folded plies of toilet paper dabbed with excess lipstick, smears of pink and red on white. When Mia tosses a paper towel into the bin, a tissue shifts, and she sees a corner of something solid and clear beneath the featherweight papers and disposed-of kisses. She digs through the bin and finds a syringe, its barrel cracked as if it's been stepped on. Smashed on purpose in some symbolic act of disavowal? Or freshly used—for injecting, for extracting, before breaking? She can't tell, can't touch, but her unease sends her out of the bathroom, down the hall to her room, feet out of slippers and into a pair of low heels. She scribbles on the marker board on her door, a message to the boy, the location of the party where the girls have gone. Perhaps he'll come and find her, perhaps not.

The party is at a townhouse that sits behind the campus rec center. A high fence bordered by low trees separates the row of townhouses from the center's outdoor pool. Right in front of the door, a couple is in the midst of a slurred argument, him with his fingers twined melodramatically in his own short hair, her saying, Derek, please, I know it sounds crazy, Derek, but I think you really . . . can be in love with two people at the same . . . time, and, and I think I am.

This party has clearly been underway for some time, though it's barely ten thirty. All around her swirls the frantic joy of amateurish, gluttonous consumption—no recognition of etiquette, no perceived need for moderation. Total abandon. All around her are healthy bodies, strong bodies, normal bodies, all contaminating themselves as thoroughly as possible, and as quickly. For a moment Mia forgets—not for the first time—whom she's supposed to be studying.

The floor is sticky and in a corner of the living room is a blow-up kiddie pool in the shape of a turtle filled with a wicked-looking purplish brew into which students are dipping red plastic cups. They lift the noxious liquid to their lips. A ping-pong ball hits Mia upside the head and ricochets into her handbag. When she reaches down in the dark to remove it, she realizes she's forgotten her notebook.

She finds Crystal, Skye, and another Waif Wing girl stationed outside the bathroom, redirecting people to the second toilet on the upstairs floor. Three more of them inside the bathroom, where a girl has apparently just vomited and is now lying on a bath mat before the toilet, propped against the tub. This girl is not one of her girls. She's normal; she's healthy—or she was. Upon seeing the girl, Mia's heart rises, and she is alarmed by this rise, by the extent of her relief upon finding that this ailing someone is not one of *her* someones.

The line's so thin between here and there—sickness and health, better or worse, the things we place insistently, arbitrarily, at opposite poles. It's an invisible boundary, a breath, a syllable, a prefix—*un*—we can attach to almost anything: unwell, unhappy, unready, uncertain.

The girls are fused around their patient like a fortress. They're in their element, the world of the infirm, and know just what to do. Chiara holds a cloth to the girl's forehead and ties back her hair. Lauren draws water from the tap, fills a clean red cup, and holds it to the girl's lips. Here, rinse your mouth. Take a sip, just a small one. Water helps.

When the girl leans over and retches again, nothing comes out. Chiara dives into position by her side. It's okay, she says. She rubs the girl's back. It's okay.

Mia watches, notebookless. She observes how no single girl's pain has desensitized her to others'; in this way, at least, her hypothesis has been wrong. Self-indulgent patients, it seems, make generous nurses. She forgets about the syringe in the trash bin. Her girls are okay.

As she turns to leave, the boy appears in front of her. One of his friends joins Skye in lifting the sick girl from the floor, wrapping arms about shoulders and elbows about waists, and carrying her home.

Let's get out of here, the boy says, dumping his cup full of the purple concoction into the bathroom sink, down the drain. This stuff tastes like medicine.

CONCLUSION

Mia and the boy leave the townhouse, Lauren tagging along. On the other side of the gate and row of trees, the rec center's outdoor pool lies empty, its walls painted a garish shade of turquoise and lined with small lights meant to illuminate evening swims during warmer months. Though it's been drained for the winter, the lights are on, and the pool is a cavernous pit of light, blue and thirsty.

Through the trees, branches catching on skimpy tops, scraping too-tight jeans. They boost each other over the fence and slide down the other side. Lauren and Mia hop over the dry pool's edge and descend along the sloping floor to the deep end, where they sit with their backs against the glowing turquoise-blue wall. Above and behind them, the fiberglass tube of the waterslide twists like a great intestine. Mia feels light, free, proud of her girls; she feels herself glowing like this pool with possibility. Crystal, Chiara, and two of the boy's friends join them, the friends each bearing a six-pack of beer whose bottles they slip through the fence and then roll down the cement incline to Mia and the others. About half of the bottles fan outward and clink daintily against the pool wall.

They've been down in the yawning blue pit of the pool for over an hour, talking and drinking, when the boy's friend takes one of his empty bottles and spins it, hard and fast, on the pool floor. When it comes to a stop with its mouth pointing to the shallow end, to no one, the seven of them rearrange themselves into a circle, knees touching.

It's late. Mia knows she ought to be the responsible adult, usher them complaining back to their rooms, where they will fall asleep in minutes, wake up strong instead of with the beginnings of bugs, sniffles, sore throats conveyed by kisses. They have papers to write, exams to take, just as she has conclusions to draw. Go home, Mia tells herself. Rest. Analyze.

But the glass bottle is spinning, and the blue glow and the beer have filled her with an underwater sensation that slows her movements and halts her breath. When the bottle stops, pointing to the space between her and Crystal, Mia leans to the side, shifts away from the girl. Dodges contact. She declines her first spin. One of the boy's friends kisses Crystal, who kisses the boy himself, a shy, dry peck. The boy and his friend refuse to kiss. Mia looks on, smiles, leans against the pool wall, looks up at the mazelike coils of the waterslide hibernating overhead.

Then the bottle is pointing at her, its insubordinate O facing straight-on the place where her folded ankles cross in front of her. She had figured it would be the boy who would take what was left of her so-called professional distance and squash it between his flawless fingers, compress it into one single, dense, frenetic atom. He's without his cube tonight and needs something in his hands: her. To sort her out, put all her pieces in order. But when Mia looks up to see who it is that's waiting to kiss her, it isn't the boy; it's Lauren.

There are forty-three quintillion places Mia could be right now, but here she is: here. There are forty-three quintillion things she could be doing, paths and detours she could have taken, wedding vows and starched shirts and objective scholarship and babies, but she hasn't taken any of them, she isn't doing any of that.

What she is doing is leaning forward as Lauren takes her face between her cool hands, smiling as if this moment were inevitable. On her lips are forty-three quintillion microorganisms, ready to infect and to heal. In her mouth is Crystal, Chiara, the whole Waif Wing.

In her mouth is the boy. Traces of everyone she's touched and loved and everyone they've touched and loved and so on and so on, endless permutations of affliction and abandon, tongues and fingertips reaching for each other—all packed into the heat of this aqua-lit, glass-on-asphalt second.

Mia opens her mouth and lets them in. Lauren pushes a strand of hair back from Mia's forehead, pulls her face closer to her own, runs her tongue along Mia's top lip, surprisingly, drunkenly assertive. Mia kisses back. Chiara and Crystal shriek and giggle. Mia feels the magnets of the boy's open eyes on her closed ones. She traces a finger down the notches of Lauren's vertebrae, pressing into grooves, persuading pain—because it's there, always lurking, in marrow, between pages, on the other side of closed doors—away. Fragile, fevered, they mash themselves together. This is it, Mia thinks. This is the only way out, the only possibility.

In two days, she'll sit on the pea-green plush chair in her dissertation director's office, the beginnings of a cold tickling her throat. Inquiries will be made. Progress will be evaluated. Conclusions will be requested. And all Mia will have to offer are questions, puzzles, disjointed and subjective observations: why an unprofessional kiss should rejuvenate her like no other has in years, how often the sick, in their way, become healers, unafraid as they are to suck venom from others' wounds. How much she would like to protect these subjects—her girls, her boy—how she would hide their needles, break their syringes, hold back their hair, wrap them in her arms when they're at their weakest, though they're not her children, not her lovers, not even—for the purposes of this study—her friends. How badly she wants to believe, naively, that she will never abandon them, nor they her. How can a sociologist, a psychologist, an any-kind-of-ologist make sense of this?

Tell me, she might ask, in what realm can we be scholars of ourselves? Behind what screen, what soundproof glass do you hide until the data is gathered, the numbers calculated and scrutinized, the conclusions drawn?

In what cold jar do you place your own sick and hungry heart until the study is through?

Ripped

CIRCE'S GETTING ripped and asks me to be her "before" picture.

She wants to post the photos online: the new her, lean and radiant and scantily clad—even in the dry chill of an Idaho autumn, as the rest of our state prepares to paunch itself in parkas and down vests—and the old her, the worse her, glad for the shelter and the excuse of bulky winter wear, played by yours truly: her twin. Two figures in swimsuits, identical except in degree of desirability. She wants to enter them in a contest whose winner will be awarded a trip to Orlando and a free one-year supply of whey protein shake powder.

I look worse than she ever did. We still have the same face, and I could pass for the old her to someone who didn't know better, but the truth is since she's gotten in shape, I've fallen out of it. Next to Circe, who's nearing the end of her thirteen-week Superfit Goddess Challenge and who's taking up bodybuilding, cutting out red meat and fruit juice, guzzling meal-replacement shakes and krill oil, I'm blubber.

We both know I'll do what she asks, but I put up a fight anyway. "It's cheating," I protest. I enjoy my show of dignity; it is almost convincing. "Why not use your own before photo?" I know she has one. I took it twelve weeks ago.

Circe is busy flipping oatmeal pancakes, dry oats mixed with egg whites. Now that she's getting ripped, each meal is a careful ritual of counted calories and precisely measured and weighed ingredients. My mother and I eat separately in scenes of culinary degeneracy: pizza ordered in, frozen vegetable lasagna in creamy béchamel.

Circe says, "It's not cheating. I completed this challenge with flying fucking colors. I just need the picture to reflect that. It's"—she flips a pancake—"dramatic effect."

I say nothing. I know a thing or two about drama myself.

"Look, I followed all the other instructions to a tee," she goes on. "I want that trip to Florida. I'll take you with me. Please, Iris?"

"So I'm the evil twin?" I push. "The ugly doppelganger? I'm your Mr. Hyde?"

"Mr. Hyde," she says, removing cake from pan and spreading on top of it a tablespoon of organic peanut butter, a small indulgence. "What did he teach, again? I don't think I had him."

I know she's read the book, but I don't press her. I know she's defensive about her mistakes. I know because, of course, I am too. I know everything about her—or I did, before she began the Superfit Goddess Challenge. Sometimes we laugh in perfect unison. I'm convinced I've had her hangovers; she'd drink all night while I stayed sober, yet I'd be the one to wake up sick. We've even dreamed the same dreams: one in which the roof lifts off our house to reveal our father, who left when we were two, giant-sized. His legs are as long as the walls are tall, and he bends and lifts us with manicured hands through the opening left behind. Another in which our skin turns to tree bark and our feet become rooted to the ground.

After pancakes (Circe's) and Pop-Tarts (mine), I strip. I don the two-piece swimsuit she instructs me to wear. I slouch, for dramatic effect. We're going for frumpy but not too far gone, dissatisfied but not yet hopeless. Circe molds me, corrects me. Then she hands me a newspaper dated from the day she began the Superfit Goddess Challenge.

"You saved this paper? You had this planned all along?"

She flashes me a wicked smile. The mischievous, welcoming kind of wicked that invites you into itself, that's full of cushions and companionship. A comfort, a delight, to be implicated.

I'd kill for her; my sister, myself.

I ask, "How did you know I wouldn't get ripped too?"

But Circe doesn't answer. She snaps my picture, then molds me again, this time into a version of one of the poses I've seen her strike before the full-length mirror in her bedroom: hands on swiveled hips, upper body pivoted straight toward where the camera will be. Chest pushed out, waist twisted and diminished.

"No one stands like this," I complain, wobbling.

When she's got me where she wants me she stops breathing, as if afraid she could blow me over, and slowly, tentatively, removes her hands from my body. I'm a tower of blocks about to fall. My architect backs away, stepping lightly so as not to shake the ground beneath us, and reaches for her camera.

"Smile," she says, "but not too much."

I do.

Later I go to meet him where he waits for me: in a lakeside cabin surrounded by ponderosa pines, a man in flannel with his shirt tucked in and a host of unusual requests that I fulfill of my own volition and after which we play board games, drink coffee, cuddle, talk. Stefan. It started with little things; he wanted to watch me clip my fingernails, brush my hair. Tonight, on my fourth visit to his house, he invites me to remove my jeans and panties and stand in his living room next to his woodstove. He asks me to prop one foot on a stack of firewood and insert and remove a tampon while he watches. So I do.

What? Don't judge. We don't get to choose what turns us on.

We met when he came to take down a dead tree in my mother's front yard. I was home alone, watching from inside, and after the tree fell, bare branches flailing, some weird force—I'll never know what or why—made me go outside in parka and pajamas and offer him a drink. He shook his head but lifted his protective eyewear and removed a glove.

"I don't have pink eye," he said, holding out his hand.

"What?"

"My eye?"

Only then did I realize it was bloodshot. "I wouldn't have noticed if you hadn't said anything."

"But aren't you glad I did?"

A red mark at the bridge of his nose where his goggles had rested. Orange foam plugs in his ears. He spoke loudly without realizing it. I shrugged. "What's the difference? If it's not pink eye, why does it matter whether I notice it or not?"

"What?" He pulled one of the plugs from his ears. He must have sensed my loneliness—Circe at the gym, working out with her new meat-hunk of a trainer, Ted; my mother in Boise protesting something or other; earlier that day, the first timid snowfall of the season—and he offered me a stick about a foot and a half in length and the chance to use it to mark the fallen tree trunk with a giant pink crayon while he followed behind me with his saw, slicing the places I'd marked. I did, tramping through the frosty, damp yard in my boots and flannel sleepwear, bending to streak bark with smears of soft pink wax, relishing my usefulness. And he—of course, what else?—he watched, then loaded the cut pieces of the trunk, ringed and equal in length for easy stacking, into his truck. Now it's piled in a shed by the side of his cabin, chopped and ready to be burned in the very stove in front of which I stand on display.

We have little to nothing in common, me and the tree removal guy; our conversations move in tight, dizzying circles. But I'll tell you this: when he tells me to do things, I burn in the best way. I become very aware of my teeth in my mouth, of each fine hair on my arms, of my toenails, my quiet breathing. I swear I can feel my own fingerprints pulsing. I wake up.

Tonight, though, doing the tampon thing, my pleasure in his voyeurism wanes.

"Why would you want to see this, anyway?" I demand. "Tampons—I don't know why you'd bring them into your life if you didn't have to."

He shrugs. "I can't explain."

I toss the spent tampon onto a piece of newspaper. Behind the woodstove's sooty windows, orange flames blaze.

"Typical," I grumble. "Men. Everything's here for your pleasure, isn't it?"

"You didn't have to do it if you didn't want to," he says. "I wouldn't push you."

He's right, but I'm suddenly overcome by an awareness of the gross ridiculousness of the whole scenario, my standing by his stove in a wool sweater and no pants, the tampon. What am I doing here? Who am I?

I would love to ask Circe, but she doesn't know about Stefan. Since we finished college last May, despite still living together under our mother's roof, we've seen less of each other than ever. Between her time at the gym with Ted, her job at the bank, my job at Firehouse Coffee, and the separate meals she eats for the Superfit Goddess Challenge, we hardly overlap. I meant to tell her one Sunday after submitting the last of my law school applications, while she labored over her weekend meal prep, filling individual Tupperwares with matching, equal-ounced arrangements of grilled chicken, spinach, and cubed sweet potatoes, but something deterred me. A certain gusto in the way she moved her body, the body that used to be *our* body, a new and confident vitality that was foreign to me. Now here I am pantsless in a highly sensitive Libertarian's log cabin with no one to tell about it.

I pull on my underwear and lay down next to Stefan on the couch, which is old-looking, made of an odd, braided brown material, but clean and surprisingly comfortable. Everything in his house is clean and surprisingly comfortable, including him. He wraps his arms around me.

"I'm fat," I sigh. The fire spits and crackles. The front of the stove reads SPRINGFIELD.

He sweeps my hair back from my face. "Why would you say that?"

I press his finger into a crease in my side where a small but soft roll of flesh has formed. I'm frumpy if not too far gone, dissatisfied, not yet hopeless but on the verge of losing hope.

"Circe," I say. "She took these pictures of me." Earlier, when she offered to show me the photos, I declined, but now I see them anyway, in my mind.

"Your sister."

"Twin. Did I ever tell you how we've dreamed the same dreams? One about the roof coming off our house, and our father . . . and another one where we're trees. Sometimes we laugh in unison. I've had her hangovers."

He asks about our names, a common question. Our mother, the feminist earth goddess, devotee of Marlo Thomas, didn't give Circe and me rhyming names or dress us in matching outfits or do any of the cutesy, homogenizing things some parents of twins do in order to play up their children's identicalness. No, Circe and I were "free to be . . . her and me," girls whose individuality was emphasized as much as possible, girls named after goddesses. Circe got the stranger name but the better goddess: a sorceress, worker of magic and maker of potions, who transformed men into swine. My name, Iris, is feminine and normal and doesn't instantly give me away as our weirdo earth mother's daughter; on the other hand, my namesake is run-of-the-mill as far as deities go, personification of the rainbow and messenger of the gods.

"A messenger's not a bad thing to be," says Stefan.

"Depends on the message."

We begin a game of Scrabble. He requests that I play in bra and panties, so I do, and his eyes shine the way they did when he pulled off his goggles that first day and took me in, my plaid pajamas, my mother's frayed pink knit cap that I pulled off a peg by the door in a rush on my way out to see him. What is it that makes me present myself to him utterly as I am—my oldest, ugliest clothes, my rolls and curves, my insecurities?

When I shiver, he drapes me in a fleece blanket. He says, touching my shoulder, "You're beautiful the way you are, you know."

I don't know why it infuriates me: that it sounds cliché or that I must have been fishing for it, the canned compliment, going on about my chub and flab.

"How after-school-special," I snap. I stand and whip the blanket around my body like a toga.

"Why are you angry?" He looks chastised, genuinely confused, and I feel queasy, first with a rush of power, then with a dull sense of shame for having rebuked him for being, of all things, kind.

"You're not in a book, you know," I say. "You're not in a movie. You don't have to talk in lines to me. Just be real with me. Please."

"I am being real. Why is it so crazy that someone could like you as you are?"

"You sound like my mother."

My heart's not in the game, now, and when it wraps up and he offers to feed me dinner, I refuse. That night, returning home and telling my mother I've already eaten, I skip my first meal.

Circe places second in the Superfit Goddess Challenge, earning the supply of protein shake powder but not the trip to Florida. The day she gets the news, she registers for the Idaho Iron Muscle Showdown, announces she'll be hiring a posing coach, and rush-orders a custom-sewn royal purple crystal-studded competition bikini. The bikini will feature clusters of light-catching amethyst crystals, a rhinestone back connector, and three-dangle crystal bottom connectors that will join at her hips and hang against her skin like strings of smiling, sparkling baby teeth. It costs four hundred dollars, and it will be delivered in a leopard-print carrying case made of two side-by-side breastlike plastic domes beneath a fabric handle with a strip of lace running across the domes at their highest point like the top of a bra or bustier. She shows me a picture of the case online. From the front, it resembles a blinged and unusually bulbous contact lens case.

Our mother takes Circe's measurements, sulking as she wraps a measuring tape around Circe's ass, complaining, "This isn't what we fought for," meaning the feminists, both the old ones she marched with in the seventies and the ones she still marches with now. "Beauty pageants. You weren't there when they crowned a sheep Miss America. You weren't there for the freedom trash cans!"

"It's not a beauty pageant," Circe says.

"Bodybuilding," I offer.

"Thirty-five," our mother reads.

Circe writes the number down. "It's just the bikini division."

"And who will judge you? Some panel of men?" Mom asks.

"People who know about fitness. Healthy people."

"Some panel of men! You'll let them line you up and tell you what you're worth?"

"I know what I'm worth."

"You'll let them put a number on you? You'll be an ass in a line of asses? A cut of meat?"

Circe colors, red as a raw steak, indeed.

"She's just trying to protect you," I intervene. My stomach growls; I skipped lunch, smuggled most of my dinner into the trash.

Our mother pulls the tape tight beneath Circe's bust. "Ain't she sweet, making profits off her meat!" she chants.

"There's no profits," Circe huffs.

"Ain't she sweet, making profits off her meat! Ain't she sweet—"

"Jesus," Circe says. "All you get is a trophy. And I know I'm not meat, and the only person saying I am, Mom, is you."

Mom lays down the measuring tape. "Promise me you won't use steroids."

"I won't use steroids. Anyway, it's not about being manly. It's about being feminine and strong."

"Can makeup hide the wounds of our oppression?" Mom quotes. "Can muscle?"

"How much is all this going to cost?" I ask. The plan was that we'd use this time at our mother's to save money, then move together to wherever I got into law school. But now there are heels and jewelry and $400 bikinis to be bought, a coach to be paid, and gods know what else.

"It's my money," Circe says, pulling on her clothes, spandex workout pants and a loose-fitting thrift-store shirt bearing the name of a beach we've never visited.

"But no steroids," Mom pipes up again. "You know the clitoris can grow into a penis-like appendage? You know that, right?"

"I told you, no steroids."

"No room for a floppy clitoris in that bikini bottom," I contribute. Mom titters and pokes my arm three times the way she always does when we make her laugh.

"Look, both of you, this is important to me." Circe moves to the kitchen island, opens a small bag, and counts out eighteen almonds. "It's my choice," she tells our mother. "Isn't that what you always wanted? For us to make our own choices?"

Our mother steps back. She is small and wiry and has looked the same for as long as I can remember, except for the graying of her hair. She looks at Circe, looks at me, and I know she is mystified by our bodies: what they've become, what we've done to them. We started our periods on the same day, on the solstice of our fourteenth year, and she threw us a First Moon party where we and her friends from her NOW chapter drank red fruit punch and ladled strawberry compote onto angel food cake. Bedazzled tampons studded with super-glued red sequins hung from the dining room chandelier and tossed ruby light like spots of spilled wine onto the walls. We were embarrassed, but the embarrassment was halved between us, as most things were, and more bearable because it was shared, as most things are. Only recently have we begun to diverge. Only recently have our bodies, which clung to each other even in the womb, interfolded before birth like the fingers of hands clasped in prayer, begun to forget each other.

"I just didn't think you'd choose this," Mom says.

Circe shrugs.

"I want you to be happy."

"I am," says Circe. "And you want me to be strong, right? You've always said so." She flexes. Her bicep bulges obligingly.

So even our mother is on board. Even she will agree to send Circe off to be a roasted-looking collection of muscles stuffed into a crystal bikini, rated, dehydrated, evaluated. The sentimental turn the conversation's taken makes me squirm, so I elect to ruin it.

"Ain't she sweet," I start again, "making profits—"

Circe throws the bag of almonds down on the island and storms out of the kitchen. On her way past me, she stops and glares. "I don't need this from you, too, you know," she says.

"I don't see why you need this to be happy," I say. "You weren't happy before? You weren't strong before?"

"Not really, no."

"Bullshit."

"Iris," Mom scolds.

Circe stares at me. She touches my face, the way she does sometimes, tenderly, and looks at me with pity. "I do not understand," she says, "why you're so angry."

I move to slap her hand away, but she's too quick for me, and I end up slapping my own cheek. Even in this, I read a confirmation of our sisterly synchronization, but I keep it to myself.

Is this the form our telepathy will take, my attempt to strike stymied by her anticipatory recoiling? Her awareness of my anger?

Later, sorry, I visit a competition gear website and order Circe a gaudy competition bracelet made of four rows of tiny rhinestones. I go to the kitchen, reopen the bag of almonds, count out seventeen. I chew them slowly, trying to be satisfied. Then I open the freezer and unwrap an ice cream sandwich.

The next day she comes into Firehouse after work, still dressed in black slacks, hair in a neat bun, on her way to the gym. She orders a dark roast to go.

"And something for Ted," she says. Her new fitness coach. He's twenty-eight, five years older than we are, and Circe's crazy about him. She's shown me and our mother pictures from his website, gushing. "One of those smoothies."

She waits patiently while I blend. My coworker Nance, at the register, praises Circe's figure, and Circe thanks her.

"You two are so cute," Nance says. "Stand side by side." She flaps her hands, beckoning for us to move closer together, and screeches as we do, Ted's smoothie in my hand, lidless. We get this a lot. "Look how cute you are."

"Thank you," Circe says again. "I bet Iris has told you how we dream the same dreams," and Nance nods, tickled.

When she turns back to the register, Circe says, "Issie, I'm sorry I upset you."

"I'm sorry too." I snap the lid onto Ted's smoothie, the special healthy one we call the Green Giant.

"I need your support," she continues. "I need to know you're with me on this."

"Okay."

"So you are?"

I think of the time in ninth grade when her first boyfriend, Max, came over, the trick we played on him. He rang the doorbell one day, I answered. I kissed him square on the lips, and before he could respond, I turned and shouted into the house, "Circe, Max is here!" She popped from behind the couch where she'd been hiding, and we both erupted into a fit of giggles, hugging and dancing and spinning and laughing, and Max said, bewildered, "You girls are *weird*." And the time when we were seven, playing softball in summer, too young to have numbers on our shirts and therefore interchangeable, and she batted for me one day at the end of a long season, knowing how I clammed up in games. I was a terrible hitter, but that day when the coach called, "Iris! On deck!" Circe got up, took a few practice swings, and proceeded to send a ball zinging into left field, a double, my savior.

"I'm with you."

"Good." She sips her dark roast sparingly, takes the Green Giant from my hand. "I'll get you a backstage pass. Okay? Will you come with me, be my moral support? Carry my bag, all that?"

"All that?"

She smiles. "Help with my butt glue, rub me down with cooking oil. All that."

I feel my nose scrunching and battle to unscrunch it.

"Please say you'll do it," Circe says.

So I do.

One week out from Circe's show, her posing coach, Jennifer, evaluates her form over Skype. Through Circe's cracked bedroom door, I see her posing in heels and the same swimsuit she used for her after photo, hips and feet twisted to one side, one knee slightly bent, glutes lifted.

"The butt is the tiebreaker," Jennifer says. I can't quite make out Circe's whole screen from the door and experience Jennifer only as an orange-ish smudge in the corner of the screen that's visible to me. She tells Circe that whenever a contest is too close to call, it always comes down to the butt. She tells her to eat a spoonful of honey an hour before going onstage to boost her muscles.

Circe turns and poses, feet just wider than shoulder width apart, butt facing the screen.

"Feet closer together," Jennifer says. "Closer. No. Too close . . . that's better. Now bend forward . . . not too far, now, let's keep this family friendly!"

That night, I do an impression of Jennifer for Stefan. "It's all about the X factor!" I parrot in the sunniest voice I can muster. "Sculpted shoulders! Muscular butt! Tiny waist! Strong legs!" I toss my hair over my shoulder, place my hands on my hips, and give my head what I think is a sultry little shake. I flash him an enormous grin.

"I don't get why it bothers you so much," he says. "It's her body. To each their own."

"Okay, Ayn Rand." I complain about the cost of the tickets (eighty dollars apiece) to Circe's show. Her competition bikini and its case have arrived, and she rubs the inside of a banana peel against her teeth each morning and evening after brushing to whiten them. She drinks a gallon of water a day and works out with Ted.

"You should see this guy Ted," I tell Stefan. "He's, like, the kind of white guy who'd get Chinese symbols tattooed on his back that he thinks mean 'strength and perseverance' but that actually stand for, like . . . 'contagious fungal nail infection' or something."

Stefan laughs. Then he asks me to take off my top and let him watch me brush my teeth. He pushes open the door to the bathroom, which adjoins his bedroom, and waves me in. A new toothbrush rests on the faux marble by the sink, still packaged, next to a tube of red cinnamon toothpaste. He sits on the bed, and I go to work. The sink is a gleaming white with not a speck of gunk or old toothpaste anywhere, the fixtures polished, the mirror shiny and free of spots; his deodorant and shaving gear are lined up in a neat row on a shelf on the neighboring wall, arranged in what I assume to be order of operations. What does he see in me?

I try to limit the jiggling of everything but my breasts, which I endeavor to jiggle as much as possible. Despite frequently skipping meals, I've lost little weight, replacing the missed meals with covert handfuls of potato chips and semisweet chocolate chips straight out of the bag. After a few seconds, Stefan interrupts me.

"Just be natural," he says. "Don't try so hard."

I resume brushing, but my mind won't go hollow like it's done before. I move around, turn to the side, imitate one of Circe's poses, parting my feet to just less than shoulder width and bending forward, butt out, resting an elbow on the ledge of the sink.

What? I'm allowed to be curious.

"Stop," Stefan says.

"What?" I demand through a mouthful of foam, turning and putting down the toothbrush.

"Who is it you want to be looking at you right now?" he asks. "Because it's clearly not me."

I spit pink froth into the sink. "I just thought I'd try something different."

"Well, don't."

He points to the corner of his mouth, and I wipe a smear of toothpaste from the corner of mine. Then he pats the bed next to him. "Sit down."

So I do.

He pulls me close to him, opens a drawer in his nightstand, and takes out a pen. He pulls the skin on my middle taut, a few inches to the right of my belly button, and begins to draw. His pen strokes are smooth and cold, a series of parallel lines, swirls, and little circles that form an abstract figure no more than an inch in diameter. Then he caps the pen and returns it to the nightstand.

"What does it mean?" I ask, studying the figure.

"Strength and perseverance."

I shoot him a skeptical look.

He grins, shakes his head. "I have no idea."

He kisses me. The kiss is perfectly lovely. Then he says, "I'd like to meet your family sometime. Your mom, Circe. What if I went with you to her show? For moral support?" He pauses: dramatic effect. "Would you like that?"

"I don't know." I pull back. "It's like a two-day thing, the show, there's prejudging in the morning, we'll be in a hotel the night before, and I'll be busy helping Circe backstage. You'd hardly see me."

He smoothes the bed's rumpled comforter, a gesture he seems to think appears casual but that I take for the opposite: anxious, obsessive preening, performed nonchalance. "Do they know about me?"

"No. Does your family know about me?"

"Sure. Why shouldn't they?"

I feel some shell around my heart unfasten and open. Timid little mollusk, be still, be safe.

"Look," I say, "I've told you not to get attached. I'm getting out of here. I'm going to law school. Circe and I—"

"Yeah, Circe and you." He stands and crosses the room.

"What?"

"Why do you want to be her so badly?"

"I don't. I just want to be . . . with her. I've never not been."

He shrugs, shakes his head, holds out his hands, palms up. "You're a grown woman," he says. "What are you going to do, marry her?"

I jump to my feet, pull on my shirt. The heartshell clamps shut; the muscle constricts. "What am I going to do, marry *you*?"

I collect my phone and keys, and I leave.

The day before her show, Circe drinks her last glass of water. She will not drink again until after the show, when she'll indulge in the extravagant cheat meal about which she's been fantasizing for weeks, dreaming of double bacon cheeseburgers, fettuccine in buttery alfredo, sweet moscato, mountains of donuts. She gathers her things: a small cooler full of her premade, premeasured meals; a bag of rice cakes, package of dried bananas and pack of sugar-free gum; the bikini in its leopard case; a set of baggy sweats to wear after her spray tan; clear plastic four-inch heels; sewing kit; bobby pins and hair glitter; a bottle of oil labeled Juicy Flex, still plastic-sealed, that I'm to massage onto her skin before sending her onstage; a special glue to stick the seams of her suit to her flesh; rubber gloves; and a host of other items of whose purpose I'm still ignorant: a tower of Dixie cups, assorted bottles of mystery vitamins, Vaseline, a bungee cord, a set of old tie-dyed sheets and pillowcases from our childhood bed.

We drive an hour to the event hotel and check in, and Circe goes to a preshow meeting with the other contestants to be weighed and measured and briefed and given a number. Our mother will join us tomorrow for the evening show. I haven't heard from Stefan since our fight last week. I know I'm the one who owes an apology, but I can't bring myself to issue it.

What would it be like to carry him with me into the future I've been imagining for myself since I was young—law school (I should begin hearing back any day now), court decisions that make my mother proud, that make this mean old hulking world a little lighter? To have my every mundane movement inspected and admired—dabbing the glued rim of an envelope with my tongue, writing a check, boiling an egg, setting a mousetrap beneath the basement stairs—for all of it to be potentially erotic, ever under scrutiny? Such pressure, to be thought beautiful; such labor, to love. His obsessions, his old truck, his unfinished associate's degree. I have a vision of him offering my mother a copy of *The Fountainhead*, of her curling up and withering in response like a slug in salt; I have a vision of myself in a judge's robe and jabot; he approaches the bar in his flannel, tells me in a loud, clear voice to show him my tits, and I do, the frilly bib of the jabot hanging limp and lacy between them, a scandalized murmur ascending in the gallery. The bailiff chiding, Order; order!

The hotel door opens, and Circe enters, jumpy, going on about other girls' hamstrings, holding a small white disc with the number 121 on it, fussing that she'll be late for her first spray tan appointment.

"Come with me," she begs, so I put away my thoughts and follow her to a small room downstairs in the hotel, windowless and with a worn red carpet printed with disproportionately majestic yellow fleurs-de-lis, where two pairs of portable plastic tents are set up and women in sweats and robes mill about, hopping up and down and eating dried figs and texting and talking and stretching and waiting to be dyed. After a few minutes, a woman with a horrifying looking spray gun calls Circe's name, and she enters the first tent, strips, places a cap over her hair and steps onto two footprinted pieces of cardboard in the center of the tent. "Not my face," she tells the woman with the spray gun, then motions to the second tent, on the other end of a small, curtained corridor, where she'll go to dry, and tells me to wait outside it with her change of clothes.

Through the barely opaque plastic I can make out the shape of Circe's body, as can all the other women in the room, waiting their turn or being sprayed in the other set of tents in the opposite corner. A buzz of eager conversation, a general din of things being dropped and picked up and set down, orders being given, calls received and sent. The hiss of the spray gun. Ten minutes later, Circe comes out of the airbrush tent shivering and into the one where I wait for her. "It's so cold!" she says, shaking her hands crazily. I hold out her sweat suit, but she waves me away, still wet with tanning solution, and fights the urge to huddle, holding her arms out from her body, bouncing on the balls of her feet before an electric fan completely naked, waxed, hairless, and animal brown. A Barbiefied, baked-looking version of the body I once knew best now made alien to me. When she is dry, she dresses in the loose-fitting black sweat suit, and I swing her bag over my shoulder so as not to let the strap rub off her tan, and we leave the room, excusing our way through crowds of women and, beyond the women's spray tan room, massive painted men.

"Ted's going to be here," she says. "He told me he'd come."

"Competing?"

"Watching. He doesn't compete anymore now that he's coaching. I gave him our room number," she says.

Great.

Back in the room, she spreads the old tie-dyed sheets from home over the bed to keep from staining the hotel sheets with her tan. We watch TV side by side, both with right foot crossed over left ankle, hers sculpted and streaked with vein lines, mine plump and winter white. After a while, she gets up, takes the tower of Dixie cups from a bag, and goes into the bathroom. Seconds later, I hear a shriek, my name called, and I hurry to the bathroom and open the door.

There she is in front of the toilet with her sweatpants around her tanned ankles and a half-full Dixie cup in her hand. The insides of her thighs are spattered with drops of liquid, beneath which pale spots of skin have appeared.

"So that's what the cups were for."

She dumps the cup into the toilet and tosses it into the trash.

"It can't get wet," she says. "You're supposed to pee in a cup so you don't get a toilet seat mark on your butt. Everybody said to do this. This is what you're supposed to do!"

"And you missed?" I try not to laugh.

She pulls a huge length of toilet paper off the roll and wads it into a cumulus puff of cloud in her hand. "I need you to go down and ask them if they can touch it up for me."

"What do I say?"

"Just say I splashed water on my tan." She wipes herself frantically with the toilet paper, but the spots on her skin turn to streaks.

"Okay."

"Wait," she says. "Don't go yet." She holds the wad of paper in one hand and, just as I start to laugh, begins to cry. Here it is again, unison.

"I can't wash my hands," she moans. "The tan will come off."

"For Christ's sake, Circe." I grab a fresh fistful of toilet paper, bend down in front of her, and dab at the pale white streaks on her legs.

"Ohmygod," she sobs, "ohmygod, I'm crying . . . oh, Iris, catch it!"

With a trembling finger she points frantically at her face, where a crystal droplet streaks her cheek and perches on her perfect jawline, gaining mass. I drop the toilet paper into the bowl and catch the tear with a tissue before it can stain her tanned neck or the back of an even-browned hand.

"It's okay," I tell her. "You're okay. Just calm down."

She continues to cry while I hold tissues against her cheeks, which will be painted tomorrow by a makeup artist to match the muddy tone of her body.

"It's okay," I say again. "They can touch it up. It's not the end of the world."

She sniffles, blinks, eyelashes clumped with her tears. She pulls up her pants. "Did you see some of those girls down there?"

I tread carefully. "What about them?"

"You know," she says. "Did you see the thighs on some of those Physique ladies?"

"No, I really didn't."

"And their biceps?" She holds her palms apart as if clutching an invisible basketball.

"But that's not even your division. They aren't your competition."

"I know. But the bikini girls, too, some of their waists . . . " She shakes her head. "I don't know what I'm doing. Iris, what am I doing here?" She raises her arms, gesturing to the room around us, the toilet, the crumpled tissues in my hand, her body. "Who am I?"

"You're a Superfit Goddess."

"I'm scared."

"I know." What a relief to hear her say it. "I am too."

She stares at me, confused, and I sit down on the edge of the tub. "What do you have to be scared of?" she asks.

"There's a guy. I think he really cares about me. And I think I screwed it up. And I can't think of a way to move forward without screwing up again."

For a moment, she says nothing. "You've been seeing someone?"

I nod. "And I want to do the strangest things when I'm around him. Like . . . he'll ask me to do things, and I do them. I want to do them."

"What things?"

"Just, like . . . brush my hair."

"Brush your hair?"

"Yeah. Or, like . . . do these everyday things, like clip my nails or spread jam on toast or play cards, but, like, in various states of undress."

Now she recoils. "Why?"

I don't answer, manage only a slight shrug.

A line appears on her forehead, a little cut between her neatly plucked brows. "Does Mom know about him?"

"No."

"And you didn't tell me."

She makes a move toward the sink but stops herself, gently wipes her palms against the fabric of her pants. "Since when don't you tell me things?"

"I didn't think you'd approve."

"So what? You don't *approve* of this"—she motions to the room, her tan—"but I don't try to hide it from you."

"That's only because you can't."

"No, it's not, Iris." She gives me a look of disgust, disappointment. "It's because I love you."

She leaves the bathroom and grabs a key card from a table by the bed. "I'm going to see about my tan touch-up."

"You're mad at me?"

"No."

"Do you want me to go with you?"

"No, I can do it myself."

She isn't gone long. When she comes back, she lies down on the tie-dyed sheets, still in her sweats. She sets the alarm on her phone; she has to be up for her second layer of spray tan at 5 a.m. When she turns out the light, it is bright as day in the room, light from the hotel parking lot pouring through the open curtains. I close them and move to curl against her, the way I would in the bed we shared when we were kids, but she says, "Don't." She turns onto her side. "The tan."

After her second spray tan, hair, and makeup appointments the next morning, I look for her backstage with one of her prepacked bags over my shoulder. I've just crawled out of bed and devoured a syrup-softened hotel waffle. Groggy and nervous, I wander through a long hallway with plastic draped along the walls, peeking into a series of small rooms (one labeled MAKEUP, one HAIR, and one full of weights and bands labeled PUMP ROOM), steering clear of the corridor labeled MEN. The hall and rooms are bustling with women, some still in loose-fitting workout clothes, most already in their glittery bikinis, all in similar, borrowed shades of brown, even the naturally dark-skinned girls glowing with spray tan, dark slashes and caverns opening up in the valleys between muscles where the overhead lights don't hit. Stretching, listening to music, propping full-length mirrors against the walls to examine themselves, posing for photos, touching up makeup, consulting with coaches and friends. A green-bikinied woman meditates on a beach towel laid out near the wall. Each contestant wears the white disc bearing her competitor number. A few lost-looking men wander in and out of the hordes, dazed.

At last I find her, coiffed and chestnut brown, wearing her purple bikini, her lips shiny with pink gloss, and her hair falling over her shoulders in curls. She takes the bungee cord from the bag and pulls on it, flexing, sending blood to her muscles, gathering her hair over one shoulder so that the muscles in her back work visibly and her shoulder blades seem to open and close like wings. She's made friends this morning and chats with a few other women about supplements while I wait to be called upon to rub her down with Juicy Flex before sending her to prejudging, which begins at 9 a.m. and where the judges will assess her before announcing their decisions and awarding trophies at this evening's show, where I'll be joined by our mother in the audience. While I wait, I duck into the women's restroom and find it swarming with ladies applying lipstick in the mirrors, flossing, bumping into one another, taking selfies. Implants abound, bobbing in bikini tops, perfectly round, like overturned bowls. The trash and the metal sanitary boxes in the stalls are overflowing with Dixie cups.

"There you are," Circe says when I return. She asks for help with her heels, and I bend down and fasten the tiny clasps at their sides while she rests a hand against the wall for balance. I uncap the Juicy Flex, put on rubber gloves, and rub her up and down, her skin turning glossy. She's hard and firm and smooth, her muscles seeming to pop from beneath her skin, tectonic plates shifting, earthen shapes rearranging themselves like new, strange continents. Is this what's underneath me, this landscape, submerged? Do I want to know?

I stand up and take her in, the finished product: four inches taller than usual and four degrees darker, the crystals on her bikini glinting in the chaos of the backstage lights. She's flawless. And she's strong. Not bulky like some of the girls in the other divisions, the militant-looking Physique women with their broad shoulders and burly arms, their thick thighs; she's sleek and feminine and confident. I search her face for a trace of last night's vulnerability but find none. No silent plea for reassurance, no indication that my superfit sister is not already one hundred percent certain of her goddessness. We've never been less alike than we are right now.

"What do you think?" she asks me, but the question is perfunctory, and I simply nod.

"Help with your glue?" a staff member interrupts. Circe hands her the bottle of Bikini Bite. The woman ushers her to a corner where heavy paper has been taped to the floors to catch drips. She spreads glue on the inside seam of Circe's bikini with a popsicle stick and holds it in place for about a minute, Circe holding still in a pose, until it adheres to her skin.

"Is this your twin?" the woman asks, handing the glue back to Circe. "How cute," she says, giving us a citrusy smile before moving on to the next contestant whose ass is in need of adhesive. Another staff member shuffles by with a megaphone, belting out orders.

"Your tan looks good," I say, glancing meaningfully at her unspeckled inner thighs. I know I'm risking offending her, but I can't find anything else to say. I feel pathetic, desperate for Circe's confirmation that the insecurity she showed last night was real, that I'm still someone who can validate her, who knows who she is. Someone she needs to see her so that she can know she's real.

"Look, Iris, I need to tell you something," she says. Another contestant in a yellow bikini with gem-studded straps like elongated infinity signs stops her, asks for a photo, and Circe poses and smiles. Before the woman walks away, Circe continues, "Those dreams, the ones you always talk about when you're telling people we're telepathic?"

"The tree bark," I supply. "The roof lifting off the house—"

"Those, yes. Here's the thing, Iris: I didn't have them."

"Yes you did."

She shakes her head. The stones on her bikini straps fling grains of light into my pupils.

"You had them," I insist. "I woke up, I told you about them, you were so amazed, you kept saying, 'Yes, I saw that too!' You were so excited. Plus, you added details from your own memory; you added the one about Dad's fingernails being painted pink . . . "

"I made that up."

"No, you didn't. And even if you did, it was in the dream . . . "

"Was it? Do you remember the dream? The actual dream? Or only the things we said about it after you woke me up?"

"We woke up at the same time."

"Yes, because you woke me up screaming, 'Put me down, put me down!'"

I shake my head. "You might not remember, but you had them."

Circe shakes hers. "I don't remember because I didn't have them."

She takes my hand and holds it. On her wrist is the rhinestone competition bracelet I gave her, shimmering and fake. She says, "I just thought you should know."

She thanks me for my help backstage. Then she lets go of my hand, uncaps a jar of Vaseline, applies a thin layer to her teeth, and smiles.

The prejudging lasts three hours. I pop in and out, read, and half watch while I wait for Circe's group, Class C Bikini. A steady stream of contestants walks out, stands on little taped Xs on the stage, hits a series of poses. "Half turn," the judges drone. "Quarter turn." The contestants obey.

So she didn't have the dreams. So what? What does it mean? And can she even be sure? Can she even remember? What dreams might we have shared without realizing it? What common visions might have gone unexpressed?

When it's Circe's turn, I watch her walk like a model, long strides in high heels. She and her sister competitors arrange themselves in a long line, and although they're hourglass-shaped and comparatively petite, much smaller than the women in the brawnier divisions, I wonder how much they can bench collectively, what they could lift or build if they stepped out of their stilettos. I imagine them all in coveralls—riveters, Rosies, assembling aircraft propellers or erecting buildings. Then I blink, and the coveralls fall away. What's Rosie wearing, anyway, underneath that blue-collared uniform? A red sequined bikini?

The degrading Mindless-Boob-Girlie Symbol—I know my feminist history; I listened when my mother spoke. But Circe isn't mindless. A judge calls her number and she raises her arm and switches places with another girl. Two people sitting in front of me turn to each other and mumble, ripping the contestants' bodies apart. I hear something about cellulite. I hear Not lean enough. But except for the rosy love lens that colors my sister superior, I see no way to rank the women, nothing that sets any of them apart as fitter or finer than the others. The whole thing is over in a few minutes, and the women process offstage single file.

I return to our hotel room and change out of my jeans and into a pair of black stretchy pants. I sit on the bed and, much to my annoyance, begin to cry. I miss her. I miss our mutual dreams. I miss Stefan. I miss our mother telling me I was powerful; I miss believing her. I miss the way things were before we began to wonder what else we could be.

Circe will be back before long to wait out the break between prejudging and the show, and I fight to get my shit together before she gets here. After a few minutes, there's a knock at the door, and I wipe my cheeks and open it. It's Ted.

"Oh," he says, and for a fleeting moment I imagine he thinks I'm her. "Circe here?"

I shake my head no, but he looks past me, searching the empty room. Then his eyes settle on my face, the red-nosed wreck of it, and he softens.

"What's wrong, Circe's twin?"

I turn my head away, but he turns it back so that I'm looking at him, lightly pinching my chin between his thumb and forefinger. He asks me to tell him my name, so I do.

"Don't cry, Iris," he says. "Don't worry."

He hugs me, and I'm not sure what to do. He holds me for a while, his heavy arms like bars weighing down my shoulders. I don't hug back, but I don't pull away, either, my hands just sort of hovering behind him. He smells like mint gum.

"Don't worry," he says again. "Anybody can be beautiful." He reaches down and gently pinches a bit of loose flesh on my side. "You just have to try."

His hand moves from my side to the small of my back, where it stops for a second, and he smiles at me. Not unusual, I tell myself; innocuous touch expected, even required in weight training, his bread and butter. Normal. The hand descends and rests itself on my right butt cheek, and I see red, as if the blood has rushed to my eyes. He smiles. And here's the thing: I smile back.

So his hand dives beneath the line of my pants, my panties, and gathers a handful of flesh, and squeezes hard, and lifts. Smiling. This is what Circe's been wanting, I think, this contact, for his touch to tip from practical to playful. He's still smiling, like we're sharing a joke, ha ha, and I could pull away, but I don't. I neither fight nor fly; I freeze. I smile. I let him.

No, I see, we do not dream the same dreams, my sister and I, nor will she sweep through this door and save me, sensing distress, the speed of my heart, but one thing I swear here and now: this man will never touch her. He gives me a second, punctuating squeeze, then pulls his hand out of my pants and gives my ass a hearty slap, still smiling, and I smile back, and it's all over within seconds, and he says, "See you at the show, gorgeous," and leaves. The hotel door swings shut behind him, sweep of wood against carpet, click of bolt into latch, and I unthaw.

What? Oh, sure, *you* would never have let him; you'd have been too strong for that. But let me ask you this, Mother, Circe, Stefan, all of you: How do you know?

How certain are you that you control your body, the snug, smug little house that keeps you warm while you think and dream? Guess what: there's only one of you, and no real precedent to show you what you will or will not do, what weight you might pick up one day and not put down again.

Don't judge me.

What It's Like to Be Us

EARLY THIS MORNING the blackbirds fell from the sky, hammering onto rooftops and parked cars, pavement and windshields. It happened in what our parents call the wee hours, the thumping on rooftops that shook us from sleep. Today we girls sit glossy-lipped at our desks at school while men in gloves buzz around outside, shoveling bird carcasses from the lawn, and we pick polish from our nails, passing notes and pretending to be bored while at the same time trying urgently to outdo each other in grades, in answers, in looks from boys.

Except for the birds, it is an ordinary day.

Though no one can explain why they fell, in some ways the birds—for us—seem like a great equalizer. Because *every* day, for us, brings a small event that in some way upsets the world the way the birds do for everyone else today: a strange look from a boy, maybe, or the stranger, more critical looks we give each other.

We love each other. We go way back. Our priests and pastors tell us to be kind, and our parents tell us to be grateful. They make casual commandments that we struggle to follow and, when we fail disastrously, denounce as unfair. No one knows what it's like to be us.

Our teacher tells us to be proud. We are really going to go somewhere someday, she says. But where? When? And where are we now?

Outside the classroom window, a steady drip from the gutter, diamond drops of water refracting light. It snowed a little last night, unseasonably, and the papers say maybe this is why the birds fell, mistaking snowy parking lots for bodies of water, avenues for rivers, and attempting to dive headfirst into them. They navigate by starlight and, at night, might mistake for stars the artificial lights of a town like ours. There are other possibilities, too, the papers say: disorientation from fireworks at a venue outside town, the inscrutable hand of God.

The birds, their bodies on the sidewalks that we picked our way around this morning on our walk to school, make everything suspect. When our teacher tells us that one number multiplied by another equals another, we are unsure whether to believe her. We watch those dainty crystals of water drip outside the window, redirect the sunlight. We pass notes, pick the color from our nails.

Our teacher, Ms. Kendall, is beautiful and flawless as an actress on a magazine cover, though she wears a turtleneck that reaches up high and sits snug just beneath her chin, a sweater that smells of wool, a smell we inhale when she walks by, a smell like being tucked beneath a warm blanket on a frost-lined morning. While men wander outside our classroom window, retrieving feathered bodies from the grass, we look at them, then look at her. We see them watching her through the window with blackbirds in their gloved hands and wonder if it's true, what the boys say—that she's a stripper after school gets out, that friends of their brothers' fathers and fathers of their cousins' friends have seen her, her knee crooked around a silver pole in a dark room.

"They've seen her," the boys say. "*Everybody* knows about Ms. Kendall."

We sense the untruth of the rumor, its cruelty. We see that Ms. Kendall looks at home in her pinstripe slacks, sheathed in her wool turtleneck. And yet, too, we understand intimately the ways in which people change: rapidly, without warning, the way these blackbirds with the iridescent oily sheen on their wings, with their wiry claws, fell from the sky in the still-dark hours of morning. We have been sinking our own claws into each other's flesh for years. We love each other ferociously, and we hate each other ferociously as well. We swing between these two positions pendulously. We are best friends. And we are all alone.

MARY LOUISE

This morning Mary Louise's mother used the pool skimmer to scoop dead birds from the lawn and the bushes. Then she threw them, and the net with them, into the trash.

She said, "It's time we started listening to the Lord."

Mary Louise's mother says the birds are a sign that the end is near. She sent Mary Louise to school this morning with an unfashionable umbrella, protection against further falling birds, and a gold crucifix around her neck. Mary Louise scoffed and jammed the folded-up flowered umbrella into her backpack, tucked the cross beneath the neckline of her sweater.

Mary Louise knows her friends laugh at her mother, with her droopy eyes, her formless eyebrows, and her piety, so Mary Louise laughs too. Still, she worries that her mother may be right. All around her things are awry: there is the still-new and surprising smoothness of her legs, to which she has recently and clumsily begun taking her mother's razor. There are the birds. There is the vision she can't help but consider of Ms. Kendall's skin lit by the fragmented flashing of a disco ball, her motions slowed by strobe lights. There is the fact that, this afternoon, when she pressed the button on the school water fountain and lowered her head to drink, no water came out, just the dry resonance of empty pipes straining. ("Broken water main," a janitor had said as she'd stood with her thumb on the button, waiting.) There is a thing called a water main, of which Mary Louise was previously unaware, and a host of other things, cogs, mechanisms, all hiding.

There are lovely things too. That same smoothness of her legs and the new skirt that clings to them, this short yellow skirt that her mother hates, with the pleats, the fabric that swishes.

If the world did end, where would she go? What would she wear, and who would go with her? Who would judge her, and what would be the verdict?

This last question makes Mary Louise flinch as she ponders it, waiting for the second hand on the classroom clock to tick its way to the end of the school day. When it does, she gathers her books and magnets together with her friends in a tight huddle, her back to Tiff. Tiff, the outcast. Chubby Tiff with that awful blot of red on the back of her jeans yesterday, the one everyone saw and that left a faint smear on the seat of her chair, Tiff who falls asleep in class and has become a burden. Tiff should control her body and her gossip; she should not have whispered that comment to Lannie, which was passed on to Jane, then passed in a note to Mary Louise, about Mary Louise's yellow skirt. Or that comment to Mary Louise, whispered to Jane, then phone-called to Lannie, about Lannie's—what was it, again?

Tiff deserves what is coming to her. For Tiff, the Judgment Day is already here.

It isn't Mary Louise's fault Tiff has done what she's done. Mary Louise has been out too, the outcast, and she has not gone to all this work to claw and scrape her way back into this circle of girls for nothing. It's hard being Mary Louise, hard in a way no one understands, not her mother, not her friends. So she ignores Tiff's desperate gaze, which she can feel crawling on her like ants. She pretends not to feel the tickle and sting of those ants on her bare, smooth legs, beneath the spectacular yellow skirt. She gathers her things and, with her friends on either side of her, she walks home.

Mary Louise has warriors and heroes in her blood. A long line of them with justice in their eyes and weapons in their hands. She thinks of the folded flag in its triangular case on the mantle next to the photo of her grandfather, his medals; she thinks of her father with his dust-colored clothes, the cuffs of his pants tucked into his heavy laced boots. (The last thing she said to him before he went away, again, to the desert: *Can't you untuck them? They look so stupid this way.*)

Some wars are just, and at the end of the day, you have to fight for yourself. On airplanes you attach your own oxygen mask before helping anyone else secure theirs.

Pinched between her friends—her loyal friends—and deliberately snubbing Tiff, Mary Louise walks home thinking of her mother in her house, washing her father's already-clean socks over and over again, folding them carefully. She thinks of the other mothers who bring her casseroles and offer to pray. She thinks of the front page of this morning's paper, of a small photo in the bottom corner dwarfed by the article about the birds. In the picture, a woman was crying, a black scarf covering her hair, a wide open mouth like a bottomless hole, and Mary Louise imagines tumbling into that mouth, falling down, down, like Alice into Wonderland, like the first rejected angel into the depths of hell. Who killed that woman's husband? Who blew her child to bits, bits of child swept under sand and pecked over by birds? Do they have birds in the desert?

(*It's time we started listening to the Lord.*)

Mary Louise shakes off the thought. She nods at what her friends are saying about Tiff. Traitor, loser. If that woman is crying like that, then she must have done something to deserve it. (*Can't you untuck them? They look so stupid this way.*)

If you are going to be on top, someone else must be on the bottom. Tiff is walking home half a block ahead of the rest of them, occasionally turning around. Mary Louise ignores Tiff in the way she ignores her mother's hideous umbrella and the face of the screaming woman in the news. She feels a rush of power; she smooths her pleated skirt and tucks her hair behind her ears. And she feels, also, a sadness spreading inside her, a terrible blossom, when she thinks about how Tiff has always been around, how they all used to be such friends, so happy. She recalls the time they held a pretend Olympics in Tiff's muddy yard. They made medals of cardboard and craft ribbon and dressed in skirts and slippers and leaped and turned in circles in the grass while their parents sat in lawn chairs drinking iced tea and clapping half-heartedly after each girl's performance. They took turns winning gold. Everyone got one chance to win, and everyone had to take her turn losing.

(*They look so stupid this way.*)

And then there were those good old days when they had killed each other in all manner of violent and delightful ways. Mary Louise had crossed herself after each girl slipped from the imaginary cliff's edge, mouth agape with a theatrical scream, or bled the last drops of her imaginary depleted veins, like the dry pipes of the school drinking fountain, from imaginary gashed-open wrists. Could it be, Mary Louise wonders, that this was our way of being glad to be alive together?

Mary Louise steps over the body of a blackbird and remembers her mother's warning: the end is near. But she believes that endings are less grandiose than her mother suggests, that the real danger and the real surprises are in the world's simple things, the things that seem safe and normal, the way strangers in stories entice with candy, the way a dull blade cuts the deepest. Mary Louise rubs at the cut on her leg where she nicked it last night before the birds fell. She senses that the world will end slowly, that it has been ending for a long time, that part of it, in fact, is already gone. Gone. And this very moment, now: gone. Now: gone.

There have been no ceremonies for the things Mary Louise has lost: that bit of flesh now sliced from her thigh, the familiar scruff of her father's chin. And those days, Mary Louise thinks, when we danced in the yard in slippers damp with earth, in skirts that our mothers did not look at with their eyebrows creased or their lips flat with disapproval.

TIFF

Tiff, pudgy and squishy, cheeks like a chipmunk's, the outcast of the week. Tiff covets Mary Louise's blinding yellow skirt with an energy that can't be contained, not even in a body big as Tiff's.

Tiff walks home with her little brother, half a block ahead of her best friends, her only friends. Occasionally she hears their witchy laughter in the distance, and she whips around, frantic, and tries to examine the back of her jeans, to take herself in in one critical glance. There are so many things that could be wrong, so many things wrong with Tiff. Her body is heavy, lethargic, uncooperative. Lately, she feels always half asleep. *Iron deficiency anemia*, the doctor said. He had spoken to Tiff's mother instead of to Tiff herself. *This girl is losing too much blood.*

Tiff has been out of these friends' circle before and knows to bide her time before attempting reentry. Still, she panics at the possibility that this time she could be out for good, alone. But Tiff has been the dead one resurrected, and she holds on for more. We used to play the strangest games, she remembers. We used to play funeral, dragging each other up the stairs of our houses and burying each other in our bathtubs. Tiff remembers playing dead, how soothing it was, what a luxury to relax her limbs and close her eyes and feel herself being borne through space by the others. She was weightless, then, her skin summer brown. Two of us held me by the ankles, Tiff remembers, and one of us held me by the wrists, and I went up, up, Mary Louise singing a hymn and the others pretending to cry, or maybe really crying. They laid Tiff in the tub, her hands crossed at her chest and her feet smashed against the watermarked faucet. They said solemn words about what a great girl she'd been. Tiff can't remember those words, now, but she remembers the soft feeling of the blanket they spread over her just after Mary Louise crossed herself, crossed Tiff, and laid a tiny pink soap in the shape of a rose, plucked from a wicker bathroom basket, at Tiff's chest. Tiff remembers the waxy texture of the soap, its ridges into which she dug her fingernails.

She would like to crawl back into Mary Louise's bathtub and sleep there forever, small and flat with rose-scented wax beneath the crescents of her nails. What a good, nice, beautiful girl she had been. How many lives she had touched. How profoundly she was missed.

We used to have so much fun, Tiff thinks. And now—now, we hate me.

"Did you ever hear about the president who was so fat he got stuck in his bathtub?" she asks her brother.

"No," he says.

"There was this president," Tiff says. "He was so fat he got stuck in his bathtub in the White House. They had to lift him out with a crane."

Her brother asks, "How did they get the crane into the White House?"

"I don't know," Tiff says. "That's not the point."

Tiff isn't sure what the point is, but she knows that this story has everything in the world to do with her. Everything in the world has to do with her, and no one understands. She knows that she is immobile and too large. She knows that suddenly her insides seem to be leaving her at an alarming rate—too much blood—at the same time that the outside is coming in, stretching, expanding her. She knows that the ring her mother bought her for her last birthday—amethyst, her birthstone—no longer wants to slide over her knuckle, that she used to wear it on her middle finger but now wears it on her ring finger, the middle one too huge, too horrifyingly, hideously, monstrously enormous to fit inside that inflexible hoop of gold.

Tiff's mother gave her the ring in February because, she said, Tiff was getting big enough to have nice things. Big enough. Tiff recalls standing with her mother by a glass case full of gold and silver and a spectrum of gems, her mother pointing at a cluster of regal purple stones set in shining metal: *Choose one*. Her mother's fingernail against the glass, so pink.

Tiff's mother has gold legs and glossy painted fingernails like hard candy. Tiff thinks of eating her mother's pink fingernails, one by one.

She thinks of letting the nails, smooth pink candy slices, rest on her tongue and slowly dissolve, or of grinding them with her teeth. Strawberry flavored and sweet. Her mouth waters. Tiff bites her own nails down to almost nothing.

There are her fingers, her nails ragged-edged and too short; there is her body too big, too tired; there is her little brother walking next to her humming something Tiff doesn't recognize, a song from school that he accompanies with exaggerated hand motions.

Tiff bats at her brother's head. "Stop that," she says, "you look retarded." She wiggles and yanks the gold band at the base of her finger. She pictures her mother, gold, pink, kicking, punching, and jumping. When Tiff was little, she and her brother used to accompany their mother to the aerobics classes she led at the Y. They'd sit back to back under a table eating strawberry fruit snacks and laughing at the fat ladies in the back row heaving and rippling. Tiff blushes. She has seen her mother standing still, cool and statuesque, plenty of times, like on the day she put her pink nail to the glass and told Tiff she was big enough to choose. But in Tiff's mind her mother is always moving. Cardio! she shouts. Get that blood pumping. She springs back and forth in her side-to-side warm-up bounce. She jogs, gold and pink, feet on springs. Kicks and punches.

Tiff twists and pulls the ring up over her knuckle. *Big enough, big enough, too much blood.* And she hurls the ring into the sunlight, she launches it into the birdless sky.

For a second as the sun catches the gold, Tiff feels free. Then she hears the metallic clink of the ring against the pavement somewhere (where?) and is hit with a renewed disgust with herself, a shock, a dizzying embarrassment at this display of destructive emotion, like when a man in a movie punched an angry hole in his bedroom wall, then stood still and stunned rubbing his bloodied knuckles, like when a child in a supermarket threw an epic tantrum over a package of gum, then looked around to find no one listening.

LANNIE

When Lannie sees the sun glinting off a shining speck in the sky, she thinks that maybe Mary Louise's mother is right. Maybe we are on the cusp of something, she thinks, something big. The sudden flash of gold in the air seems like an image out of a dream.

Lannie is going to be a writer someday; in fact, she is something of a writer already. Ever since she learned to write, she has kept a journal next to her bed in which she has ritualistically recorded the details of her dreams. It was her mother's idea. Each day at the breakfast table, Lannie's mother asks her for her dreams as if they are tickets or currency and quietly stirs brown sugar into oatmeal and scribbles notes in shorthand while Lannie narrates. When Lannie can't remember, she makes things up. She spoons oatmeal from her bowl and wedges of grapefruit from the rind and watches her mother's eyebrows move as she relates and fabricates. This moment at the breakfast table is Lannie's favorite part of the day, her mother listening so attentively. And it thrills her to flip through the book by her bed when she first wakes up, the Book of Lannie, full of metaphors and flourishes. Though she is unsure of what her words mean or what they say about her, the writer, the dreamer, Lannie likes the way they sound in her head when she reads. She practices different handwritings every few days, looking for one that best fits her dreams, that fits her.

In this morning's dream, Lannie and her friends were gathered at a party at Jane's house. From the ceiling fan in Jane's big living room there hung a piñata shaped like a person; it hung so that Lannie could not see its face. All at once, she and her friends took up baseball bats and swung them, crazed, battering the piñata from all sides, flecks of tissue and crepe paper chipping and flaking from its shell until it burst like a bomb and out of it, instead of candy, poured shrapnel made of ripe, luscious fruit.

This was where the memory of the dream ended and the lines in Lannie's journal trailed off in points of ellipsis. At the breakfast table, while her mother's pen moved rapidly over the page, Lannie popped a piece of grapefruit into her mouth. Perhaps, she thought, she dreamed the beating of the piñata to the rhythm of the blackbirds striking the roof over her sleeping head. Perhaps the line between dream and reality was really that blurry.

"And then?" Lannie's mother looked up, pen poised, expecting more.

"And then," Lannie said, imagining, "a giant rhinoceros burst into the house and left a rhinoceros-shaped hole in the wall. I made a lasso from the stems of daisies in a vase and swung it through the air and looped it around the rhino's neck. The rhino left pulpy fruit tracks on the white carpet, and when I reeled it in, it lifted me into the air and tossed me in circles, around, around, till I woke up, all dizzy."

Lannie's mother put down her pen and raised an eyebrow. She popped a round, white pill into her mouth and swallowed. Lannie watched as she reviewed her notes.

"Well, Mom," she said after a while, "am I normal?"

Her mother looked up, surprised by the question. She poured Lannie another glass of apple juice. "Oh, honey," she said, brushing Lannie's cheek with the back of her hand and then picking up the newspaper. "There is no such thing."

After a moment, glasses on the tip of her nose, Lannie's mother read aloud about the birds and the snowy parking lots. "Mass accidental suicide," she read, taking up her pen again and twirling it between a finger and a thumb. "When all of a sudden there's light all over the place, they don't know which way is up anymore." And Lannie could practically see gears turning in her mother's head, analyzing those birds, their fantasies, their latent avian longings.

Lannie pictured her mother's words in her own latest handwriting style, thin with pointy letters like the turrets of a castle. She pictured them in pencil on a clean, lined page. Even now, hours later, walking home, she feels them in her chest. *Oh, honey, oh, honey, there is no such thing.*

Though Lannie's mother reads minds, or at least comes close, piecing together fragments of dreams and dialogue to arrive at diagnoses and interpretations, Lannie is sure that her mother does not understand her. What *do* her dreams mean, and why does she dream them?

It gets lonely having dreams like puzzles that no one else has ever had, a world inside the blackness of your head that is yours and yours only. Lannie wants to share the dreams that form in her head during the day, the conscious ones, the questions, without fear of rejection or betrayal or analysis. Lannie wants everything out in the open, on the page, in words, in answers. Lannie wants no secrets. But everyone has them: herself, her friends with their crushes and their venomous gossip, her mother who spends evenings behind her closed bedroom door watching *The Bodyguard* or listening to Carly Simon and crying but in the mornings looks so fresh, her hand so steady stirring hot oatmeal and popping her little round pill. Is it always so hard to decipher oneself? When Lannie was little, she dreamed up a twin, Frannie, who accompanied her in her lonely moments, but as she grew older, she let the fictional twin dissipate. When Lannie was little, she and Mary Louise had fit together into a single flannel sleeping bag, snuggled together at a sleepover, a movie that Lannie has long since forgotten flickering on the TV screen as they chattered and huddled in that small space. We're too big for that now, Lannie thinks. We are too secretive.

A few streets down, on the corner, Lannie and her friends spot the homeless man who hangs around the neighborhood, shaggy-haired, with his plastic bag of trash. His only possession: a makeshift wooden flute, hippie-sounding, which has sometimes roused Lannie from her dreams.

"There he is," Lannie says to the others, and plugs her nose dramatically.

"Scum!" Mary Louise shrieks. "Trash!"

About a block from where the man stands, mumbling, flute in hand, Lannie and the others come across Tiff sniffling, blubbering, a sheen of snot above her quivering lip. Traitor.

Jane asks, "What's your problem?"

"My ring," Tiff sobs. "My ring!"

Lannie and her friends look at each other, roll their eyes.

"What'd you take it off for?" asks Mary Louise.

Tiff just sobs and sobs. Lannie despises Tiff for her sloppy body; she seethes at Tiff's comment about her—what was it? It was infuriating. And it hurt, a real hurt that Lannie remembers and relives poignantly, a hurt that perhaps propelled last night's dream of beating and batting and bursting. At the same time Lannie remembers, once, eons ago, playing a duet on Tiff's piano, Tiff's right hand, Lannie's left, making music. *Traitor, loser*. The loveliest music.

"All *right*," Lannie says, "We'll help you if you'll just shut up, okay? Will you shut up?"

Tiff nods. Lovely music, slender fingers over ivory keys, Tiff's mother standing by in pink sweatpants, a metronome ticking. Is it a memory or a dream? A dream or fiction? Is there a difference? Lannie can't be sure. Whatever it is, though, it feels entirely real.

JANE

While the others scour the sidewalks for Tiff's ring, darting into the street between passing cars, Jane scuffs her feet along the pavement and thinks of music—angry, glorious, furious music.

She has so many things she'd like to say; she envies Lannie her gift for words, her As in English, her journal full of dreams, like she envies Tiff her amethyst ring. But Jane's words, unlike Lannie's, come out stiff and bland, so she chooses music, her yet unformed band. There is still the problem of lyrics, but Jane is working on these.

For her birthday this year, Jane would like a guitar and a voice. An electric guitar and a voice that projects. She wants to sing a sad song, and she also wants to shout, so she'll design a song that will marry the two. A song with which she'll sing a truth so true. She is searching for rhymes and plastering them together, rhymes in the sun and in cloudy weather.

She pokes at a bird with the toe of her shoe. It feels startlingly rubbery. Wings askew. Jane decides to write a song for this bird, a song that she will drag out of the depths of herself with her electric guitar and that she will sing in a black gown, her eyes deep, doomy pits ringed with shadow.

"What's that noise?" she hears Lannie ask. Jane hears the noise, too, a noise like wind in a tunnel. Like many small beads in a funnel. She shrugs and pokes the bird again, imagines herself shrouded in black feathers.

Jane is in no hurry to get home, though she doesn't particularly care to be here either, looking for someone else's ring. At home her stepmother will accuse her of sulking, will remind her to stand up straight. You've got it pretty good, princess, her tidy little stepmother likes to say. Jane resents the misnomer; her stepmother has got it all wrong, with her Martha Stewart magazines and her collection of picture frames and useless knickknacks with inspirational sayings inscribed on them: "Dance like no one is watching." "Shoot for the moon; even if you miss, you'll land among the stars."

Jane is no wordsmith herself, but she knows that these platitudes are pathetic.

At school Jane would like to hide, and at home, while her stepmother tells her that the good old days are here and now, that she should live every day like it's her last, she would like to hide as well. When Jane is alone, when no one is watching, she does not dance; she has taken to lying on her bed, staring blankly at the ceiling, rhyming, in a kind of trance. At school, Jane clings to her friends for shelter, lets them wall her in. She finds it hard to speak in the company of others, except these dull old friends she's known forever but who, even while familiar, she recognizes as amorphous, inexpressible. Her favorite part of the school day is the half hour Ms. Kendall allows the class to read uninterrupted, during which Jane slips beneath her desk, into a hollow place, an open vampire book spread before her face. Ms. Kendall keeps a hamster, Buster, in the classroom, which she allows one student each day to hold during the free-reading session, but Jane hates Buster and his disgusting furry body. She imagines pitching Buster out the window. She imagines little Busters raining from the sky to their deaths like these blackbirds.

What is wrong with her? Jane's stepmother asks her father, about Jane. Jane bookmarks her novels with a photograph of her mother from the seventies, holding a sign at some protest, surrounded by other women glazed over with determination, brave and outraged and beautiful. The sign is turned sideways, and Jane can't read the words, but she can read the intensity in her mother's eyes. Whatever her mother was protesting, Jane is protesting it too. She has rubbed the photograph back and forth in her fingers so many times they are engraved with paper cuts, with threadlike scars.

Friends are forever, Jane's stepmother says. You've got to have friends. Jane's stepmother brings casseroles to Mary Louise's mother, sits beside her on the couch, speaking gently.

Jane struggles to speak gently like this, or to speak at all. Jane would like to scream. She enjoys beating the punching bag her father has hung in the basement. She beats it sometimes in his big punching gloves and sometimes with her bare knuckles: bam! slam! But Jane knows, on some level, that her stepmother is right: she needs these friends, though they are sinister and a bore.

"Well," she hears Mary Louise shout at Tiff, "which *way* did you throw it?" And, a few seconds later, "What do you mean you don't know?"

They would make, Jane thinks, lovely backup singers. At the very least, without them, who would fill the seats at her show?

Of course, she knows, deep down, that there will be no show. No show, no go. She rubs the tips of her fingers together, feels the grooved scars there.

Jane doesn't notice the homeless man until she hears Lannie shout her name, then turns and finds that he is upon her, his knotty hair, his torn plastic bag. He holds out his hand, and in it, something gleams in the sun. Jane opens her mouth and finds that she is screaming. She imagines the gleaming thing a blade, like the ones parents check Tootsie Rolls for on Halloween. In the split second between the moment the scream begins and the moment it ends, she imagines this blade slicing her, gashing her open, slashing her veins and severing her tongue. She imagines her mouth filling with blood, and just like that, the scream is over. She reacts the way she does in her father's basement, before the punching bag: she strikes, hard and fast, and then she feels a girl (she isn't sure which one) grab her, and they turn and run. Jane spots Tiff, a blur, and grabs her, too, and she is running full speed and has traveled several blocks before it occurs to her that the object in the man's hand, that thing catching the sun, was gold.

We run as fast as we can even though we don't know if the man is following us. We run in shoes that squeeze our feet, with backpacks full of heavy, jostling books. We pump our knees and run and run; we hurdle over birds' bodies. The sound that Lannie pointed out grows louder, but we run on because we are as uncertain about what might be behind us as we are of what's to come. We fall back, we pull ahead, we gain and lose ground on each other. The noise gets louder and the curbs become suddenly wet; we splash through puddles. We half forget why we are running, and we are not sure whether this is a race that anyone will win, or whether we want it to be.

We round a familiar corner. Around it, we find an unfamiliar world: water exploding out of the street, spraying high into the air, shooting into the sun, choppy waves frothing at the base of the spring, rippling streams rushing down the pavement.

We collide with each other as we stop short and watch the geyser surge into the branches of overhanging trees, spray power lines and darken telephone poles. Someone cries out; it doesn't matter who—our voices are indistinguishable and muted by the noise. Our feet and socks are soaked, and mist gathers in our hair and beads on our skin. Everything is inverted: water in the sky, birds on the ground. We reach out, and somehow, our hands find each other. We stand like this, fused like a chain, for a long time, because it seems less perplexing to be perplexed together.

On the other side of the strange fountain, through a spectrum of color that radiates from the spray, we can make out some shadowy forms moving, running, splashing. Vague faces in mist. We wonder if they are girls like us, girls with new shoes ruined and hands touching.

As we watch, shoulder to shoulder, a police officer approaches, materializing through the whiteness. This street is closed, the officer says. Broken water main. He motions to the gushing water, our soggy feet.

"Where you girls headed?" he asks.

We look around as if we just woke up, the water and the sun in our eyes. We try to reconstruct a normal walk home, try to recall that place on the route we thought we'd memorized, that point at which the road forks, at which our paths split and we separate.

Fake Mermaid

Sometimes she feels like a third gender—preferring primary colors to pastels, the radio to singing. At least she's all mermaid: never gets tired of swimming, hates the thought of socks.
—MATTHEA HARVEY, "The Straightforward Mermaid"

THEY WERE packing up the car to drive to Madison, where Luna had a mermaid gig, when Noah said, "I think maybe it's time we started thinking about talking more seriously about possibly having a baby."

He was laying out Luna's twenty-five pound silicone tail on the back seat with a tenderness that testified to his parental potential, folding over the limp points of its wide, ornate monofin, stuffing a pool noodle into the scaled bodice to preserve its form. The tail was custom fit to Luna's body, covered in iridescent orange and gold scales, and it had cost fifteen hundred dollars—Noah's dollars. A web developer and designer who worked mostly from home, he could afford what Luna—part-time mermaid and author of two failed novels—could not, helping her chisel away at her mountain of student loan debt, springing for her tail and, two weeks ago, an engagement ring that she had somehow not seen coming and that she twisted off in her sleep, her first night wearing it, waking up in a panic to find the stone sleep-shoved beneath her pillow.

Luna stuffed her inflatable clam shell into the trunk, then climbed into the passenger seat. She wore swimsuit bottoms underneath a pair of gray yoga pants and a copper clamshell bra with a string of fake pearls twisted through one strap. She flipped down the mirror, touched up her waterproof eye shadow. Brushed mascara onto lashes, combing out clumps. Suggested they go for lobster rolls after the party, changing the subject, evading. She was hungry already, and thirsty, but it was an hour's drive to their destination—the home of a woman named Vida Heathershorne who had booked the Mermaid Luna online for her daughter's fifth birthday party—and her lower half would be sheathed in skintight silicone for another hour and a half once they got there, so she did not drink.

She unfolded the paper copy of Vida Heathershorne's reservation and read: daughter named Ava Rose, house with an in-ground pool on Long Island Sound, nine children RSVP'd. A typical gig, no special requests, paid in full. Luna would be presented to Ava Rose on the inflatable clam shell, would swim with her and the other children, apply glitter tattoos to their arms and legs, and hand out sparkly mesh pouches in which the children would collect plastic gemstones that Luna scattered on the pool's tiled stairs and on the floor of its shallow end.

For a while, she and Noah drove in chummy silence through a chaos of green foliage. This was what Luna had always loved best about being with Noah: the way they could share silence. They rarely argued; he was thoroughly housetrained, and he cooked and cleaned. With him, there was none of the combat and debate that had defined Luna's last serious relationship (college, a woman named Shay, a volcanic four years of heat and periodic eruption), just smooth swimming. The ring had seemed to glide onto her finger without effort or ceremony, as if deposited there by the tide, and another woman in Luna's position, a better woman, might certainly have declared herself ready for a family.

Noah tried again. "Seriously, Lu. Let's make a baby."

Luna winced. *Make a baby*—she pictured an infant mashed together from papier-mâché or molded from a heap of sweaty, dead-gray clay, misshapen, grotesque. Or an origami baby, all sharp edges and potential paper cuts, or one sewn, Frankensteinish, and stuffed with down and cotton like a quilt, stray innards escaping white and hairy through holes in fabric. He knew she disliked the expression, that and the word "trying" when applied to sex; she had no interest in effortful intercourse, and she'd told him so. When they met, four years ago, she had unloaded her eccentricities onto him, and he had accepted them gladly. But he was older, forty to her thirty-one, his biological clock set to another time zone. That the idea of reproductive sex discomfited her so made Luna wonder, not for the first time, if she'd gotten herself wrong—if she did not belong with a man.

But no—she loved Noah. And not just platonically; she desired him; she loved his body, the six determined little hairs that populated his otherwise bare chest, his odd brand of humble vanity, the approving nod he gave each morning after inspecting himself in the bathroom mirror. He was not one to brag and would never confess to the steady, low-volume sense of satisfaction she knew he derived from his appearance except for a few stray, understatedly arrogant observations in dressing rooms: "I guess I look really good." She loved his strange, near narcoleptic gift for sleep, how he'd glide out of consciousness in the oddest places—on a rock-strewn shore with his head on a block of granite, on the chair swing ride at the fair. She loved their quiet, companionable rapport, how it extended into the marine world she loved, how he'd go anywhere with her, on land or underwater; she loved that he dove with her, off the New England coast and on trips to tropical waters, spearing lionfish with a pole spear in scuba gear, reaching out with a gloved hand to pass her a perfect sand dollar. Part of her had even come to love the sense of contented boredom she'd developed at home with him in recent months and of which she became conscious one day, sitting at her window watching him mow the lawn, back and forth, back and forth, back and forth, the same number of strides each way. Perhaps, she thought, this was happiness, this pleasantish, yellow-winged numbness, and she should catch it and cage it to keep it from flying away. Or perhaps it was death, creeping toward her, stealthy hypnotist—that back and forth, back and forth, back and forth lulling her to sleep.

"I know, I know," he said now, "you don't like the phrase. But what about the idea?"

Luna closed her eyes and pretended to be asleep, though they'd been open when he spoke to her, and she knew he knew. He had sprung these questions on her before; it was his right. She had given back maybes, and he'd dropped the subject. What had made it rise again? What was different now? She knew: the ring.

"You're quiet today," he said, and reached over and cupped her left clam shell. She shrugged, crossed her legs, leaned close to the window glass and watched her reflection there, how it seemed to take in everything she passed, the green world blurring, passing through her like water. She opened her mouth and watched it rush in.

In Madison, they crawled along the winding, Soundside road at twenty miles an hour, passing the Beach Club, families in white tennis shoes walking along the shoulderless road with the handles of rackets poking out of backpacks, couples on tandem bikes pedaling in sync. Past the Beach Club the Sound reached right up to the seawall along the road, the water sun-spotted and crowded with boats. Noah took a left off Middle Beach Road and stopped in front of a massive house hugged by a stately wraparound porch and sided in whitewashed clapboard. Expensive-looking cars crowded the street and lawn, and a single parking spot stood available in a paved parking area behind the house, a hand-painted sign marking it "Reserved for Mermaid!" Beyond the parking area, a gate in a literal white picket fence stood open, leading to the pool, the woodwind din of children's voices. The fence was draped with a colorful banner—LET'S SHELLEBRATE!—made of cutout letters dangling from breeze-blown twine, pink-orange scallop shells standing in for the apostrophe and the dot on the exclamation mark.

"Can you believe people live like this?" Noah marveled at the house with a naked admiration that embarrassed Luna. He took off for the pool to meet Vida Heathershorne, plug in the inflatable clam shell, and receive instructions for where Luna should change, and she knew he would praise the house to its owner, earnest, unbegrudgingly deferential.

"It's two women," he said when he returned. "The parents."

He always pointed this out to her, as if she'd want to identify all the other women out there capable of loving other women so that she might high-five them. Luna might not have been enough of a lesbian for her ex, Shay, but at times, she had been too much of one for Noah, who in the early days of their relationship used to ask her obsessively whether she thought that women they encountered—on sidewalks, at neighboring tables in restaurants, on beaches, in shopping malls—were attractive. She had replied that she could ask him the same question but didn't, and he'd responded, with a shrug, It's different.

And sometimes he would pull her sexual history into their love-making, panting out references to her past acts and partners. Underneath his insecurity, it seemed, was a half-formed fetish that he could acknowledge only within a narrow, five- or ten-minute window before climax, when he was a safe enough distance from his pre- and post-coital standards of decorum to ignore them. She let him have it.

Vida Heathershorne offered them access to a small backyard shed where they went now, Noah carrying Luna's tail over his shoulder. Inside, he spread a yoga mat and an old towel on the floor, and Luna went to work putting on her tail. She slipped on a pair of neoprene socks, hating the way she knew they'd feel once damp with sweat and water inside her fin, but deeming them necessary to prevent blisters. She lubed her legs with coconut oil, folded down the top of the tail, and sat on the yoga mat, pulling the tight material up to her knees, then her thighs, the silicone sticking and sucking. She lay on her back and pulled and wormed herself into the tail, shimmying its top up to her belly button. Ten minutes later, she was finished, sweating, and she lay still for a moment, recovering, before Noah offered his hand and pulled her vertical. She could stand but not walk, feet in fin. He counted to three and she gave a little hop, and he lifted her into his arms and carried her toward the pool.

"Remember to smile," he said into her ear. He reminded her at every appearance, ever since one of Luna's clients complained to him that Luna had not smiled often or enthusiastically enough while working at her child's party.

"I just thought the mermaid was a little . . . morose," the woman had grumbled when she paid Noah, and he refunded her a small percentage of Luna's pay. Later, Luna and Noah argued about the refund, and about his executive decision to issue it, and it was still a sore spot between them—how quickly he had conceded, how readily he'd agreed to the regulation of Luna's emotional expression, the movements of her facial muscles, the choreography of her performance of piscine glee. For her, mermaiding was about the swimming, about fantasy, about forgetting her body. That children should be present to witness her transcendent transfiguration was purely an accident of capitalism. She'd done some adult parties, some mermaid bartending, pouring champagne poolside, but had sworn it off after a few too many uncomfortable encounters and lewd, inebriated inquiries. ("Baby, where's the hole in that tail?") She enjoyed her status as sexy but sexless, alluring but unfuckable, but she preferred to contemplate it in contented solitude, not to have it up for discussion by strangers who found it maddening. What enjoyment she took from working with kids stemmed largely from the fact that they did not think too much about it.

This party seemed straight out of a parenting magazine, an effervescent onslaught of energy and color, its aquatic theme carried out with an almost pathological diligence. Kids in swimsuits wore sequined party hats in the shape of mermaid tails. On the pool deck, shaded by an enormous tilted umbrella, a table was clothed in neon pink, draped with nylon fishing net and loaded with treats: tiny cookie sandwiches made to look like clam shells, open-mouthed and filled with purple frosting and silvery-white icing pearls; a sand castle cake with frosting coated in cinnamon sugar and studded with decorative white chocolate seashells; clear bowls full of gummy fish; sticks of pink, purple, and orange rock candy in a jar labeled Coral. And for the adults, pasta salad made of shell noodles with wilted spinach and arugula "seaweed." Luna took all this in as Noah carried her past, swiping a gummy fish from a bowl and sucking it, sweet and pleasantly sun-softened, melting in the heat despite the shade. Tucked out of sight between two hydrangea bushes, a bubble machine pumped furiously, sending a steady stream of soapy orbs into the air around Luna's constantly-inflating shell, its motor humming. Children chased the bubbles, crazed, amid their parents' cries not to run by the pool, popping them and spattering the pavement with oily, rainbowed puddles, then flocking toward Luna as they one by one caught sight of her—a mermaid! A real, live mermaid!

Noah placed Luna in the blown-up clam shell's hollow center, on a white plastic stool like a giant ice cube, and the children bombarded her with questions she knew she'd have to answer once she was comfortably situated, autographing party favors in purple glitter pen—What does seaweed taste like? Can you do magic? How long can you stay out of water? Then the crowd of children parted, and the birthday girl, Ava Rose, suntanned and glittering in a tiny pink bikini top and a ruffled, metallic green bottom bearing a pattern of scales, a sort of mini mermaid skort, was brought forward, flanked on either side by two women: on the left, a stranger, hair prematurely gray with a silver streak in front in movie-star sunglasses and a wide-brimmed straw hat, body tall and slim in a pinstriped romper; and on the right, hatless in bland khaki shorts, Birkenstocks and a loose-fitting navy scoop-neck tank, bra straps showing, arms freckled as if sprayed with windblown grains of sand, squinting in the sun, was Shay. Luna's first love.

Oh God, oh God—no word for her horror, no fairy tale twisted enough to capture it. Ava Rose held on to her mothers' hands, Vida Heathershorne fawning over the Mermaid Luna, oblivious—how shiny her hair, how sparkly her tail!—and Noah looked on from a distance, oblivious, and Shay turned red as a steamed lobster, and Luna smiled, the muscles in her face trembling and resisting, head full of echoes, heart racing, resting her hands on her scaled lap so the shaking wouldn't show, and a child pushed past Ava Rose, slapped a hand down onto Luna's tail, and demanded, "How do you pee?"

They'd met at Fairfield, where Shay was a sullen prelaw legacy student, young for a freshman, having skipped a grade in high school, and Luna a first-generation tabula rasa with no major and no clue. As a student, Shay was driven, disciplined to the point of rigidity, and given to a kind of scholarly self-flagellation; she could accept nothing less than perfection from herself or from the rest of the world. As such, she was perpetually disappointed in them both, and her resulting rage was general, constant, and red-hot.

Luna had been drawn to that rage, in awe of Shay, who knew where she stood on everything, who ranted about conflicts in the Middle East and the Darfur genocide and systemic racism and patriarchy, and who sometimes wept in her sleep, overcome. Her dreams were littered with visions of failure and tragedy, from forgotten exams and missed first days of class to dropped bombs, and she slept shallowly, thrashing about, clobbering Luna with flailing limbs. Luna had loved pressing placating thumbs into the knots in Shay's tense shoulders every evening and morning, kneading. Shay was her compass, and Luna felt special, skilled, for having drilled through the igneous shell of her anger and into the magmatic softness beneath.

Their senior year, they moved together, along with a few fellow students, into an off-campus house two blocks from Long Island Sound. Luna got a job making lobster rolls at the Lazy Lobster, living off leftover bisque and packets of oyster crackers, and Shay began applying to law schools, and they adopted a puppy that Shay later took with her to New Haven, a smash-faced fart factory who slept curled at the foot of their bed, snoring. After three blissful years, their final one together was tempestuous, with things beginning to unravel when Luna confessed an attraction to one of the men in the house, and Shay dug out that old, dull blade of a line—choose a side—and stabbed Luna with it.

They had both been surprised to discover that Luna could fight back. No more Shay's starry-eyed understudy, she had watched and learned; she had reshaped herself in Shay's image. Their fights were long and strenuous, their arguments sophisticated—Shay the student of law, Luna the student of Shay—and the list of charges leveled between sides was lengthy and ever-growing: Luna's wandering eye and fluid sense of self (which Shay conceived of as noncommittal shallowness), her lack of ambition, her obsession with words and tendency to prioritize language over action; Shay's domineering streak, her dogmatic purism on matters of sexuality and love (which Luna held was drably conventional, reductive). Their troubles peaked during an argument on a friend's boat, when Luna, incensed, exhausted, dove from the deck and into the Sound in sundress and shoes.

She had taken a diving class and knew some of what to expect, though without gear or a plan the experience was far from any she'd had before. She had begun to build up her CO_2 tolerance, to train her body not to give in to the panic-inducing accumulation of carbon dioxide in her system. She had learned to manage and manipulate the desperation of long-held breath, to let her body find oxygen elsewhere, accessing myoglobin in muscle, hemoglobin in blood. In her diving class she had submerged her face in a bowl of ice water while wearing a heart monitor to activate her mammalian dive reflex, and felt her heart rate plummet. Without weights or fins, she knew, she would not sink too far, but she had not prepared for her dive properly, lacking equipment and patience, going overboard in a moment of passion. She shed her sandals and kicked until she couldn't anymore, felt a current carry her, grew afraid. Lightheadedness set in. Her diaphragm contracted in desperate hiccups. She kept her eyes closed, as if by doing so she could trick her body into believing she was still above water, that there was no need to panic.

When she came up she almost sank from fatigue and fear. She could hear Shay screaming on the boat. Shay took off one shoe, then the other, and threw them into the Sound; they plopped stupidly, one several yards in front of Luna, the other several to the right, and sank. Someone tossed Luna a buoy and she dog-paddled weakly toward it, grabbed on, and was reeled back to the boat like a caught tuna, shaking, miserable, exhilarated, and alive. She rode back to shore in Shay's arms, her head against Shay's chest, the boat's owner apoplectic. At the time, she thought her desperate act could save them, and for a few days, they clung to each other in gratitude and fear, afraid to move, but the dive had been a death throe rather than a turning point, and once she recognized this, Luna let go. She was not a social media user, and they had not kept in touch in the nine years since Shay left for Yale Law School and Luna took a copyediting job in Hartford, then moved to Boston for her MFA before returning to Connecticut with Noah. She had heard from a mutual friend several years back that Shay had gotten engaged to someone she met at Yale, but she had not asked for details.

Now here she was, the woman, Vida Heathershorne—the good lesbian, the lawyer, the high-achieving WASP on holiday, moving through children and parents handing out cups of blue Jell-O, Shay pacing in the background, back and forth, back and forth. Luna finished greeting the children, and Noah lifted her and perched her on the edge of the pool.

"What's wrong?" he whispered. "You're pale as a ghost."

But words wouldn't come, her tongue wouldn't work, and what could she say if it did? She shook her head—nothing's wrong—and slid into the water gratefully, as if it were opaque and could conceal her. Children belly flopped and cannonballed into the pool around her, but for one sweet second, she kept her eyes squeezed shut and imagined them away—imagined pool as lagoon, cement walls as atoll, swapped seawater for city water, plankton and brine for chlorine. Then she felt a child grab onto her, and she opened her eyes, put on her smile, felt the chlorine burn. Her vision blurred. She waved to the shapes and streaks of the children underwater, in goggles to protect their eyes from the chlorine that stung her own; she blew bubble rings, she turned underwater spins, she rolled her body in a wave and propelled herself across the pool, the power starting in her core and hips and flowing down her legs, through her tail. She stood on her hands and let her tail flip up out of the water, her ankles throbbing from the weight of the fin. She smiled underwater and she smiled when she surfaced, at last, having mastered the art of rising from the pool with her head tilted back so that her hair was sleek and sightly and not a tangled mess before her face.

Up for breath, she studied Vida. Could Shay be happy here, with her, living in this fairy tale? Noah was nothing like Shay, but Vida was nothing like Luna, either; it did not seem to Luna any more implausible that she should have fallen for Noah than that Shay should have fallen for this breezy, privileged, party-planning extrovert. But she could remove gender from the equation, consider chemistry only in terms of temperament and personality; Shay couldn't. Seeing Luna flirt with their male housemate all those years ago, Shay had been enraged, felt betrayed—not just because Luna could want someone else, but because she could want a man. Ever a purist, Shay accused Luna of taking advantage of her, playing at gay in order to be able to see and sell herself as "interesting"—as if Shay and the time they'd spent together had been only some great experiment, cynically conducted, and not the greatest, most transformative love of Luna's life. At other times Shay went the opposite route, belittling Luna's attraction to the man, calling it a game, insisting that through it, Luna was attempting to quash or deny her homosexuality out of fear of living with its social consequences.

Gay or straight, reality or fantasy, woman or fish: Choose a side. She could see Shay watching her from a shaded chair by the table of clam cookies, fanning herself with a sealed birthday card, and her humiliation was a lead weight. It had not been true that Luna had no ambition, only that it had been private, and that it had not come to fruition. She had imagined Shay picking one of her books off a shelf and stroking its cover with awe and approval. She had imagined critics praising her fresh, bold voice; she had imagined that people would care what she had to say and that she was capable of saying it well, and she had been wrong. She sat on one of the pool's shallow steps, children hanging from her arms and stroking her tail, and felt herself begin again to work the ring on and off of her finger, twisting and pulling and pushing it back on, fighting off a leg cramp from pointing her toes for so long, a feeling like knives in her calves.

Noah handed her her box of fake jewels. Then, to kill time, he approached Shay and struck up a conversation, still oblivious, out of Luna's earshot. Her heart hiccupped. She propped an elbow on the side of the pool as the kids clustered around her like hungry minnows, and she ordered them to the edge of the pool to wait while she scattered the gemstones through the water, one eye on Noah and Shay. When she was finished the children dove and shouted all around her, shrieking with demented joy, fighting over pieces of plastic, and she twisted her ring, twisted, pulled, twisted, until it slipped from her fingers and onto the floor of the pool.

When she dove to retrieve it, distracted, distraught, she bonked heads with a towheaded girl who immediately began to wail. She tried to comfort the girl, smiling, eyes darting back and forth between the floor of the pool where her diamond bounced and tumbled and the child's open-mouthed howls, her gullet like the long, slick body of an eel.

Vida and Shay rushed to placate the crying child. Vida helped her up out of the water, took her hand, and led her away toward the snack table. Luna studied Shay's legs and thought without trying of licking them, one at a time, bottom to top. A hot ache spread through her body. Shay was close enough to touch; Luna should say something, she knew. But what?

The breathless, goggled figure of Ava Rose bobbed up between them.

"Look what I got!" the girl gasped, panting. "Mommy, look!"

She grabbed the pool's edge, legs still kicking, hair matted, her pouch full of treasures cinched around her wrist, and held out a hand toward Shay. In her palm, twinkling, was Luna's engagement ring. Luna could see Noah in the distance, witnessing everything.

Shay bent and took the ring from Ava Rose. She examined it conspicuously, shamelessly, then closed it in her fist.

"I think that's Mermaid Luna's magic ring," she said. "We better give it back."

She slipped off her Birkenstocks and sat down, dipped her bare feet in the water. She held out her hand for Luna to collect the ring from her palm, now open like an oyster with the prize inside gleaming.

"Is that him?" she asked, tilting her head toward Noah. "He seems nice."

Luna managed a half smile. Her throat was dry and sore.

"Second thoughts, huh," Shay said. "Well, you'll land on your feet either way."

Ironic, under the circumstances. Luna propped her elbows poolside, slid the diamond back onto her finger, and looked down at her monofin meaningfully.

Shay smiled and kicked her feet, her lovely legs swinging, water rolling off her smooth skin like mercury. "I always envied you, you know. How you jumped off that boat because you'd had it with me. How you could just . . . swim away."

Luna stared through the slats in the white picket fence, past the yard and the road to the Sound beyond. A heavy cloud lurched over the sun, repainting the water, azure to iron. And with the change of light, she felt herself slip into the memory of another gray day, an afternoon at the shore, their first spring together. The tide had pushed up a wall of shells, and they walked along a narrow strip of beach at low tide intertwined, arms around hips and necks and shoulders like tangles of kelp, crunching shells beneath their feet, every now and then bending together to collect translucent orange jingle shells, the kind nicknamed mermaid's toenails. Senseless with love, mute and insulated, not feeling the cold wind that took their words when they tried to speak. Luna put her shells, paper-thin and sun-hued, in Shay's coat pockets, and Shay put hers in Luna's. Shay's pockets were warm caves at her waist, and Luna let her hands linger there, tingling.

That was the day they found the breast. Luna knelt to retrieve what she thought was a particularly vivid jingle shell, a more opaque orange than others of its kind, and found that it was slippery and spongy and had a strange kind of hump in its middle. A nipple. It was a prosthetic silicone breast form, washed up and buried to the nipple in a mound of shells. They passed it back and forth in cold hands, smooth and rubbery and realistic, its underside wrinkled, and made up stories about how it came to be lost, with Luna offering the explanation that it was a mermaid's breast.

"A mermaid's breast!" Shay cried, delighted, then, by Luna's every utterance. She wiped a clump of wet sand from the surface of the breast. Then she wound up and hurled it back into the Sound, to be swallowed, digested, and pushed out again, later.

"You are a delight," Shay said, pulling Luna's hands back into her pockets and wrapping her arms around her. "You are a dream." When she kissed Luna, their cold noses pressed against each other, and Shay pulled up the hood on her oversized jacket to cover both their heads, and the wind howled, and the tide rose and licked at their feet, and the shells rattled like coins in the banks of their pockets, and Shay kept repeating, looking at Luna like she'd just been born, like they'd both just been born, "Who are you? What are you? How can you be real?"

Oh, to just swim away. How could Shay have it all so wrong? Luna stared at the flat, steely bar of the Sound with a merperson's longing. How she'd love to kick forever toward that gray horizon, to become the foam on the crest of the waves. But first she would need someone—Noah, Shay—to lift her in their arms, to carry her limp and heavy like a sack of rice to the shore, deposit her on the sand, and then let go. Without legs, she could not get there on her own.

She felt a tap on her shoulder, followed by an impatient tug on her hair. She turned around. It was the birthday girl, upper body flopped over a pool noodle, wiggling a wormy little finger, beckoning Luna closer.

"I have to tell you something," said Ava Rose.

Luna leaned in, inspecting the girl, searching her face for signs of Shay—shape of lips, color of hair, curve of jaw—and finding none. Had she been in Shay's body, this child pinching a pool noodle with her armpits, this child cupping her hands around the conch of Luna's listening ear?

Ava Rose leaned close, her breath hot and sweet. "I know you're fake," she whispered, and cackled like a witch, and swam away.

Happy Like That

LILLIAN HAS BEEN dead for a week when Elaine remembers the slip of paper, tucked in a drawer in her desk, that Lillian gave her shortly after beginning an affair with a man only Elaine knew about.

It's been five months, Elaine calculates, since Lillian pressed the note into her hand, hurrying from work to spend a Friday night with her lover, telling her husband who knows what, leaving their eight-year-old daughter Violet in Elaine's care, as she often did. Five months, but it feels like much longer. Now Elaine digs through the detritus in her desk until she finds it: the yellow Post-it, a blackish strip of filth clinging to the adhesive on its underside, bearing Lillian's lover's name and number.

In case of emergency, Lillian had said, and Elaine had stashed the Post-it away with a nonchalance that struck her, now that Lillian was dead—killed by a drunk driver—as callous. It was a thing you said, in case of emergency, a casual precaution you took in the same half-hearted way you might locate the exit row on an airplane you assume won't crash or replace the batteries in a smoke alarm you assume will never go off. Elaine had thought nothing of it. She'd simply accepted the note, proud and pleasantly scandalized to have been entrusted with it, the neatly printed family of digits on its face, the viney cursive scrolls of the lover's name, and the secret they signified. At the time, she could not imagine a situation that would require her to put the slip of paper to practical use, but now, here is one. Does Lillian's lover know she is gone? Does he have anyone to talk to?

Elaine doesn't know. But she knows that, for better or for worse, her best friend loved this man, and she believes that the ache in the pit of her stomach, the hopeless hunger for Lillian's company, qualifies as an emergency. Who could understand better than him? Following Lillian's funeral, Elaine had grabbed desperately for every trace of her friend she could find before they too disappeared: a half-empty box of jasmine tea labeled with her name; her favorite mug, wide and rounded and painted like a strawberry, from the common area at the office where they both worked as speech therapists (private practice, Elaine a specialist in child language disorders, Lillian working mostly with adults with dementia or recovering from strokes or brain injuries). Now, she decides, she will add the lover to this list of consolatory artifacts, mementos of Lillian. She knows that he works odd hours as a K-9 sergeant with the Department of Corrections and that he, too, is married. She does not expect him to answer when she calls him just before leaving work on a Wednesday, but he does.

"Oh," he says when she introduces herself, "Elaine, yes. Lillian's told me about you. I was sorry not to meet you at the funeral."

"You were there?"

It had been in the paper, of course, on the news, but the lover lives in a different town almost an hour away, a place with its own tragedies, and Elaine had thought it likely that she'd have to break the news of

Lillian's death to him. Now, it seems, she'll be spared that particular unpleasantness. She imagines him at the funeral, skulking near the back unnoticed, grieving privately. The funeral was crowded; Elaine had clung to her husband David's arm and kept to herself. Lillian had many friends, and Elaine had often wondered why Lillian had chosen her as her confidant when so many other options abounded.

"I'd love to meet you," she says now, surprising herself. "I've heard so much about you. And it's been hard; you know—"

"Yes," the lover says. "You want to be close to everything she was close to."

Elaine nods. She had not expected to propose a meeting, but his explanation for why one is called for suits her. They agree to meet at a tavern on Friday afternoon for a late lunch. He cannot be more than a half hour's drive from the prison where he works, lest he and his dogs be called out on a chase, so she'll travel to his neck of the woods like Lillian used to do.

David had never liked Lillian, not since the two women met at Brookwood after giving birth on the same day and discovered that they had the same profession, though they worked in different places at the time, Elaine for Birmingham public schools and Lillian in private practice in the office where they later worked together. Both births had been difficult, both babies premature, both their parents' first and only children. David objected to Lillian's irreverent sense of humor, her jokes about the places tiny Violet might fit and where Lillian must therefore be careful not to place or drop her: into her handbag, in the elastic throat of a tube sock, down the toilet. When at last they were released from the hospital, again on the same day, parting ways in front of sliding doors, Lillian kissed Elaine on the cheek and said, "Can you believe it?" She nodded toward the building they'd left, cradling Violet at her breast. "They're crazy, letting me take this thing home."

This was the beginning of the friendship that would come to sit at the center of their lives.

"Isn't she stunning?" Elaine marveled to David on the way home.

"Her tiny little toes," he said, thinking Elaine meant Mandy, their daughter.

"No," she said, "I mean Lillian."

David said he had not cared for the way Lillian called her child a thing. But to Elaine, Lillian's crassness felt like honesty, not blasphemy. She had been afraid to take Mandy home, as well, into a house that had seemed cozy before but that now seemed like a death trap, with its steak knives and sharp corners, and it refreshed her to hear such apprehension expressed without having to express it herself. The truth was she had not loved Mandy right away. Instead the love bloomed in her slowly, building once the girl began to show herself emotionally human, not just physically so; Elaine had required payment of smiles, of laughter, in order to give it. Loving had been an exchange, even with her child. She would die for Mandy now, but it had not always been so.

This was the kind of thing she could not tell anyone but Lillian. David still holds that he loved Mandy madly, immediately. But of course he did: it was easy for him; it wasn't fair. Mandy had only ever given to him, never taken. And she had taken Elaine's body; she had nearly taken her life. Only Lillian understood. She had been the sole sounding board for Elaine's observations, all the things that surprised her about motherhood and marriage, the things no one tells you.

As a mother, Lillian was carefree, open, and blunt in the way she framed the lessons she imparted on her daughter—no baby talk, no euphemism. Violet had taught Mandy the word vagina before age three. And Lillian teased Elaine relentlessly about the time she would not allow Mandy to bob for apples at another child's birthday party, when Elaine was put off at the sight of the dozen grimy children plunging their faces into a large metal tub of water, trying with teeth and tongues to trap in their mouths apples that bobbed like fat, red sunbathers in a chop of waves. Elaine held Mandy on the margins, saying Mandy was ill when, in fact, Elaine was only worried about the possibility that she might become so. She did not see what was so wrong with that, why

Lillian had laughed at her, or how her friend could cheer so enthusiastically when her own daughter came up from the bucket with her teeth sunk deep into a germy Red Delicious, grinning like an imp.

Elaine had aspired to soak up some of Lillian's ease, her acceptance of her daughter's individuality. For her own part, Elaine sometimes found it distressing to watch Mandy get bigger and older and begin to show flaws that promised to make life hard for her (an insecure streak, a dislike of the sound of others' laughter, an unassuagable conviction that it must be at her expense) and to have thoughts that Elaine would never know. Her child was separate from her; it was both obvious and sad.

"I don't know," Lillian said when Elaine shared her frustration over the fact of her daughter's miraculous, awful autonomy. "I think it's kind of beautiful."

This was in the early days, on their babies' second birthday, when Elaine and Lillian threw a party that was more for them than for the girls. They wore cone-shaped party hats and ate red velvet cake from a box while Violet and Mandy teetered about and bopped each other with balloons, indifferent to the occasion, having long since rejected their own birthday hats.

"Why?" Elaine whined.

Lillian shrugged. "It's true, Violet's not me. But that's okay. She's her."

One of the girls began to wail. Lillian lifted her up and held her, rubbed a blue balloon back and forth on the child's head, then raised it up and watched as the girl's fine baby hairs followed, standing on end.

"Oh, little static baby," Lillian said. "Little Einstein. Don't cry."

They soon grew tired of the party. Elaine stood by the picture window in her Homewood bungalow with Mandy on her hip and her party hat's elastic strap digging into her chin, cone-headed and bored, taking in the houses across the street, all of which were lined with neat gardens, stately in floral magnificence.

"Who has the time?" she complained. "How do these women do it?"

She would have given in to her feelings of inadequacy, letting them pull her down, if not for Lillian. Instead they rounded up the kids and made a run to a nearby box store, bought out their stock of silk flowers, brought them back to Elaine's, and just before David came home, stuck their plastic stocks into the dirt of her front lawn. The children ate dirt, and the neighbors peeked from between curtains and slowed their cars in front of the house on their way to softball practice or swimming lessons to take in the sudden swell of rainbow blossoms, amused, aghast, and Elaine and Lillian laughed and laughed, earth trapped under the skinny white moons of their nails.

It was the kind of thing David just didn't get, like the time Elaine and Lillian swapped wedding rings (Elaine's idea) or the time they went to the derby party at Windwood with buckets on their heads.

"Why didn't you plant real flowers?" he asked Elaine that night. "Wouldn't it have been the same amount of work to just do it the right way? Buy something, dig a hole, fill it in."

Husbands. Let's be honest, Elaine thinks: you can find one anywhere, the world is bursting with them, and once you've got one you can learn from a thousand different sources what to do with him and how, though he won't really get you and you won't really get him. Anyone can tell you to plant flowers the right way. But she'll never find another Lillian. No.

On Wednesday evening, she tells David she'll be going to see her mother in Tuscaloosa on Friday. And perhaps she really will go there, she tells herself, after her lunch with the lover. It would not be out of the way. She should pack a bag just in case.

On Thursday, after work, she gets a bikini wax.

"Been a while," says her aesthetician.

"I'm so busy," says Elaine. She feels defensive, like she's being accused of something. The rip and tear of the hard wax and the seared feeling of her bare skin afterward feel punitive, but she has not done anything wrong, attending to her overgrown bush. She's near the end of her period, and her skin is especially sensitive.

After her wax, she stops at Publix and buys a package of frozen enchiladas to stash in the freezer at home in case she's gone overnight. As she waits in the checkout line with the box puddling the grocery conveyor belt, she thinks of her indispensability to her family—David's helplessness in the kitchen, Mandy's myriad quirks and needs—with a mix of resentment and pride.

On Friday, after sending Mandy to school, she showers then stands in her closet, unsure what to wear. She thinks of how Lillian will never again stand in her closet, unsure what to wear. She dons a funereal but sexy black dress, then reconsiders and, in what may be an act of overcorrection, ghosts herself in a white mock neck sleeveless sweater, an ice-blue cashmere pencil skirt, and a pair of low silver pumps. She has no plan for this day other than to think and talk of Lillian with her lover, but she finds herself afflicted with a nervous energy that she attempts to release by pacing around the room, moving her arms aimlessly, running out the clock, speaking to herself aloud: "Yes, the silver earrings" (spearing her lobes); "Oh, a goldfinch!" (looking out the window); "Definitely the blue" (reconsidering her choice of skirt, then unreconsidering). The sound of her voice in the empty house reassures and splits her: she's both a woman preparing for lunch and a woman watching a woman prepare for lunch, objectively observing her actions, putting down a record of their purity and triviality, her innocence. Nothing to see here.

She knows enough to know that this splitting and recording, this half-felt sense of censure, stems from her guilty awareness of the lie she told David about going to Tuscaloosa (but was it a lie? She might go yet; yes, and besides, why would he care? Why must he hear about every lunch she eats, every private ritual by which she mourns Lillian, who after all was her friend, not his; this grief hers, not his?), and she sees for the first time how easy it could be. How smoothly she could spin a web of excuses and half-truths, the silky threads of secrets; his trust has purchased her this ease.

At last she gathers her bag, tosses it into the trunk of her car, and slides beneath the wheel.

She should take him something, the lover. Lillian left no gift, no lock of hair, no letter.

A dozen roses, then. Red. No, white. No, red.

No. White.

She buys the flowers on her way out of town and hits the freeway, where she gets stuck behind a sewage truck, THE STOOL BUS, sluggish and yellow-painted, just taking its time in the fast lane. She passes on the right, reading, WHERE YOUR FECAL MATTERS. Once again, she has the sense that she's being reprimanded, though she's innocent of any and all definable wrongdoing other than being alive in a world from which Lillian's been taken.

On her way south on 65, she thinks of the lover. Though they've never touched, she knows that he is quiet and earnest in his lovemaking; she is familiar with his habit of twining his fingers in his lover's hair like a cat's claws. She knows that he apprehends criminals in his dreams, that once, in his sleep, he pinned Lillian's hands behind her back, dreaming of capture, and held her down with both her wrists vised in one damp palm until she screamed him awake. And she knows how tenderly he held her afterward, awake, repentant.

The lover can know no such things about Elaine. And yet, realizing that she is his only remaining link to Lillian, the closest he can come to her now, she feels herself imbued with an eroticism that is no less potent for its despondency.

Her stomach turns as she pulls into the tavern's parking lot, right on time. It is mid-May and a humid ninety degrees, and the heat hits her before she even opens the car door. She leaves the flowers on the passenger's seat. She should not have brought them.

She enters the tavern where the lover waits, already seated. A table for two, two full water glasses sweating. Two wet rings on wood.

She recognizes him from pictures she's seen on Lillian's phone, and he rises and takes her hand in his. He's a large man, tall and fit, broad-shouldered and blonde with an Alabama drawl. He used to build bombs in the army. The polar opposite of Lillian's husband Parker, who is thin and erudite in glasses, dark hair buzzed to hide his balding, a soft-spoken architect and news junkie transplanted from Baltimore. Elaine and Parker are not close, but as she pictures him now, she feels a pang of loyalty and of hostility toward this golden-fair lover who will get over Lillian, move on to someone new, while Parker raises motherless Violet alone.

Still, there's a sadness in the lover's eyes she can't deny, and a softness to his voice as he thanks her for coming to meet him, and she figures he has no one else with whom to remember Lillian. She says, "I thought you might need someone to talk to."

"It's been awful," he says. "Surreal. Thankfully, I have Kyra."

His wife. No kids, she knows, just dogs.

She takes him to mean that the loss of Lillian has renewed his commitment to his wife. She nods. "And she's a teacher?"

"Fifth grade. Convinced her not to have children of her own. But she's going back to UAB now, for her master's. Psychology. She'll be up your way this evening," he says, meaning Birmingham, "for class."

Their server comes. The lover orders a beer and some fried green tomatoes to share; Elaine an unsweetened tea. What is she doing here?

"You don't want a drink?" he asks.

"I'll be driving," she says, and they're silent for a while. The server brings Elaine her tea, and she dips a spoon in and swirls it around, though there's nothing to stir. "And you work at the prison," she says, "training dogs."

"Training them, medicating them, cleaning kennels. Driving the perimeter of the prison checking for drug deliveries. Shakedowns. I'm the knife guy," he says. "The best at finding them."

"You find many? Knives?"

"Knives, pieces of bed frame. You'd be amazed how many things you can stab a person with."

Elaine waves over their server and orders a drink after all, a glass of white wine. "And your dogs—they track runaways?"

"Every person lost in eight counties. Felons, mostly, and runaway inmates, lost children, Alzheimer's patients who wander off." He sips his beer. "And your work? It's similar to Lil's?"

Lil. Elaine never called her that and had not known that anyone did. She considers the diminutive nickname, which seems like something Lillian would have hated.

They go back and forth like this, speaking of work, their families. Elaine thinks of how, assuming she'd remain forever at a safe distance from him, she has imagined herself into bed with this man a hundred times—him amorphous and anonymous then but real and tangible now. She fights back the thought, but it rises inside her, buoyant, and she blushes.

He tells her about chasing three criminals for fifteen miles through a briar patch in Bibb County in the middle of the night, how when one man fell behind, unable to go on, his companions tried to saw his head off so he could not tell their names. He tells her how the dogs licked the blood from the man's throat as they waited for EMTs to arrive. As he speaks, Elaine begins to see how Lillian could love this man, a natural storyteller, charismatic yet unpretentious, magnetic. He tells her how his mother, after a stroke, went to see Lillian for melodic intonation therapy to aid in language recovery. This was how they'd met.

At this delayed but inevitable mention of her friend, Elaine begins to crack. "I used to hear them sometimes, singing," she says, and her eyes well up, and to her surprise and relief, his do too. MIT is not a technique Elaine herself uses, being long and arduous in implementation and awkward to perform. But sometimes through Lillian's door she would hear the up-and-down rhythms of her voice, the voice of a patient with stroke-induced aphasia rising and falling on the waves of it. Lillian would tap out melodies on her patients' left hands while they repeated the phrases she sang, finding speech through song.

"I-*love*-you," Lillian would sing. There was really no reason for her to belt out the melodies the way she did, practically at the top of her lungs with an unnecessary, operatic bravura, but that was Lillian: nothing done halfway. Her patients did their best to sing with her as she tapped and nodded and prompted—"I-*love*-you, I-*love*-you, I-*love*-my-*hus*band-and-*daaaugh*ter-and-*son*"—and if all went well, she would be able to ask her patient at the end of a session, "What did you say?" and hear the patient answer, in speech, "I love you."

Elaine blinks back her tears. After a few minutes, their server brings her and the lover a single bill. The lover is swift, assertive, so the embarrassment of negotiating it is over before it can begin. He pays. She volunteers to leave the tip, but he waves away the fold of bills she tries to pass him.

"You came all the way here," he says. "Do you have to leave right away?"

No, she says, she's free.

"You been to see the Cahaba lilies?"

Not since she was young, she tells him. They agree to leave the tavern for a nature preserve where the rare lilies grow, a fifteen-minute drive away, along their namesake river. She follows him there, the white roses shrinking from the heat in the seat beside her.

"Everyone's up to something," Lillian used to say.

Elaine always pushed back. People, she insisted, were generally virtuous. The two of them would sit and debate at the small lunch table in the converted house where they had their offices, eating avocado toast or chicken salad, or at the gym, where they went together three mornings a week. At the thought of these trips to the gym, Elaine's heart, in its staid, soldierly life-march, stutters and trips. She can still see Lillian, sweat-stained and glowing, peeling off her gym clothes without a shred of self-consciousness.

It was the same after every workout. Elaine never knew whether to look. It was both more effortful and more conspicuous not to do so; it required a gymnastic and unnatural turning away toward a distraction that didn't exist—there were only so many things you could pretend to be paying attention to instead, just tile and grout on all sides. And there was the question of what to do once you inevitably did look. Did you pretend not to have seen, or did you acknowledge it, and if the latter, how? Did you let your gaze linger as a kind of compliment? Were you supposed to comment on what you saw, the way a man might? Anything Elaine did felt sudden and wrong, and her embarrassment seemed to crystallize and settle on her in a glassy frost that shattered and cut as soon as she moved or breathed.

It annoyed her, how there seemed to be no way to move through those moments without breaking them, how Lillian constantly subjected her to them anyway, oblivious or indifferent to her discomfort. At the same time, Lillian's ease around her had made Elaine feel special, and if Lillian had ever stopped undressing in her presence, she would certainly have felt deprived. Almost everything she felt for or about Lillian was like this: layered, contradictory, complex. For instance, there had been times when Elaine felt crushed by the weight of her friend's confidence, her knowledge of Lillian's affair. But there had been many more when she had treasured it: as a privilege, as a cherished indicator of her friend's trust and of her own exceptionalness for having earned it, and also as a validation of her own goodness, a secret sufficiently dirty as to make her own life, in contrast, seem sparklingly clean.

Elaine did not undress in front of her friend at the gym but instead waited until she entered the shower stall next to her. In the shower, they passed shampoo and coconut body wash under the plastic curtain and talked. About their kids, about the lover.

"You don't feel for her, though? The wife?" Elaine asked once, snapping the cap onto a bottle of Pantene, and Lillian responded, "Feel what?"

"Bad?"

"Bad? No."

"Parker, then? You don't feel bad for him? You don't feel guilty?"

A pause from the neighboring shower stall, then, "Guilty, no. Love doesn't have to have a lid on it, you know? People ought to let a little more out."

This had sounded poetic but largely meaningless, as far as Elaine was concerned, an eloquent avoidance of the question. The conversation ended there. It hadn't made sense to Elaine at the time and still doesn't now, how her friend could be so blasé in her transgression. She tried to understand, she checked out *Anna Karenina* from the library, but things had seemed to go much more easily for Lillian, emotionally, anyway, than they did for poor Anna, and the comparison proved unuseful.

The newness of the affair seemed to thrill Lillian, but Elaine cannot imagine starting something new: the hard work of it, learning each other's bodies, introducing the person to your siblings, teaching them how you don't like ketchup or red onions, establishing how the bath towels should be folded. It has always seemed to her that to love is to make a commitment not so much to a person as to a story. A marriage, for instance—it's less a promise to a human person than an agreement, mutually reached, that in that person's mind and in yours, a certain narrative should prevail. You agree to frame everything before the wedding as the fateful twists and turns of a charmed and inevitable path to the person you're marrying, and everything after as bumps in a road cotraveled or as shining silver pins mutually placed on a shared map.

If you started a new story, what would happen to that old one? Where would it go, those plot points, those twists and turns and bumps and pins, that lived, lost time?

Elaine can't imagine, but sometimes she tries, and the fact that, according to the laws of marriage, she will never again experience a first kiss or the flitter and thrill of new intimacy is not lost on her.

A lush green carpet sits on the surface of the Cahaba River, starred with delicate lily blossoms, each of which blooms only for one day. A few other visitors mill about, families and couples. A church group in matching purple T-shirts gathers by the water and begins to pray, thanking their Lord for the beauty of nature. To escape the crowds, Elaine and the lover take a narrow path along the water. Bushes and weeds and tall grass grow along the path and extend their long arms, trying to overtake the gravel. He tells her how vegetation holds the scents of runaways, how their lost cells settle on leaves. He tells her how his beagles' ears drag the ground when they're tracking, picking up scent. He tells her that runaways cross rivers thinking the dogs will lose their scent, but the dogs can swim and track at once, are glad for the drink and the chance to cool down, and a river must be very wide to stop them.

"Wider than this?" Elaine motions to the Cahaba, the blanket of lilies, the current running rapid through the shoals. She's not dressed for this; her pumps have begun to chafe at the heel, blisters starting, and her skirt and sweater hold in heat.

"Wider and deeper," he says. "Adrenaline smells strong. The worse the crime, the smellier the criminal."

A black snake, at least four feet long, slithers across the trail. Elaine stops, startled.

"Just a little water snake," he says. "Won't hurt you."

She gathers herself, heart pumping double-time. A greasy sheen has formed on her face, and rims of sweat wet the fabric below her armpits.

"What about the ones who aren't criminals?" she asks. "The children, the lost dementia patients?"

"Harder to find. There's not the same anxiety, there's less sweat. They're too innocent."

"You don't have the dogs smell the person's clothes or belongings, find that scent?"

"These dogs aren't article trained, no. They follow the first human scent they pick up. We take them to the last place the runaway was known to be, and let them go to work."

Elaine walks beside him on the side facing the river. A dragonfly whizzes by. She imagines Lillian on her other side, wading through the rushes in a dress of woven lilies, drenched, and a chill runs up her spine. It is the first time she's thought of her friend as a ghost, as anything other than a living, breathing woman who is simply elsewhere.

She asks, "What if they chase someone else? Follow the wrong trail?"

"Most of the time, we're deep in the woods. No one else out there, no reason to be there other than to hide. Sure, sometimes the pups will pick up the scent of the cop who followed the criminal as far as he could, make a loop and end up back where they started. But for the most part, the system works."

She feels his eyes on her. Her shoulders tighten. She becomes very conscious of her hips.

She stops walking and thinks again of Lillian. She ought to do something, she thinks, besides walk and ask questions. The river at this point is almost entirely covered in a mat of greenery and the spidery white blossoms of the lilies. She doesn't want him to know she knows he's watching her, but she does want to give him something to watch, some thoughtful memorializing gesture to show her depth, to share her sorrow. She owes it to him, she thinks, to make him privy to her grief, or at least to a performance of it. It is all they have in common.

She picks her way to the riverbank, where a bunch of lilies blooms in the sunny shoals not far from the footpath, surrounded by broad, flat rocks. She steps onto one of the rocks and crouches. Feels her skirt constrict around her thighs in objection as she lowers herself. The current flows swiftly. The Southern sun beats down. She reaches out to stroke the green stocks and tall grass surrounding a cluster of lilies, to gently tilt a flower's face toward hers. The waxy filaments of its stamens reach out, tipped in wanton yellow fuzz; the green strand of the pistil lazes to one side like a straw in a martini glass. The blossom is sun-centered, yellow where its pale petals meet, and rimmed by six long, thin petal-plumes that radiate out from the stem below like insect legs. She takes in its light, then lets go. She rises to her feet.

And then the slick rock face gets the better of her, and her silver heel slips, and she tumbles sideways. The cool water takes her. One hand plunges into the grassy base of the stand of lilies, and her palm and wrist smart when they stop her fall against a tangle of roots and rock and slime. The base of her spine throbs with the impact, and she sits, for one defeated moment, in her soiled dream-blue skirt, in water that reaches as high as the base of her bra.

"Oh, *fuck*," she says, and looks up at the lover, dizzy, top-heavy with the blood in her face and her ears red and hot like the coils of a stove, her feet, still heeled, struggling to find purchase in muck.

He offers her a hand and laughs. At first, she is mortified, but she recalibrates, realizing that his laughter is her license to make light of her tumble, her clumsiness, and she lets herself laugh with him. And she sees how a new story can start at any time; she sees that all these years as her story with David has progressed, as they've slogged through its middle, she has in fact been trudging past potential beginning after potential beginning, blind to the thousand geneses that offered themselves to her but that she'd contracted never to embark upon. Here, now, is one: a tale that begins with two mourners touching. She can hear herself telling it, years in the future: I was soaked! But then he took me by the arm and pulled me up, so strong, and our eyes met, and . . .

"You're soaked!" he says. "We should get you home."

Home. Elaine considers telling him about the change of clothes she's packed but holds back. What does he think she'll do in his house, waiting for her clothes to dry? Wear his wife's things?

Let him call the shots. They head back to their cars. Her shoes squeak with each step. Her sweater sucks at her skin. After some time walking, she realizes that the thin pad inside her underwear, there to catch the dregs of the end of her period, is waterlogged, swollen, and squishing like a small diaper between her legs, and a curtain in her mind pulls back to reveal to her the full scale of her foolishness. Until he speaks, and the curtain closes again.

"You're welcome to come back to our place and shower," he says. "Borrow a change of clothes from Kyra, if you want. Whatever you need."

Just once, Elaine and Lillian fought. Not bickered, the way they sometimes did about how much screen time a child should have or the pros and cons of various forms of therapy, but argued in a way that wounded.

It happened on their most recent trip to Pearl River, where they went annually for a night between Christmas and New Years to gamble, leaving the girls with their fathers, sharing a hotel room into which they stumbled giggling at night. The original trip had been Lillian's idea, and she'd throw a bill into a slot from time to time between cosmopolitans; but it was Elaine who, to both of their surprise, sitting at a glowing machine drunk, careless, and exuberant, pulled the handle again and again. And again. Each year David forbade her from going; each year he caved under Lillian's smooth insistence that he let Elaine "get it out of her system"—"it" being, Elaine supposed, her vice.

It was the night Lillian told Elaine about the lover, whom she disclosed over dessert, a crème brûlée. She'd been sleeping with him for a month, Lillian said, and she'd been dying to tell Elaine. They tapped their spoons on the torched sugar crust to crack it. Elaine listened quietly, pensively, priding herself on not passing judgment, taking small, sweet bites of custard between questions.

"But where can this go?" she asked. "You can't leave Parker."

"I don't want to leave Parker."

"But then where can this go?"

"I don't know," Lillian said. "Maybe where it *goes* doesn't have to be the point, you know? I'd like to think we can just be here, now. What if all life isn't linear?"

"But things build, they intensify. They change. How long can it stay static?"

"I don't know," Lillian said. "But I want to find out."

They left the restaurant and entered the casino, found a pair of open machines and sat in their seats, immersed in an ocean of electronic noise, cranks and levers and spinning wheels, celebratory and taunting.

"Don't you want to be married?" Elaine pressed.

Lillian shook her head. "No . . . I mean, yes. It's not that." She sat in her leather player's chair with her hands cupped in her lap, one upturned palm folded inside the other as if begging. One foot tapping against the base of the slot machine. Elaine could not recall the last time she'd seen her friend so nervous, or nervous at all.

"So you want to be married—but not to Parker?"

"Yes, to Parker. I don't want to not be with him."

"You still love him?"

"Yes."

"It's risky. It seems dangerous."

"But maybe it doesn't have to be. Elaine, what if there's another way to do all this? Marriage, sex . . . If we don't like the rules, why shouldn't we—"

"Break them."

"No, change them."

"To what? And what about Violet?"

"What about her?"

Elaine yanked the handle on her slot machine, a game called Pirate's Booty. She won a set of free spins. On the screen a treasure chest opened, and a congratulatory mermaid swam out, breasts seashelled, and blew a kiss that floated from her face in a bubble, growing in size, then popping.

"I don't think you understand what I'm trying to say to you," Lillian said.

Elaine took one of her friend's hands in hers. "I love you," she said, "and I'll support you, whatever you do. I want you to be happy. But I also want you to be careful."

Some women walked by dressed in flare jeans with formations of rhinestones on their ass pockets, low-cut lace camisoles meant for women much younger, saggy skin, and too-tight dresses that did not flatter. Elaine said something about their breasts hanging out. Then she said, "Gross, put that *away*, you know?"

She intended it only as an offhand, camaraderie-boosting observation, but Lillian pulled back her hand. "Why do you have to shame them? Why do you have to be like that?"

Elaine balked. "They didn't hear me."

"It doesn't matter. They can wear what they want, and so can you."

"It's tasteless."

"We're in Mississippi."

"No excuse."

"Well, if you don't want to see it, don't look."

Elaine thought of her friend's brazen nakedness in the locker room and debated flinging her complaints about it back at Lillian, while they were on the subject of looking or not looking at things that ought to be covered, but held back. She punched the Cash Out button on her slot machine. "What's with you?" she said, and from there, things devolved.

"Virgin eyes, over here," Lillian said, rolling her eyes. "Who made you the morality police?"

"I just think people should control themselves. It's not that hard."

"Oh, okay, Ms. *Fifty Shades of Grey*," Lillian said. "Reading about what you're too afraid to do for real."

These books were Elaine's soft spot. They still are. She keeps them hidden in a box in her closet. For a long time that night at Pearl River, she sulked, and Lillian sulked, until in bed, Elaine wrapped her arms around her friend, and Lillian threaded her fingers through Elaine's.

"So," Elaine whispered in her friend's ear. "Tell me what he's like."

At the lover's house, an A-frame on a country road surrounded by trees and the noises of insects, she is greeted by his two howling beagles.

"Bama and Bailey," he introduces them. Born at the prison and taken home when, weak-nosed, they couldn't be used for tracking.

She decides to take the packed bag inside. She can't decide whether he looks surprised when she removes it from her trunk; all her gears and meters seem off, so she chooses to explain: "In case I stay the night at my mother's."

"She lives nearby?"

"Tuscaloosa."

His house is clean and smells pleasantly of vanilla. Upon entering it, he takes off his shoes, so Elaine follows suit, her bare feet sticky-damp and gritty with river grime. On a sideboard just inside the door sit a silver-framed wedding photo, the lover's military portrait, and a picture of the wife in a graduation cap and gown, holding her degree, in a "Roll Tide" frame. Next to the photos is a bust of a phrenology head.

"Kyra's," he says when he catches Elaine studying the head. Her own head spins. Her sopping, bloated panty liner sends another drop of water down her thigh; she asks for the bathroom.

"Did you want to shower?"

"Yes, please." She hates the way she blushes, the wrong way, all the blood to her nose rather than her cheeks. He leads her to the upstairs bathroom, through the master bedroom, a church-like, triangular space where the ceiling peaks and a round window lets in a chute of slanted sunlight that, at this hour, hits the foot of the bed like a spotlight and bends. The usable space in the room is almost wholly consumed by the rumpled king-sized bed and a wide, low dresser whose drawers hang slightly open, revealing bits of fabric. His things, hers. On the wall opposite the bed, next to the bathroom door, hangs a massive mirror.

She sets down her bag while he enters the bathroom, opens a narrow linen closet, and lays out a clean towel for her. When he leaves, she enters, closing the door and stepping into the glass-paned stall. She washes quickly, rinsing the river and dirt from her bottom half. All of the products in the shower seem feminine besides a single, flattened bar of soap, dry and cracked. He hardly seems the type to use women's body products, but she can find nothing there that isn't fragrant, floral—none of the unadorned bottles she associates with men's hygiene. Does he use only this sad soap bar to bathe? To wash his hair? Does he watch his wife shower here while he shaves, prepares for his day? Has he watched Lillian?

Through the glass, she watches the door. Will he be outside it when she comes out? Or downstairs? She should of course come out fully dressed in the outfit she's packed, a pair of shorts that show off the thighs she's worked on at the gym, a simple white cotton tank with a cluster of lace at the chest. Should she carry the towel out with her, perhaps wrapped around her head, a reminder (though surely he does not need one) of her recent nakedness? Or should she hang it on the free hook on the back of the bathroom door, perhaps to be found later by his wife? Why is she thinking about this?

There's no fan in the bathroom, no vent but the one through which the thin stream of the AC slithers, and the room steams up quickly. After turning off the water, she remains filmed in mist that she can't wipe off no matter how furiously she dries her skin, the moisture regenerating, the heat oppressive. Her clothes stick to her and the steam on her belly and back turns to sweat. She pats herself down as well as possible and turbans her wet hair, a few strands escaping the folds, clinging to her neck like baby snakes. She looks around for her bag of clothes and realizes she's left it in the bedroom, sitting outside the bathroom door, at the foot of the lover's bed.

For a moment, she stands still in the damp heat, waiting. There's no sound on the other side of the door, though she hears something distant, some noise downstairs. The beads of moisture on her skin accumulate, and she counts to ten, then opens the door. And finds herself face to face with a compact blonde woman, barefoot in a white blazer, butter-yellow blouse, and tight black slacks, hair in a high, messy bun: the wife, Kyra.

Elaine jumps, startled, and swings a limp arm across her front. Dizzy, she finds her legs locked in surprise, her feet fixed to the hardwood floor, and she stands still, catching her breath, completely naked.

"Oh!" Kyra says. "I'm sorry."

Kyra turns away politely, but before she does, Elaine feels her taking in her body, her eyes darting lightning-fast up and down her frame, curious, assessing. At the same time, Elaine moves to cover herself, right arm stretched across her chest, her right hand mashing her bare left breast; left hand dangling dumbly, shielding her groin. Her mind races, searching for words, for a way to explain her presence to Kyra.

"He got called out on a chase, left just a moment ago," Kyra says, eyes courteously averted. "I came up to see if you needed anything. A change of clothes, perhaps something of Lil's." Her eyes flash toward Elaine's bag on the floor. "I didn't realize you'd brought your own." She turns to head back down the stairs.

"Wait," Elaine says. She unwraps the towel from her head and pulls it around her body, tucking the terrycloth beneath her armpits. A drop of water licks its way down her back. A few more drip from strands of hair and plink against the hardwood. "Something of Lil's?"

"Sure," Kyra says, and opens a drawer of her dresser, and pulls out a Vanderbilt T-shirt, Lillian's alma mater. "She kept some things here. I'm Kyra, by the way."

"Elaine."

"I know. Lillian spoke of you often. I'd hoped to meet you at the funeral, but we were in and out quick. Such a turnout."

Elaine blinks, thinks, her mind stalling. "Let me . . ." she says, and nods toward her bag on the floor.

"Of course."

Kyra hands Elaine her bag, and Elaine retreats to the privacy of the bathroom, throws her clothes on in a rush, trembling faintly, her pulse beating swift and shallow. So Kyra knew; Kyra knows. Elaine recalls Lillian's words: *If we don't like the rules, why shouldn't we change them?* What was Kyra's role, then—to give permission? To participate? Does Parker know too? What is happening?

When she emerges from the bathroom she finds Kyra still waiting by her dresser, with Lillian's shirt and a purple silk slip in hand. She holds them as one might hold a baby, with a kind of tender care that borders on reverence. She runs a hand over the silk, and in that touch, that tenderness, Elaine sees everything: That it had been the woman too, it had been Kyra too, that Parker had known and consented. There is no guilt here, no treachery, in the way this woman smooths Lillian's garments before placing them in Elaine's hands.

Why hadn't Lillian told her the whole story? All this time, Elaine had thought Lillian told her about the lover because she thought Elaine could handle anything, because their friendship knew no boundaries. Instead, it seems, Lillian told her what she told her, just a portion of the truth, because—why? Because she thought Elaine couldn't handle much. Because she thought—she knew—Elaine would judge her.

And Elaine had. The fact was she had treasured Lillian's secret as though it were her friend's Achilles's heel: a vulnerability, a sign of the imperfection that, after all, she'd needed Lillian to display in order to feel that they were equals. So many nights, she turned to face David in bed and came so close to telling him, *Guess what? Lillian's*... so that she, they, could feel that, yes, they were doing okay, the two of them; Elaine and David, they were doing it right.

Had Lillian sensed how desperately Elaine had needed her to be dissatisfied? Ms. *Fifty Shades of Grey*—had she fed Elaine a half story, a scandal, because she knew how hungrily she'd eat it up, how eager she'd be, deep down, to live vicariously through her friend's treachery? The truth was surprising, yes, and alien to Elaine, but it was less incriminating, ultimately, than secret infidelity. Yet Lillian had chosen to let her believe she'd betray Parker, she'd betray Kyra. Because she thought Elaine was too much of a prude to understand, the truth too complexly spiced for her palate? Because she thought Elaine might be put off by the fact that Lillian had been with a woman? Because Elaine didn't really know her, and now she never would?

Oh, Lillian, she thinks. How sad to see this only now, too late: there was never not enough love; there was only too much.

Feeling overcome by a need to escape Kyra's presence, Elaine moves to the front door, Lillian's clothes in hand. "I brought you something," she says, and slips on her shoes, and dashes out to her car, where she retrieves the dozen roses.

She reenters the house and holds out the bouquet. Kyra takes it with the grace of a pageant queen, thanks her, removes a vase from a cabinet and moves to the kitchen to fill it with water.

"Tell me something," Elaine says, as Kyra arranges the roses. "You were happy... like that?"

"Polyamorous?" Kyra supplies.

"Yes," Elaine says. "You were happy, all of you."

She waits for an answer, though she has not really asked a question. Kyra places the vase on the sideboard next to the phrenology bust. She says, "As the day is long."

Outside, the beagles bark. The cicadas start up. Somewhere in the woods, a criminal flees the scene of his crime, or hers, the lover and his dogs hot on their heels. Kyra offers Elaine a glass of sweet tea, and Elaine accepts, anticipating the cold, sweet shock of the beverage with an eagerness that reminds her, in a way both welcome and terrible, that she is alive.

Where does the story go from here? What happens next? She will drink the sweet tea, let Kyra refill her glass. She will carry her new knowledge home with her. She will keep it from David, she knows, the same way Lillian kept it from her. She will buy groceries and get bikini waxes; she will survive. She will go to work, and she will help her patients find the skills to say exactly what they want to say. No less. And no more.

· II ·

Like This

American Moon

IT TOOK A LONG time for the foreign girl to convince us she was real. Long before we loved her, before we learned that Verona was not by the sea, that her mother and father did not stomp grapes in their bare feet and make wine in their front yard, even before she dropped out of the sky and into our deep, dark forest, we doubted her authenticity. I was twelve at the time and the most doubtful of all, full of that skepticism particular to those who have been abandoned. I was skeptical of Sadie's mother's dreams of bringing the great big world to her lackluster modular in rural Pennsylvania, skeptical of the foreign girl's name, which did not sound Italian. When the homestay program first sent Sadie the information about the girl, called just plain Anna, her face fell. She tried to hide her disappointment, but I knew she wished that the girl had been called Francesca or Giovanna, something exotic with many letters. I wished it too. On the information sheet, there was a picture, black and white, so we couldn't see that Anna's hair was actually golden-fair or else we might not have had her at all; we would've thought right then that the homestay program was a scam and said, never mind, we want a *real* foreigner.

In the picture, Anna, who was coming to America to improve her English, stared solemnly at the camera. In an attempt at optimism Sadie's mother said, "They're Catholic there, see?" and looked pleased because it was Italian. Next to the picture, the paper said that Anna liked to dance ballet, that she was an only child, thirteen, and that she had a brace. It didn't say what kind of brace, and so we imagined she'd walk funny and wear metal on her legs like Forrest Gump. We were nervous about this; she was due to stay for a whole semester at the junior high, and it would be winter by the time she left; it could get very icy here. Sadie's mother said, See, we should be thankful—they probably didn't have such good care, medically, for kids where this Anna came from, and anyway, the brace couldn't be too big, since that would make it pretty hard for Anna to dance ballet like her profile said. Still, our doubts were not dispelled until weeks after her arrival.

Because the foreign girl was coming, Sadie was expected to shine like new, always behave. The same expectations applied to me since I was with them nearly all the time, ate almost every meal at their table. Sadie's mother didn't let us forget—we were to be kind, generous, country strong. Standing on a kitchen chair, sweating with exertion and anticipation, she polished the antlers of the deer heads mounted on the living room wall, turning occasionally to look down at us over her shoulder and remind us how important it was for us to learn what it was like "out there," get some culture, make a good impression, represent our country. This was how she'd sold the idea of the homestay program to Sadie's father: tapping his national pride. A logger, he was a man who, like most of the people in our town, despite our relative poverty, saw everything in the world as ours, looked at the sky at night and saw there a great big American moon (*our* flag planted, *our* astronauts' footprints in the dust). But who, at the same time, could look around at our oil-bust town—rust and rubble and train tracks to nowhere—and understand what, out of patriotism, he would never say aloud: that even a strong thing can run to ruin. That, as Sadie's mother put it, there was a world out there, and we needed it to come into us and fill us with something indefinable, unfamiliar, but essential.

Sadie's mother gave Sadie's father strict orders about where and where not to drive while Anna was in the car, which street to take through town so as to make the best impression, where to turn to miss the dirty bars and rundown pawn shops whose junk overflowed onto the sidewalks. She told him which roads to take to avoid—as much as possible—the sites of everything unpleasant, from boarded-up busted meth labs to mean dogs, but she forgot about the school bus, which would pass all of this daily, making stops along the way.

"No matter how much you polish a turd, it's still a turd," Sadie's father said, laughing, when Sadie's mother lectured him about what to hide and what to reveal to Anna. "We don't got much; there's no hiding it. But we're good people, and there's no hiding that, either."

He didn't say much, but when he did, he had a way of making light of every situation, dismissing misfortune with a joke, then following the joke up with something sturdy and sincere and, we thought, profound. He was strong and patient and camo-and-orange, everything everyone I knew expected a good man to be, and I spent years imagining he was my father.

When the time came to pick Anna up at the airport, he took the day off and put on a brand new button-down shirt, and Sadie used her mom's eyeliner to draw thick lines above her top lashes and below her bottom ones. If you looked closely, you could see the crookedness of the lines and the places where she'd smeared them in an effort to straighten them, but from a distance, she looked refined, like a New York businesswoman. When I told her so, she drew lines on me, too, holding my eyelids open and streaking the edges of my brown eyes with 124: Deep

Navy so that when I looked in the mirror I, too, felt old, sophisticated. Then she climbed into the passenger side of her father's Ranger, and the two of them drove the three hours to Pittsburgh to get Anna. It was mid-August and ninety degrees.

There was no room for me in the cab. I stayed at the house and waited. On the way home, I knew, with Anna's bags secure in the bed of the truck, Sadie's father would crack the windows, and Sadie's hair would blow in Anna's face, and Anna's into Sadie's in some strange, primitive bonding ritual, and the three of them would sit together, sweating despite the breeze and their clean hair and faces. Arms and knees touching. I imagined myself there, in Sadie's new shoes, pressed awkwardly against Anna. Her skin would feel strange, warm, Mediterranean. Foreign. We would talk about the weather, and I would ask, casually, "How was your flight?"

Flight. I couldn't have imagined it if I'd tried. It was a luxury that was out of my reach—not just flying, but mobility in general. This Anna was mobile; she had been in the sky; she was practically a constellation; we had dreamed up story after story about her, and now she was descending, down through the canopies of our trees. I pictured her in goggles and a brown leather jacket, a silk scarf fluttering in the thin air just beneath the clouds, red lipstick, dramatic dark hair and *Ciao*. Ciao *Bella*. Lamborghini-Pasta-Pasta-Mafia-Mamma-Mia.

In the back of my mind I couldn't help but think: the joke was on her. She didn't know where she was landing. America or not, I couldn't see anything in the least beautiful or romantic or even educational in our hometown. Someone should have told her: "Here bears trail your trash through the yard, eating it, and if the animals aren't making a mess, the people are; your father, drunk and morose, throws empty bottles out his bedroom window; you step on the pieces as you run through your yard in summer, you cut your feet on brown glass. Here tractors drive down back roads pulling old washing machines and pieces of cars to trailers where they're displayed in overgrown side yards, and you might observe your neighbor riding his cow. Here kids cook meth in rundown houses, and cops interrupt lessons on your proud oil heritage to tell you and your classmates all about the stuff, what it does, how it's made, and what with so you *won't* go and make it. Here your peers drive their four-wheelers screaming down the road at night, drunk or high or both or neither, and slam into your mailbox, crash into your ditch, into trees, into your dreams, into each other. You are well-versed—or will be, eventually, inevitably, here—in extraction, collision, destruction, ammunition. Your local paper entices with urgent headlines like, 'Fall Falling All Ready? First Red Leaf of Season Sited in Yard of Local Teacher.'" You had oil once, and wealth, but now you have only trees; you are ferociously American, and yet you have, too, the secret, haunting half-sense that America has left you behind.

Someone should have told Anna all of this. This was where she would learn her English; these were the people whose words she would add to her vocabulary. If I'd had a chance to fly away, it was when my mother drove west and didn't take me with her ("Baker, CA," read the postcard she sent me to say, *Be good, Jeannie J*—"Home of the World's Largest Thermometer and Gateway to Death Valley National Park!"). I don't know if she ever made it to LA, to the ocean, where she was surely headed. But that's not the point. The point is, I'd never known anything but my town: the same houses, same sadnesses. You didn't have to be a genius to know there was nothing here for a foreigner.

While Anna plunged out of the clouds in her silk and leather, I waited at home—at Sadie's home—and watched her mother swab the insides of mounted deer heads' nostrils with a damp Q-tip. Eventually, she handed me the fly-swatter, sent me out to the deck.

"You see any skeeters," she said, "swat 'em good, Jean-girl."

Her blonde hair was a little greasy. She was tall and thin, but she looked strong and moved gracefully; it was clear she was a dancer. There was no sign of a scarf or a brace, and I was surprised to find that it was not a dark complexion or a chic sense of style but only her baggage, with perfect bows tied from flowered ribbon around the handles to mark it as her own, that labeled her something "other." If I'd seen her from a distance, without her luggage, I never would have known.

"The treese are-a beut-iful," she said.

We stared. On her teeth were shiny silver braces—the "brace" she had mentioned in her profile. "Your 'ouse ees beut-iful."

It wasn't. Just a house, clean but dingy. Peeling paint. I looked at Sadie's mother and saw her squirm with delight, giddy like a rich kid on Christmas morning.

As she spoke the words, Anna threw her arms around first Sadie's mother, then me. I stumbled with the impact and noticed a few freckles on her nose and cheeks. Dazed, I looked over her shoulder at Sadie, who shrugged, unable to explain this sudden intimacy. I was not sure whether to be alarmed or moved, but I maintained my position against the girl's chest and tried to convince myself that this contact was normal. It was hard to do; I was unaccustomed to touch.

We entered Sadie's house through the front door, not the kitchen, since it was a special occasion. We wanted Anna to feel welcome. I was a kitchen-door guest. It had been a long time since I'd been through the front door, but it was no wonder we used it that day. Entering there, the first thing you saw were the deer—Sadie's dad's trophy bucks, the ones worth keeping, the ones that made his friends say, tracking their boots across the shag carpet, *Nice rack*. There were three deer, their heads turned slightly toward each other as if they were engaged in conversation; they were heads to be proud of, and Sadie's dad was proud. It took me and Sadie years to convince him to let us string blinking colored lights in their antlers at Christmas.

When we were little, Sadie named the first two heads—Jenny and Princess Star Prancer.

I remembered the day of the naming. It was during my silent year. My mother had disappeared, and at the time, she was still in limbo; it would still be a few weeks before the Baker, California, postcard would arrive. I was seven and had already learned to go to Sadie's when I was hungry. I'd scratch at the kitchen door and Sadie's mother would let me in, call me Jean-girl, talk to me in a slow voice and feed me, trying to get me to speak, and I wouldn't. I didn't remember how to talk to grown-ups. I suppose I feared them—their anger, at least, and the words that came with it, and the noise.

My dad didn't say much himself after my mother left. When he spoke, it was only ever a mumble and hard to tell whether it was meant for me at all. He didn't yell at me. He never touched me or hit me or even threatened to, though Sadie's mother questioned me about this frequently, and my silence in response only made her more suspicious. Sometimes I heard him curse under his breath, and this alarmed me—I never knew what provoked the words. They were mysterious to me, and I memorized them quickly. Alone in my bedroom with the door closed and the lights out, I would recite them before bed, one at a time, over and over. *Fuck*, I would whisper to my stuffed animal, an unnamed blue bear, and I would wait for a feeling to come. I expected, each time I tried this, a faint thrill like that of having a secret. But the words sounded strange in my voice. My blue bear stared up at me from my bed. I apologized to him each time.

I never spoke to strangers during that year and rarely even to Sadie, though I always knew I could. She was nine months younger than me and always a few inches shorter, but she stood with her arm around me as we waited for the bus to school, brought me an extra knit scarf in winter, tucked it around my neck in the cold the way her mother had tucked her own. Still I didn't speak. I was afraid of what I had discovered words could do. And when Sadie named the deer heads on her father's wall, and her mother stopped her and said, "Let Jean name one. You want to name one, Jean-girl?," all I heard in my head were the words that I practiced by night in my bedroom at home.

"Fuck," I said under my breath, shy.

Sadie's mom gave me a sideways look. "What . . . what'd you say, baby?"

"Fuck. Fucker," I said. I was loud this time, speaking clearly. "This one's Fucker."

"Jean!" Sadie's mother clapped her dishpan hands over Sadie's ears. "Don't let me hear you say that word again in my house, Jean, understand me?" She paused, stewed in her concern. "And if you hear your daddy use that word, J, you come straight over here, understand? Understand?"

I was too confused to reply.

So Sadie named them. Her father came home from work that day, and his trophies' names were Jenny and Princess Star Prancer because Sadie said so. Her mother smiled, hugged her, said what a great imagination she had, went into the kitchen and peeled potatoes.

When she had left the room, I faced Sadie.

"Those deer are boys," I said.

"They can be girls if I want."

"They can't. You can't make something a girl if it's a boy. And you can't name a boy a girl name."

"I can name them what I want to," she said. "They're mine," and I knew she was right. Aside from my worn blue bear, I had nothing of my own to name.

Now it was Anna's turn to meet Jenny and Princess Star Prancer, as well as the most recent addition to the wall of heads, a buck from two years earlier called Just Buck (named by Sadie's father). Their corresponding framed newspaper clippings hung beneath their heads, yellowed with years: Sadie's dad hoisting the heads—still attached to limp bodies, slit down their middles—into the air with an unpretentious half-smile. Mounted on the wood paneling of the side wall, a pheasant posed frozen in takeoff.

Sadie's father conducted the living-room tour with pride, his face flushed, talking at Anna about the sound of the dead pheasant hitting the ground while his wife brought out a big plate of Oreos. *Was . . . she . . . hun*-gry? Sadie's mom asked Anna, drawing the words out like yawns. She spoke so loudly that Anna jumped and dropped an Oreo on the floor, which Sadie's mother promptly scooped up, still grinning.

Anna glanced from deer head to deer head to deer head to pheasant, and we watched her, waiting, and Sadie's father asked what kind of animals did her father hunt in Italy, and with what kind of rifle?

Anna's eyes were wide, and her face was blank; we thought she must have been tired. This was the conclusion we drew when, after a few moments, she didn't answer.

"Want to meet my dog?" Sadie's father inquired. "She's out back." Tracker, the English setter, lived in the backyard. She was a bird dog, well loved but utilitarian.

Anna's eyes grew huge and she turned to face me as Sadie's dad led us back outside.

"Ees-a the dog . . . alive-a?" Her voice was barely a whisper.

"Huh?"

"The dog. Ees . . . alive-a? Yes?"

Oh!

Sadie's mother overheard Anna's question and took hold of me as I began to laugh uncontrollably. "Jean!" she exclaimed, then, "Yes, Anna, of *course* Tracker is alive!" and, in temporary horror, "Oh, sweetie, have the deer bothered you?" and, running ahead to catch up with her husband, a loud whisper: "Alan, she thought the dog would be *stuffed*!" Then, sheer elation. A dog, stuffed! *Stuffed!*

This embarrassed us a bit, and shortly after she'd met Tracker, Anna announced that she was very tired-a. We were afraid we'd made her feel uncomfortable, but I guess, more than that, we feared looking stupid, too backwoods, unimpressive. So the next thing she said came as a relief—we had forgotten about the time difference. In Italy, Anna said, it was six hours later already.

I tried to imagine this. I imagined it being the middle of the night, right now—now!—while the sky above me was still a deep evening blue like a vast ocean over our heads. A different time, at *this* time. It seemed impossible for the sky to be so multicolored, dark-blue here, black there, tinted orange with the sunrise somewhere, oranger with the sunset someplace else. It was like we were not all of the same world.

Like there were many earths. Many suns. Many moons, all of different shapes and sizes. I thought of ancient Greeks and aliens. Impossible.

I pictured Anna's parents fast asleep in some villa with vines and purple flowers climbing its crumbling walls, overlooking the sea. There would be a big wooden vat outside where they would stomp on grapes in their bare feet and make wine in good weather, in the sunshine. And there would be a crucifix on the wall and one of those funny guitar things playing in the distance.

I asked, "At night, where you live, can you hear the sea?"

Anna looked at me, and I blushed, debating whether to repeat the question in the same loud, slow voice that Sadie's mother had assumed when speaking to her, like the voice you'd use to speak to the senile.

"Verona ees not on-na the sea," Anna said.

Sadie and I helped her carry her things into Sadie's bedroom. We stood and gaped at her for a few moments and then said a simple good night before I headed back through the trees to my own silent house and silent father, leaving Sadie's mom to fuss over Anna, tuck her into Sadie's bed, and make sure she had everything she needed. For the next four months, Sadie would sleep on a cot in a cleared-out storage nook in the basement, her books and shoes and clothing in cardboard boxes, an old grape juice–stained tablecloth tacked up in the empty, unpainted doorframe for privacy, a few yards from the woodstove. Underground, she would shiver during the last weeks of summer, when it was still hot above ground and silly to light a fire, and she would sweat during winter when the heat of the flames was almost more than she could stand. She would come upstairs some mornings during that November and December dressed in a short-sleeved T-shirt and jeans, no jacket. Throughout that winter, I would meet her at the front door in my donated winter coat and gloves to get the bus; Anna would usually answer, and Sadie would ascend the basement stairs behind her, huffing and puffing, red in the face, dressed for another season and another climate.

• • •

Once Anna had gone to bed, I retreated through the line of trees that separated my real home from my substitute one. My father sat at the kitchen table with a TV dinner, no lights on. It was the same scene that always met me at night when he was home, which was not all the time. He didn't tell me where he went most nights, and I didn't ask.

I approached him. "Hi," I said.

He looked up at me and held my gaze for a few seconds, which was more than I usually got. In my years of wondering why my father seemed so averse to looking at me, I had settled on the explanation that I must look like my mother. This was pure conjecture; I could recall neither the shape of her face nor the color of her eyes. He'd kept no pictures of her.

"What's that on your face," he said.

"It's makeup. Sadie did it. She has a foreign girl—"

"Take it off," he said. He tossed a beer bottle into the kitchen sink, stood up, and stalked out of the room, slouching. I heard his door shut.

So, I rationalized, my mother must've worn number 124: Deep Navy at the periphery of her eyes, whatever color they were. The women probably all wore it in Baker, California, home of the world's largest thermometer. I scrubbed it off.

Throughout the first few weeks of her stay, we tested Anna's authenticity when Sadie's mother was not around, making up pretend English words and watching to see whether she'd let on she understood. She usually did, and we laughed so that she believed she'd agreed to something inappropriate, answered yes to an embarrassing question or consented to some kind of dare without knowing it. She passed all those tests out on Sadie's back deck—the made-up words, the meaningless questions. Sometimes she would excuse herself politely and run into the house and we would hear, through the window above and behind us, the shuffle of her dictionary pages turning as she searched for meanings that did not exist. She was real.

School started. We were nervous because she looked so normal.

Because we could claim her as ours, we wanted her to look as exotic and interesting as possible. She was our key to popularity.

"This is my foreign girl, Anna," Sadie said when introducing her.

She wouldn't have had to. What was not obvious about Anna at first glance was plain as day when she did things like dance through the hallways and kiss people she'd just met on the cheek—and, of course, when she spoke. It wasn't just her accent that made people point at her as she walked away, lean in close to me or to Sadie, and ask in a low voice, "Is she, like, *from* somewhere?" She used strange words that we didn't. Strange *English* words. She called nice kids and cute kids "beautiful." She called a kid who bumped into her in the hallway and did not apologize "smarmy." We had never heard it, and we didn't think it was real.

I figured she was reversing the games Sadie and I had played on her, making up words just to fool us, and I was determined to get to the bottom of the business. After school on the day Anna used the word "smarmy," I sat on the cot in the basement while Anna showered and Sadie did her homework. Under the privacy of the juice-stained sheet-curtain, I opened the pocket dictionary I'd found buried at the bottom of one of Sadie's cardboard boxes. There it was, smarmy (*adj:* 1: marked by false earnestness; unctuous. 2: of low, sleazy taste and/or quality).

"What're you doing?" Sadie asked from behind the curtain.

"Nothing."

I looked up "unctuous."

One day she told us she was in love.

His name was Matty Carpenter. In first grade, I had kissed him on the cheek. We had sat on our carpet squares on the classroom floor while Mrs. Davis read to us from an Eric Carle book, and I had snuck in unexpectedly and pecked him on the cheek, then turned my cheek, expecting him to do the same. He didn't. I punched him. He cried. His mother picked him up in a baby-blue minivan.

And now he was Anna's true love. As they walked to her locker after algebra one day, she said, he took her hand and kissed it. Trying to be romantic. European or something. I could see it in my head: Matty, awkward, a solid four inches shorter than Anna, trying to be suave (*adj:* 1: polite, charming, smooth. 2: well-groomed and having a sophisticated appeal).

"He drop-a my hand," Anna said, "and he look eento-a-my ice. Ah, Jean, hees ice are so blue—blue like-a the *Cinqueterre* sea! Ah, Jean, hees-a so *beut*-iful!"

I rolled my eyes. "I don't know about that," I said. "Kind of cute, maybe. I guess."

Throughout the semester, he courted her, slipping sheets of notebook paper through the vents in her locker. They were elaborately folded, printed in smeared pencil with lines of bad poetry that I caught him copying off a computer screen in the library. Before she left, she gave him a lock of her hair. She cut it for him, right in the middle of the hallway, with a pair of scissors swiped from the art room. She snipped a good three inches of blonde curl from right at the front, by her face, and laid it in his hand with a dramatic sigh. Her head tilted. Her eyes watered. The assistant principal confiscated the scissors.

She slipped me notes in class, the letters short, fat, overlapping. "Jean!" they said. "Matty = beutiful." She spelled it this way every time, even after she'd been here long enough that she ought to have learned to spell it the right way. Beutiful, without the *a*. A long word made short, an intimidating word—so flowery—made accessible, made simple.

She made dinner sometimes, and over dinner, we talked. Her accent rose and fell in waves and swayed back and forth, back and forth while falling; she spoke the way a loose sheet of paper floats to the floor. Sometimes, just from being around her, we found ourselves talking like her without meaning to, when we wanted her to understand, like we were singing. Around the dinner table when Sadie's father got home from work and sat down in his old plaid shirt and dirty jeans, bits of sawdust still stuck in his hair, we would chat with Anna and notice our voices taking on the cadence of her own; the same musical pulse would beat through our own language and make it into something different, alien, and smooth. This was how we reached her, through this rhythm like a lullaby we'd never known we knew how to sing. Even Sadie's father, red in the face and smoking like a chimney, would begin to draw out his vowels, to slow down the words that came between puffs on his Marlboros as he tapped the ash on the side of his plate. Through the haze of smoke and the thickness of the yellow light in Sadie's kitchen, his words came, scratchy, hoarse from years of smoke and work, and floated: "Ann-na, pass-a me the pep-per."

And despite Sadie's mother's initial censorship of our town, our house, and us, Anna took an interest in our ruins. The cluttered messes around town and the empty spaces in between seemed to fascinate her. There were a few abandoned refinery tanks along a back road on the way to town that she liked to walk to sometimes, to sit and think—she did a lot of that, just sitting and thinking. We would circle the old tanks, pace the pavement beneath them, now barely discernible through the grass and weeds that grew over it, hinting that everything here was bound for erasure.

"Piece of shit," I said on the first day we visited the tanks, kicking one.

But Anna touched the tanks, rubbed the iron flakes they shed between her fingertips. She found beauty in our rust, girl from the land of gladiators.

In time, as we continued to frequent the tanks, her genuine interest in them made me begin to think differently of them too—hints of a better time, suggestions of the lost potential of home, here. Our little Colosseums.

Her fascinations did not die out. Every day when the school bus picked us up, she commented on how beautiful it was. She took pictures of chipmunks and lawn mowers and pickup trucks and sent them to her parents. And every evening we sang at the dinner table.

• • •

Fall was hideous, brown, soggy. It rained for weeks and didn't snow until a few days before doe season. When the first snowflakes began to fall, Sadie's father sat by the living room window with us and watched.

"It keeps snowing like this, it'll be perfect for spotting deer."

Sadie agreed. For her twelfth birthday, they'd gotten her her own rifle. (They got me a book, *Where the Red Fern Grows.*) She was set to go out with her father on the first day of doe; school was cancelled that day; no one would have gone if they'd had it. It was an important event for both of them, a rite of passage for Sadie.

To everyone's surprise, Anna asked if she could go.

Sadie was annoyed at first. Her patience was short with Anna sometimes, when she couldn't understand questions, when she hugged and kissed Sadie's parents far more than Sadie herself would have ever thought of doing. Her annoyance was mixed with amusement.

"You know I'm gonna *shoot* one," she said to Anna, grinning.

"Yes."

"It's gonna *die*," Sadie went on. "There's gonna be blood."

"I know."

"My dad's gonna cut out its heart."

"Sadie," I said. "Stop."

"No," Anna said. "Ees true. But I want-a to come."

I was invited too. I had never been hunting before; I had no one to go with, and it had always seemed dirty to me, a sad ritual of a sad place. But when the day came, I summoned my courage and let Sadie's mother wrap me, like Sadie and Anna, in a bright orange scarf, a loose, torn camouflage jacket, an orange knit cap that held the smell of woodsmoke. I imagined explosions of smoke and guts, body parts and violet insides flying through the air. I was afraid to see it. Sadie was afraid not to. It was the first year that we were old enough to kill.

There was hardly enough light to see by when we set out that morning, but we could make out the silvery smoke of our breath in clouds around our faces. It had snowed enough over the past few days that the ground was completely covered and the dead leaves beneath the layer of white were frozen and crunched under our boots. It was the only sound we heard. Unlike the crashes and bangs of the primitive hunt of my dreams, this sound was regular, peaceful, like a pulse, and the smoke around us was not smoke at all but only vapor. Our excess life, expelled from our lungs, crystalline. The cold burned in my nostrils and filled my throat, dry and clean. We walked slowly, Anna and I close behind Sadie and her father, Sadie's short legs pumping, stepping twice for every one of her father's strides as the morning grew clearer.

Several times, Anna tried to speak. Each time, Sadie or her father hushed her. She looked at me. Her cheeks were red and her skin was shiny; snowflakes caught in her eyelashes, melted, shimmered. She wiped her nose. Ahead of us in the dim light, Sadie held her rifle like a soldier. Anna slipped her gloved hand into mine, and we walked that way for a long time, crunch, crunching through the snow, not speaking.

We'd been waiting for an hour at the spot Sadie's dad had chosen by a boulder shaped like a dinosaur, sipping hot chocolate from a shared thermos, when the deer showed up. She was alone. Sadie's father motioned for her to wait. For a clear killing shot.

I watched the doe and never saw Sadie raise the gun or pull the trigger. When she did, the sound was a sharp, tearing blast that broke the air around us, shattered the silence.

More than the destruction of the body, I had feared that the doe would suffer; in the fraction of a second between the sound of the bullet and its impact, this fear welled up in me again. I knew how hunters followed trails of blood, sometimes for miles. But as the bullet entered her body right behind the front shoulder, clean and sharp through the lungs, the lack of gruesomeness startled me more than any amount of gore could have done. It was less than a minute before she collapsed. In the meantime, between the impact and the end, there was a dance. She leapt into the air, spun, landed unsteady on her feet, took one wobbly step, and went down, all with barely a sound. She was dainty, dignified in this dance of death, which she seemed to have practiced for years.

This was the secret behind the heads on the wall. I'd never felt so involved in the place where I lived, in the only arts it had ever perfected: the art of dying and of watching things die.

Sadie's father whistled, laughed like a boy, picked Sadie up, and twirled her around. We made our way over to the deer.

Her eyes were open. Her legs had buckled under her and were bowed in strange directions, snapped sticks.

"What do you think, girls?" asked Sadie's father.

No one spoke. Anna leaned over the deer's face. I expected a soliloquy of some sort, a dramatic sob; I waited for her head to tilt the way it did in moments of melodrama.

"Will-a you keep its face?" she asked.

"Nah," Sadie's father said. "Not a doe. She's pretty, though, ain't she?" He drew his knife from its case. The blade gleamed in the sunlight.

We hadn't warned Anna about the way the knife would slice through the doe's underside, bottom to top, the way Sadie's father would roll her onto her side, his hands steady and efficient, and sever tissue, letting organs and intestines slide free of their frame. I had heard about all this before, seen the carcasses hung from trees. But just before the doe's insides seeped free of their casing, I found myself reaching for Anna's hand.

"Maybe you should close your eyes," I said.

But neither of us did. The same silence that had been with us all morning, through the sunrise, through the falling snow, descended again, and the body lost its shape. In the cold, the organs steamed. Like our breath that vaporized around our faces, clouds rose from the cut and from the vacant carcass. The lungs, which the bullet had broken, oozed blood and melted the snow beneath them. The red dripped into perfect, bright circles. From where we stood, we could feel the heat rising from the body, both its shell and the former interior, which now lay in a heap, strangely neat and mostly intact. I did not think that I could look at a real heart, plump and unbroken, and not look away, and yet there it was. And there I was.

I dropped Anna's hand and stepped forward. I stood in the clean snow by the deer's disassembled body. I touched her face. Then I removed my glove, extended my hand and held it over the carcass, now empty down to the base of the ribcage. I moved my fingers, white with cold, in the steam. I thought I moved them gracefully.

I can think of a hundred words, now, to express that moment—the heart on the snow, my hand moving in the heat of an open body, my fears behind me. In the moment, though, language failed me. I looked at Sadie, smiling, and I was proud of her. I stood, and Anna took my hand again, and we waited together as Sadie's father finished his careful work and finally took the doe by her legs, hauling her back the way we'd come.

At the time, I thought it was only the presence of Sadie's father that steeled us and kept us from turning from the sight of the blood, closing our eyes as knife severed hide, and running away. But now I'm sure we would have stood there either way, whether he was with us or not, the three of us girls, holding hands in the snow and the silence.

Sadie's father said that after a few hours, the organs would freeze. Eventually, he said, coyotes would take care of them. In the meantime, songbirds would pick at the fat and sing. He butchered the deer himself, and the meat lasted until long after Anna left near the end of the month, just a few days before Christmas.

I asked Sadie's mother for some of the venison. I could tell she was surprised, but she didn't ask questions. I took it home and stashed it near the back of the freezer.

It was only a matter of weeks before Anna would return to Italy. We braced ourselves for the change the same way we had in August, but though her arrival had been sudden and shocking, her departure seemed to occur in bits, stretching themselves across a period of weeks. At times, our voices slipped back into song even after she was gone. Matty Carpenter came over the night before she flew away, gave her a crimson rose from which he'd carefully sliced the thorns with his pocket knife. He tied three scraps of fabric around it—green, white, red: the colors of the Italian flag, which we had not known four months ago. When we returned to school after Christmas, he brought an identical one in and laid it on the floor at the base of what had been Anna's locker. It was one of the corniest things I'd ever seen. She would have loved it.

She promised to write, and for a long time, she did. Her letters were verbose (*adj:* 1. using or expressed in more words than are needed; loquacious) and full of exclamation points and love and "very beutiful." She promised me an Italian home and family, a family I had never met and figured I never would meet. I went back to imagining her, her house, her family, and their everyday lives, more realistically now—not stomping grapes, but a lawyer and a teacher in a second-floor apartment in a town that was not by the sea. Blonde.

On the day she left, I took the venison Sadie's mother had given me out of the freezer and let it thaw. I could cook well, thanks to my time at Sadie's, my years of handing her mother spices and wooden spoons and watching her without talking. By the time my father came home—he was pumping gas then, I think, at a Kwik Fill—it was nearly ready. It was dark outside.

His face was blank when he saw me. "Don't they want you over there no more," he said.

I shrugged.

He stared at me for a while and then sat in the living room. I heard the TV click on.

I served the venison on old plastic plates. I sat down across from him and we ate in silence. On TV, the History Channel, Neil Armstrong was walking on the moon.

"Dad," I said after a while.

He looked up.

"This deer?" I said. "Sadie shot it."

He nodded.

"I watched it die."

He didn't say anything, but he looked at me for a long time. He looked old.

I had slept in my own bedroom in my father's house nearly every night of my life, and yet I couldn't remember the last time we'd eaten dinner together. I had an urge to tell him things, then, in my new language.

But I didn't. And I didn't tell him about being eight years old, sitting on my bed, wondering whether I should slam my arm hard against the doorknob or run an untrimmed fingernail down my face and pretend he'd hurt me. I'd thought about this every time Sadie's mother asked if he had, yet I never did it. I guess, even then, I knew what the consequences of such an action would be. I guess I never really wanted to be taken away from him.

On TV, 1969, Neil Armstrong planted the American flag on the moon and bounded across the surface, playful, like a cartoon. Then the scene changed, and he was sitting in an armchair, many years later, talking about what it was like making contact with what he, what everyone, had seen, stared at, dreamed under for so long from across such a vast, empty distance.

"That's something," my father said.

"What?"

"The moon." He motioned to the screen.

Yes, I thought, it *is* something—something shared with all the world, though it's right outside our window, throwing shadows over our yard. Beautiful.

I guess I fell asleep because, the next thing I knew, I was waking up. My father was sleeping in the armchair across from me. I looked at the clock on the wall, 7:30 in the morning. I thought of Anna, six hours ahead where it was already afternoon, and of my mother, in Baker, California, home of the world's largest thermometer, three hours behind, where it was still dark.

Make Yourself at Home

ANYWAY, THE ADDRESS on the package was her own—at least for now—even if the name was not. Surely that made opening it less dishonest. Caroline knew better, knew the box was none of her business; still she found that her hands folded back its cardboard flaps and sifted through tissue like two ill-behaved friends whose peer pressure she was incapable of resisting. Her hands located the shape of something hard, ceramic, and fractured: a blue bowl, a broken blue bowl not meant for her.

Caroline knew the responsible thing would have been to leave the box for Meredith's return or forward it on to Boston, to its rightful owner—Meredith under bright lights, trying on wedding gowns—no questions asked. She pictured Meredith times three or four, multiplied in the mirrors of a boutique fitting room, turning to evaluate from all angles the flattery of the cut and the fabric. Everything in the world to be gained, or else gained already.

Caroline pulled each chip of the ceramic bowl from the box with care and assembled them on the table. Then she searched every drawer in Meredith's apartment for glue.

When Meredith had left the apartment, heading to Boston to spend the next three months with her new fiancé, a law student at BU, she'd taken with her all the belongings she could fit into two suitcases and left the rest behind. She'd shoved aside the clothes that still hung in her walk-in closet to clear space for Caroline's and told her to make herself at home. It had been challenging at first. Meredith, an old college classmate of Caroline's, kept her apartment bejeweled with framed photographs of herself that seemed to stare at Caroline as if waiting for the answer to some unasked but urgent question. On the day she left, Meredith had handed Caroline the keys, shown her how to jiggle open the lock on the front gate, and instructed her to place fresh bay leaves by pipes and drains to keep roaches away. But she had neglected to arrange to have her mail forwarded. *Everyone who knows me knows where I am*, she said when Caroline called her after a few days of receiving her Victoria's Secret catalogues. *Just throw whatever comes in a pile; I'll deal with it when I get back*, she'd instructed. Less than a week later, the package arrived. It came from North Dakota, and what made it so irresistible was the fact that, although their addresses were different, the receiver's name at the center of the box—Meredith's—and the sender's name in the upper corner were exactly the same, down to the letter, even the uncommon Polish surname with its many consonants and single vowel stuck among them as if the name were a child's puzzle: Which of these letters is not like the others? Which one does not belong?

Inside the box, among the fragments of pottery, was an envelope—*To Meredith From Meredith*—which Caroline now turned over in her hand. And slid her finger under the edge of the flap, and tore.

• • •

Before coming to Meredith's, she'd been living alone in a house on a country road outside Fort Collins, a rental surrounded by pines, set away from the commotion of the university where she'd studied and where she still worked. The house sat against a hill where a mountain lion ranged, sometimes screaming at night like a woman being stabbed. Otherwise, it was silent, and since her father's death, Caroline had taken to leaving the radio on all day for the noise. She listened to conspiracy theories, depressing stories about civil unrest, uplifting stories about cancer survivors, strange stories about spontaneous order, bioluminescence, conjoined twins fused at the hip or sharing a common heart. But in Denver, she had no use for a radio; there was the noise of the building's tenants, the clamor of the street, other people's doors opening and closing. It was less possible, there, to forget you were in the world.

She had come to the city for a change of scene in the wake of her father's death. She would spend late summer and autumn at Meredith's, an hour and a half from home, close enough that she could run back if necessary, far enough away to feel fresh and strange, subletting while her father's house sat empty. It had been Fat Man who'd told her, You've got to get away, kid. He'd been kind enough to grant her a leave of absence for the fall. And why not? She was replaceable; grad students would do her work while she was gone; she'd compose a draft of Fat Man's next article from afar, and as usual, he'd be first author of all her published words. Caroline was a detail. She was "et al."

During her father's last months, she'd told herself it was only the stress of his sickness that was keeping her from quitting her job as a lab manager for her former advisor and moving on. But now, supergluing the shards of Meredith's blue bowl, watching two sisters approach the apartment building in step from her window—left, right, left, right, as if one was a body and the other a mirror—she understood that this had been a lie. She had become the ugly stepchild of her department: the hanger-on, the petrification, and it was her own fault. Some people got married, some people had babies, some people went to work in power suits or got fancy industry jobs or tenure; Caroline simply held on, and barely. Fat Man—the title was more a statement of fact than of judgment or malice—got the grant money, credit for the publications. Caroline was Skinny Man, responsible for ground work, as much a mechanic as a researcher, passing on data, running around haggard. She had finished her PhD in plant physiology three years ago, and now here she was in the same department at the same university, labeling plastic bags, surrounded by pruning shears and chainsaws, calibrating pressure bombs, measuring chemical concentrations in leaves. She kept a sleeping bag rolled in the space underneath her desk on campus, a flaccid pillow and travel-size toothbrush in a drawer. She was her own handyman and her own housewife, and it wasn't the job itself she was unhappy with, it wasn't her life, necessarily. It was just the sense of stagnation. The running in a circle, gathering things she felt always about to drop.

Her friend Paula, whose dissertation was considered more significant than Caroline's, had just snagged a Forest Service job in an industry with low turnover rates, run by men who didn't let go of their posts until they had to, men who died in the saddle, so to speak. She had removed her things from the office she shared with Caroline just a few days before Caroline left for the fall. "It'll happen for you, Caro," Paula had said, leaning over Caroline's shoulder while she mounted cores on pieces of wood and measured their rings under a microscope. "You know how it is—it's all just waiting around for some old white guy to die. And they do, eventually."

"Ha," Caroline said.

She had imagined that in the city she'd be different, more like Meredith, maybe. Zipping around in taxis wearing heels. She'd become a coffee drinker, maybe adopt a cat. But already a week in, and the late summer scorching too early the leaves on the trees, a premature autumn, she'd settled into lethargy—hair unwashed, wearing mismatched socks, opening somebody else's mail.

Was she nothing without someone to take care of?

Meredith,

I Googled my self yesterday and was surprised to find I was not the only me. I know this might be creepy but I saw you were getting married (saw you're online registry) and wanted to send a gift. I found you're address in a web database. Hope your not too freaked out 1.) that I'm out here and 2.) that I found you. I am 27 and recently out of rehab the second time, trying to stay clean. We'll see how it goes this time around. I am working on getting back in touch with my self, you might say. I got toxic things inside me I need to let out.

I live in N. Dakota and work in a restaurant and am an artist. I'm sending you this bowl I made and best wishes for your wedding and a happy future. No need to write back, I bet your busy, but for some reason it's a comfort to know your out there, like discovering a long lost twin, even though I'm sure your not much like me. But it's not like we're both named Jane Doe or John Smith. I always thought I was so unique, and so alone.

I suppose names are just outside things, like coats of paint or glaze. Besides you'll probably be changing yours soon, and then it'll be just me again. I don't know. What do you think?

I hope you like the bowl.

Take care,
Meredith

Caroline set the letter on the table, flushed with the sense of having irreversibly committed to something large. To ignore the letter seemed cruel; Meredith was an addict, after all, or had been. She needed support. Caroline sat for a while at the kitchen table where the reassembled bowl sat healing, glue drying. She had seen the letters *MP* scrawled in the unglazed clay of its base. It was probably cold in North Dakota, even in summer. Caroline had never known anyone who'd lived there or imagined that anyone actually did. She pictured Meredith, the new one, in sturdy boots on a farm, face a hazy blur like something censored. In the morning, she milks cows, and the raw milk in the bucket is swirled pink with blood. She lights a cigarette—no, only considers it in a fleeting moment of weakness; she's stuck a nicotine patch on her arm, another attempt at wellness. Her pottery studio is a small, cold lean-to on the side of the barn. She sits down at the wheel, blowing puffs of moist air onto her thin fingers, and throws down a chunk of clay the size of a softball. She watches it spin. An urge to use—whatever it was she'd been using—and she rolls the impulse off with a shiver, plunges wet hands into the clay. The slip gathers under her nails. She does this because she loves it, because she's cleanest when her hands are this particular type of dirty. She does it so as not to do something else.

You couldn't just leave someone out there like that. Caroline dug through Meredith's desk—Meredith of the wedding gowns and the many self-portraits—for paper.

Dear Meredith,

Thank you for your note and for the bowl. I have filled it with strawberries and it has brought a cheerful splash of color to my kitchen. My fiancé and I are house hunting, and when we find one we plan to paint the walls cornflower blue. It's as if you knew this somehow. He is an entomologist, and for our honeymoon we will travel to Malaysia to watch thousands of rare fireflies flash in unison in a forest of mangroves. He studies insects, and I study trees—we're a natural pair, I suppose. We met in Banff, researching.

I sincerely wish you the best of luck in your rehabilitation. I myself have had a positive experience with recovery, recently; my father has survived cancer. Last year there was a tumor the size of a golf ball in his lung and this year he is up and about and currently hiking the Continental Divide Trail. Am sending you positive energy.

Positive energy? What was that? A cheerful splash of color? Who was the writer of this letter? Not Meredith, certainly, but not quite Caroline either. There was no fiancé, for instance, and there had been no tumor, and of course there was no hiking the Continental Divide, though the thought of it made Caroline smile: her father tearing open a bag of granola with his teeth.

Except he wouldn't have eaten granola. Too hippie, too green. Homemade jerky, probably, sliced along the grain and dried in the oven with the door cracked, and not too good in all honesty, marinated too much or too little. And he didn't have cancer; he'd died of a neurodegenerative genetic disorder, and it had been—it still was—terrible. Shortly before his death, Caroline had gone alone to the hospital to be tested for the gene that caused the disease. The results were negative. So she was in it for the long haul with herself, and she was supposed to be happy about this.

They had always loved each other like they were the only two people in the world because it had seemed to them that they were; Caroline's mother had died when she was young. This was not to say that there was always peace between them. But still. Even though Caroline knew, logically, that she and her father had had their share of battles, it was becoming harder and harder to recall them. Already her mind was replacing them with fonder memories, better images, the kinds of familial anomalies you celebrate, not the ones that kill you. Like this: they used to eat in the dark. He was a bad cook and she a picky eater. When she could see how his meals turned out, unsightly, too runny or clumpy, she refused to eat. And, as her father often said, she was sticks and stones already—knobby knees and shoulders, twig-thin legs. He put a small dinner table on the lower floor of the house, mostly underground and where little sunlight reached, closed the blinds on the narrow window there, and turned out the lights.

"What's in this?" she would sometimes ask, hesitating.

He'd say, "Food," and leave it at that. They ate without speaking and without seeing, and she grew.

Caroline returned to the letter she'd written the new Meredith. She kept the bits about the splash of color and the positive energy but cut the part about the synchronized Malaysian fireflies. She had heard a story about them on the radio a few months back but now thought the lie about traveling to see them seemed too showy, too arrogant. For all she knew, Meredith might never have left North Dakota. Needles in her veins and nowhere to go.

She went to her laptop and typed in Meredith's name, scanning the search results, careful not to write anything in her letter that would contradict what limited image the new Meredith had been able to form of her namesake. She found only the old Meredith's wedding registry and a record of her time in a half-marathon she'd run several months ago. Caroline rewrote the letter with a casual reference to long-distance running, then rewrote it again with a few nonchalant questions for Meredith—about her interests, about North Dakota, about pottery—and signed it with a name that wasn't hers.

Was there another *her* out there? Someone braver, someone who'd do better, know better? She couldn't help but wonder. When she'd jumped off a bank or leapt from a diving board as a child, was there another her who felt, at the moment Caroline's body began its plunge, the sensation of vertigo in her gut? When Caroline scraped her knee or had her hair pulled on the playground as a girl, did the other her, by instinct, scratch at the pink skin on her kneecap or smooth her tidy hair? Even now, as Caroline sat by the window with the sun blazing in, watching orange and yellow leaves toss on the quaking aspen outside, did another her, in some cool room somewhere, feel suddenly warm and fan her reddening face with the flat of her hand? She pictured herself on an escalator, slowly descending, hand on the railing, eyes straight ahead. And another her on the other side, in ascent. Eyes straight ahead. Going somewhere else—where? At the midpoint the two cross, unknowing.

"Hello," Caroline whispered to the empty room, to the air, to anywhere. "Hello, Caroline," and she collided once again with the profound realization that she was alone.

. . .

There was Daniel, of course.

His fraternity brothers had given him the nickname Boog, but it didn't fit. "Boog" was big, blubbering, sloppy. Daniel was small, lively but secretly vulnerable. Like a puppy minus the loyalty.

He was six years younger than she and had been her dendrology student back when he was a sophomore and she was about to defend her dissertation. He'd performed poorly on most of his quizzes, and whenever he was completely uncertain of an answer, he would fill the space instead with some bawdy tree joke involving hardwood or with a pun: I can't seem to get to the root of the problem. She'd covered his quizzes in red Xs. But later, when he signed up for an independent study in Fat Man's lab and was assigned as Caroline's field assistant, he revealed another side. He was motherless, like her, seeming to have sprung from the dirt, and he kept his eyes fixed steadily on hers when she spoke. They worked together, measuring water stress in the stems of leaves, and they sometimes camped in the field, waking up every few hours to take water potential measurements. She brought him with her to carry the machinery, and that was where it began: the two of them twisted between flannel-lined sleeping bags. He often brought along a case of beer, and on one particular night, she had drunk too much and he just enough, and they made—not love, but a kind of rough sketch of it, like a rehearsal. Afterward, she pulled on a pair of fleece pajama pants that sparked when she climbed under the covers, and he, drunk and childlike, marveled at the blue lightning flashes she produced with her movements. "It's like a storm under there," he said, blankets over his head. "Do it again," and she shifted her knee against the flannel, glowing.

He said, "You are *literally* electrifying."

They were not in love, yet she sensed that he needed her, and if that wasn't love, it was at least familiar. It was enough to keep her answering his calls and making a few of her own. It had been three years, and now, a super senior, he was about to graduate.

They had worked together on an extension of her dissertation research, an examination of what caused trees to die in droughts. She'd spent years comparing the processes of carbon starvation and hydraulic failure. The first is like holding your breath until you're dead, impossible for a human but possible for a tree that, starved, defoliates and dies. The second, like sucking a straw when there's nothing in your glass but air and that awful slurping sound. Capillaries fracture, leaves curl and drop to conserve carbon and water. The processes are interconnected, largely simultaneous, and have the same outcome, which was why her project was not considered particularly consequential. Ultimately, no one cared what made an individual tree die, whether a clot or an inability to breathe—either way, other experts said, what's dead is dead. Shouldn't we, they asked, be concerned with the threshold level of water stress at which the tree dies instead of the mechanisms that do the killing? Caroline felt that her research did matter, that it mattered immensely, but she couldn't explain why.

Maybe this was why she liked Daniel: he valued her work because he'd been in on it, albeit marginally. And she had the feeling that somehow Daniel had seen inside her, as well, had seen what she was made of.

After dropping her letter into the outgoing mail slot in the lobby, Caroline returned to Meredith's apartment and paced about, not knowing what to do next. There was a message on her phone from Daniel that had been there for two days. She opened the door to Meredith's closet and stared at the modest collection of her own clothes hanging limply at the end of the rack next to Meredith's abandoned ones. Flannel shirts, some of which had been her father's. Nylon pants that unzipped at the knees to become shorts, practical but unfeminine. The fact was she spent much of her time shooting down foliage samples with shotguns from high parts of trees, or climbing in ascension gear to cut down segments needed for study. She drilled into trunks and drew out ringed sample tubes. Or she cut whole trees down, took cookies—inch-thick slivers of the trunk—back to the lab, labeled them. She dressed appropriately, her body forgotten under fabric.

From among Meredith's clothes, she selected a turquoise sleeveless dress made of material like water that refused, when she slid it from the hanger, to be gathered into her hands. It was unlike anything she'd worn in years. She spent many minutes collecting its folds and ripples into a ball and then tossing it in the air, watching it unwind fluidly, a dress again for just a second before it pooled formless on the floor. When she pulled the dress over her head, squirming in its clingy grip, she stepped back to evaluate herself in Meredith's full-length mirror. She shifted her hips, yanked at the dress's straps, and turned in a circle, letting the hem stroke her calves. She kept the dress on, sifted through some of Meredith's left-behind jewelry, picked out a turquoise pendant, and fastened it around her neck. She returned to the closet and dug around on the floor for a pair of heels, finding a scuffed and spent-looking pair and slipping them onto her feet. Then she called Daniel.

"Boog here," he said when he picked up the phone.

"Why do you answer like that?" she asked. "You know it's me."

Meredith's next letter came soon enough that she couldn't have waited more than a day to reply to the one she received from Caroline. Caroline could already tell that the two Merediths were nothing alike; there was no supernatural connection between them, just an accident of nomenclature. If the new Meredith's letter had found its intended recipient, it would probably have gone unanswered, the fragments of the broken handmade bowl thrown away, clay pieces sent back to the earth. It wasn't that the old Meredith was unkind, just that she was . . . busy, too confident and too comfortable to really need anyone, let alone to need broken pottery. She and Caroline had never been close, even when they'd lived in the same dorm as undergraduates. Caroline envied both Merediths a little, in different ways. On the one hand, the feeling of "finding oneself," whatever that meant. On the other, the sense of not needing to.

Yes, I do enjoy my job at Elroy's. Most of the diners are regulars and we serve there coffee for free. The owner (yes Elroy himself) has been nice enough to take me back several times, despite everything. Although lately I been thinking I'm ready for a break from the place, maybe I'll get out of town. I don't deserve his kindness, and besides it's hard trying to live different in a place where every thing has always been the same, where you're surrounded by enablers and so many people who have seen the worse of you. I've given up social media for this reason, trying to remake myself away from old ties.

A while back I had a stand at a craft fair in St. Paul and liked it there, so maybe I'll head that way. Who knows. All I know is that for miles around here you can drive and drive and still feel like you haven't moved an inch, like your stuck on a treadmill. You'd think the world would seem bigger with a horizon that empty and the sky so wide. But it just seems small. There's no distant mountain or city skyline to focus on, not even a tree sometimes to put stuff in prespective. How did we ever think the earth was flat? When I look at the horizon I see it's edges curving clear as day.

A fun fact about North Dakota? We have more churches per capita then any other state. Personally, I don't attend a one of them.

The letter went on to tell of the death of one of Meredith's close friends, a woman whose overdose had propelled Meredith back into rehab, this time with a genuine determination to recover. To recover from several things, she said. *I know her death wasn't my fault, but I still feel like it was,* Meredith wrote. *I wasn't planning to tell you, but when I picked up the pen I found the words wrote themselves.*

It surprised Caroline that Meredith should open up like this, speaking of her tragedies to a stranger. But there was an intimacy to the whole thing that she felt working on her as well: the exchange of letters, with their creases, ink smudges, and imperfections. She wished she hadn't said that thing about her father, about the Continental Divide Trail.

She wished she could say to Meredith, *I know how you feel.* But she was engaged, happy, house hunting, and traveling the world, as far as Meredith was concerned.

She put on the turquoise dress and heels again the day Daniel drove down from Fort Collins. As soon as he got there, he retrieved a stack of papers and envelopes from his car and tossed them on the kitchen table: his graduate school applications.

"I need you," he said, gesturing to the pile, then to the turquoise dress, its thin straps, fabric pulled tight across her breasts. "Where'd you get *that*?"

Caroline shrugged. "Oh, I've had this for years."

She poured them each a glass of water and set Meredith's bowl, now intact and full of grapes, on the table. She sifted through the papers, the mailings from various universities, all out of state. She picked up a copy of his application letter, blank but for a few generic and unimpressive sentences. Then she opened his laptop and sat down. "How would you describe the work you did as a field assistant?"

He shrugged. "Glorified pair of shoulders." He plucked a grape from Meredith's bowl. "What happened here? You broke this chick's bowl?"

"No," Caroline said, "I didn't break it. I fixed it. And you've got to do better than that. Pair of shoulders, I mean."

"Well, I carried stuff," he said. "I wrote down numbers. I clipped leaves from branches and handed them to you."

"Experience working both in the field and in the lab," Caroline said, typing. "Understanding of the start-to-finish process of research. Problem solving—"

"Sometimes I turned on the GPS," he said.

"Familiarity with instrumentation," she went on, "and . . . advanced navigation techniques." She remembered their nights under the trees, his stupid answers on his dendro quizzes: It would be a re-leaf if I knew the answer. She drank from her glass. He yanked grapes from their stems.

"I made up a joke yesterday," he said.

She was losing him.

"Rare plant identification," she said, typing. "Remember when we found the twinpod?"

He nodded. "Why was Godzilla so upset?"

Physaria obcordata. Frail yellow flowers, rosette leaves. Threatened and, Caroline feared, doomed to die.

Daniel's fingers drumrolled on the edge of the table. "He had *a reptile dysfunction*."

Caroline shook her head. She typed away on Daniel's letter; her fingertips spun phrases. Big-picture thinking. Short- and long-term research goals. She had a knack for this, it seemed, composing euphemisms and half-truths. And lies, too, plain old lies.

"Hey," Daniel said, suddenly serious. She became aware that he'd been watching her, studying her shape in Meredith's dress. He reached over and brushed a strand of hair behind her ear. "You clean up well, Caro." His voice was soft. She knew he knew he would have been lost without her these past few years, professionally anyway. She knew that in a few more, he would be capable of making someone happy. And she knew that it wasn't going to be her.

He was moving up, away. She felt certain that, between the independent studies and the euphemisms, he'd get accepted somewhere. Outside the window, a church bell clanged, and the changing leaves trembled in a breeze; she heard them crunching under a passerby's feet, and she sensed that it was time to disengage.

He had her address the manila envelopes in which he'd mail his applications; his own handwriting was a child's, a Boog's. Caroline crossed each *t* with care. The next day, before he left, she stacked the envelopes and handed them to him.

"Daniel," she said. "That Godzilla joke? It's funny."

He grinned. "A keeper?"

She closed the door behind him.

• • •

She hadn't been there when her father died.

His dementia began as simple absentmindedness and escalated into more dangerous forms of forgetfulness: confusing the symbolism of colors in traffic, running red lights, rear-ending another car on the freeway. She brought him out to live with her in Fort Collins, thinking she could take care of him, but after a while, his limbs swung at her uncontrollably, muscles like sticks tied to some sick puppeteer's strings, and by the time she admitted she could no longer care for him on her own and hired a nurse, he'd stopped bathing and was newly bruised and damaged at the end of each day from falling down, running into things. He remained, though, just lucid enough to realize what was happening to him, enough to be ashamed, and that was the saddest thing.

He had always been a model of resigning himself to things, making the best of them. Even raising her—she always knew he loved her, but still, when she imagined what it must have been like for him to find himself alone with her, a five-year-old . . . there must have been times he wanted out. She followed him into the woods and became like him, boyish, maybe, but what did it matter? She learned that the inner tips of the heads of red clover flowers tasted sweet on the tongue. She learned to shoot a .22 at an old Folgers can balanced on top of a wall he'd stacked from wooden planks. He tried to be a mother, too—attempting to style her hair, for instance, on picture day or the first day of school, fingers catching there incompetently.

For a few weeks during deer season every year, he drove from butcher shop to butcher shop with two wildlife biologists prying open discarded, severed deer heads with a knife and a steel jawbreaker. It was only seasonal work, a temporary duty, and the only part of his job as a forester that he hated. But he did it; he accepted it as part of a bigger, better job. He studied their molars to determine their ages, review the health of their herds, set license allocations. At the end of those days, he scraped brain from between the treads of his boots with a stick. He left his boots on the porch and hung his coveralls over the railing. He picked ticks and keds from his skin, showered, and cooked her dinner.

He didn't complain, just described. And she didn't flinch during the telling, just learned, and things that other girls might have feared became commonplace to her: insects, soil, organs, death.

And he had died alone in the dark. She'd been asleep at the time. A nurse had found him. How could she have let him down?

I know it wasn't my fault, Meredith had written. *But I still feel like it was.*

Caroline picked up a pen. *I can only imagine how you feel*, she wrote. *I had* . . . she hesitated. How to put it when, in this fantasy, she had a husband-to-be and a father cured? *A dog*, she wrote. *It might sound silly and my loss is clearly not comparable to the loss of your friend. But he was loyal, my most constant companion. I had him put to sleep a few months ago.* She paused again. *You have to forgive yourself, Meredith. You have to move on.*

The Meredith she was impersonating did have a dog, a Pekingese that reminded Caroline of a gargoyle. But he was still very much alive. Meredith had considered leaving him with Caroline for the summer and letting her dog-sit in exchange for half off the rent, but at the last minute, she'd taken the dog with her to Massachusetts, smuggled it into her fiancé's townhouse.

But the dog didn't seem like enough.

> *It looks like I have a new problem of my own. I found a lump. The doctors say we've caught it early enough that everything should be okay. Of course, you never know. I keep asking myself: Why me? Especially following so closely my father's own battle with cancer! My fiancé has been wonderful, so supportive, but I can tell that the news has placed a new strain on our relationship, created a new distance between us. I'm full of doubt and fear, but these letters give me hope. I'm glad I have you to talk to, that we can support each other from afar. Meredith, do you ever feel the world has been unfair to you?*

Caroline ran downstairs and posted the letter before she could change her mind.

So she was in deep now. It was as if her pen had moved independently of her body, concocted this lie without her full consent. Yet this new lie felt more real, less treacherous than the other smaller ones she'd told—more in keeping with the way she truly felt, somehow. The problem now was how badly she wanted to tell Meredith everything. The truth, even in the form of a lie, if that was possible. The North Dakota Caroline imagined now was not violently cold, only comfortably chilly, and Meredith was not on a farm but in a small and tidy apartment. This Meredith leaves the apartment and walks not into a blizzard or a barn but onto a road that bisects an open field, dead grass the color of sawdust on her left, on her right. She wears mittens knit by a relative and sets off jogging down the road, gravel crunching under her feet, whitewashed churches with pointed steeples on the horizon. A chill reddens the tips of her ears, the part where the flesh curls in on itself, neatly finished as the lip of a clay pot.

There were so many things that Caroline wanted to broadcast there, into the soft drum of Meredith's ear where an ache forms from the sting of cold air. Her name, for one. And what she did for a living, and the way tree rings resemble great thumbprints, and the fact that she could use some tips on recovery. The fact that, had her parents known about the deadly gene her father carried, they'd likely not have had her at all; his decline was so inevitable and the risk so great of his passing it on to her. The fact that she had escaped this fate by some fluke of nature and could not figure out why, or what to do with life, with health, a gift that had been thrust at her. The way that love felt, for her, hard and dense like a fist in the gut, her heart like a rock carried in a fraying sack. Was she alone in this? She would like to ask Meredith. How do you start over with yourself?

Sign your own name to your letters, for one, Meredith might say.

It was true: she couldn't keep this up forever. At the end of the fall semester, she'd return to Fort Collins, and obviously, the real Meredith could never know what she'd done. She could tell Meredith in North Dakota she was moving, give her her own address, and continue receiving mail as someone else. But even then, how long could she go on?

Meredith's reply to the lump letter was nurturing, kind. *So sorry . . . terrible . . . if there's anything I can do . . .* And Caroline believed her—believed that Meredith would, really and truly, sweep to her aid somehow if she needed her. She imagined the two of them banded together, facing the world and what it threw at them.

No I don't think the world has been unfair to me, Meredith wrote. *I just think I've been unfair to my self.*

Hours after reading the letter, Caroline stood in front of Meredith's bathroom mirror. She removed her shirt and bra, folded them, and set them beside the sink. She lifted each elbow and massaged each breast, fingers moving with care and precision in small circles from armpit to center. Then she lay on her back, one arm at a time over her head, and pressed each one again, softly, then firmly. No lumps, no knots of any kind.

She wasn't surprised, exactly, and yet she felt a curious sense of relief, as though she'd half expected, subconsciously, to have summoned ill health, to have conjured disease, death, psychosomatically through her letter to Meredith—to find that the lie she'd sown there had sprouted into some real, malignant thing. She knew this hypothesis was unrealistic, indeed impossible; she'd known better, she, a scientist, a biologist, and yet she had tested it, and the results had, on some visceral and undeniable level, startled her. She pulled her shirt back over her head.

I'm responding well to treatment. I am, as my doctor suggested I should be, cautiously optimistic. At this point, I'm as concerned about my relationship as I am about my health. Things haven't been so great, lately—I'm afraid we're drifting apart, even as the wedding draws near. Sometimes the shock of nearly losing someone you love—or of nearly losing yourself—is almost as strong as actually losing them.

They'd been writing for two and a half months when Caroline decided to come clean. They should meet, she decided. She would tell Meredith everything. The lies wouldn't matter in the end; Meredith herself had said that a name was nothing but a layer of glaze applied to the outside of something. What would matter was that they'd connected, regardless of titles, details. So she wrote it: *Perhaps we can meet.* Then she folded the letter, sealed the envelope, and ran it to the mailbox, allowing no time for second guessing.

Their letters must have crossed in transit because she received another from Meredith just two days later.

> *Have you thought about what it would be like to meet? I've been considering it. The thing is (don't laugh), I come to picture you as me. When I imagine what you might look like I see my own face. I know its probably stupid, but I'm superstitious. In Norse folk tales like my gramma used to tell me as a kid, to see you're other self, you're double, is an omen of death.*

Caroline began a new letter. *You're right about not meeting. What you said isn't stupid at all. Forget that I proposed it.* She paused, unsure of what to say. *Besides, I have good news*, she wrote. *The cancer is almost gone.*

Her phone buzzed: a text from Daniel. Apps in the male! Thx for ur help! She deleted it.

That night, she woke with the immediate and illogical sense that she was being watched. She thought for a second she'd heard the mountain lion scream, but then she looked around and remembered where she was. The room was empty, the blinds closed. She'd dreamed of walking through a dry field parched from sun, a color like tarnished brass, a few naked trees with arthritic arms, branches like the graphite strokes of a well-sharpened pencil. In the dream, she'd held her hand before her face, between her eyes and the sun, and watched light gather in molten puddles in the rounded webbing between her fingers. Little

Us of red-orange flame. Behind her hand, a sudden motion, a flash of something. She put down her hands, squinted, and there in the field, she saw herself standing facing her. She thought the horizon might be made of mirrors. So she stepped forward and reached out, expecting her fingertips to brush glass, but there was only autumn air dry with heat and electricity—no mirrors, no walls, no angles, no instruments of reflection, nothing but raw reality.

To see one's double: a deadly augury. Caroline shook off the thought, embarrassed, and switched on the radio. It was a broadcast she'd heard before, a story about an elderly postal worker who, for twenty-five years, withheld postcards mailed from loved ones to loved ones, hoarded them in her house, pasting them picture-down to the walls. Twenty-five years of unreceived wish-you-were-heres assembled and adopted by a woman whose job description read, "Distribute and collect incoming mail. Collect and process outgoing mail." When they caught her, she said, I didn't do anything wrong. Her husband was dead, all her children either dead, too, or estranged, and the thing that made Caroline laugh from out of her borderland consciousness was that even after the program host revealed these bits of biography, he still found it necessary to ask the old woman why she did it.

The next day, she got in her car with a small and hastily packed overnight bag. She took out an atlas. She planned a route to North Dakota and traced it with a yellow highlighter.

She didn't know what she was going to do once she got there. She wedged Meredith's blue bowl against her overnight bag on the passenger's seat, and she drove.

Everything Meredith had said was true; the world did seem smaller, the earth did visibly curve in that wide open place. Gradually, in the distance, wind turbines began to spread across the horizon, spaced and angled so as to catch currents of air, turning almost in unison, almost to the beat of the music playing from Caroline's radio. It was a song she'd never heard before, and she drove on, wind rocking her car, the turbines increasing in number, ranging from faint birdlike flecks on the horizon to massive open-armed angels cartwheeling by the side of the road. They looked like enormous samaras of the kind that pinwheel from maples on a breeze. It was a ballet, a ceremonial, and she thought if she watched long enough, there might come a moment when they all lined up—when, for one split second, they synchronized. Perfect.

For the last two or three hours of the drive, the fields along the highway were flooded, the wash sometimes running over the road, spraying up alongside the car as she passed through the overflow. Too dry at home, the height of autumn, thirsty roots, and here, more water than the ground could hold. What few trees there were stood in clusters part-submerged under floodwater with no roots in sight and the clear sky mirrored all around them so that they seemed to shoot out of the sun. She viewed their bare branches with a sensation of recognition. Where the water stretched to the roadside, she could see her car, her window, her face behind it reflected from out of the blue. No double, no twin, no omen, just her own small self and the sun.

It took twelve hours and twenty-one minutes for Caroline to reach the little town where Meredith lived. She had left when the sun came up, and by the time she pulled into the parking lot at Elroy's—gravel, no frills—it was ready to go down again. The journey didn't seem foolish to her until it was over and she remembered the blue bowl on the passenger's seat, which she had strapped in somewhere in Nebraska, fearing that it might fall and crack again. Now, climbing out of the car, she stashed it out of sight, not ready, yet, to give herself away.

Caroline realized that Meredith might not even be at the restaurant. She didn't live there, after all, and though Caroline had her home address, it would be too invasive to look for her at home, too clandestine and creepy. She'd made the decision to come on the fly and, even during the twelve hours in the car, had driven as if hypnotized. Now the facts of her situation began to solidify in her mind, and she feared that if Meredith wasn't here, now, she'd never find her, never find out. Reason would take over, and she'd flee back home, back to the familiar.

But she was there. She was the first person Caroline saw when she came in the door. On her chest was a red plastic nametag. She had a round face, healthier-looking than Caroline had expected, sturdy legs, thick blonde hair, and a perfect, round mole like a gem at the center of her unpierced earlobe.

"You can seat yourself, love," she said.

Caroline sat at a round table near the center of the room. In the corner, an old man was raising a fuss, his voice growing loud: "There's a tooth in my pot pie. There's a tooth in my pot pie." The walls were paneled with engineered wood, and the table was draped in a red-and-white checkered tablecloth. Paper placemats marked each setting, and a small ceramic cup holding a handful of dull crayons stood at the center of her table next to an almost-empty sugar caddy. In a glass vase next to the crayons was a magnolia flower standing in about an inch of water. Caroline reached out to touch its petals—fake, but even she was fooled at first.

"Yep, fake," Meredith said as if reading her mind, motioning to the silk flower. She held a menu and a pitcher of water smashed against her breasts. Her nose was endearingly freckled, and her hair frizzed at the temples. "But they fool people all the time. I put a little water in there just for fun. Magnolias don't grow here, but it's Elroy's daughter's name, so."

Caroline ordered a salad and sandwich, and Meredith poured her water with calloused hands, a potter's hands. An ice cube sloshed out of the metal pitcher and onto the table.

"Waitress," the old man in the corner called, "your tooth is in my pot pie." His wife and a younger woman—probably his daughter—shushed him, but he only spoke more loudly: "That girl lost her tooth in my pie!"

"Gene, please," said the man's wife.

"Daddy," said the young woman.

"It's Meredith," Meredith said, approaching the man, hand on hip. "You know my name, Gene. And it's not *my* tooth. I got all my teeth right here, see?"

Caroline turned back to her table and the white placemat in front of her, picked a crayon from the cup, and began absentmindedly to draw. Someone's face. It felt warm in the room.

"Gene," the older woman said in a low voice, "it's *your* tooth. Just check and see."

He grew quiet then and left the restaurant shortly after Caroline finished her salad. "I'm sorry," he said to Meredith on his way out, his wife and daughter holding him by the arms. They were mourning him already; it could not have been more plain if they had decked themselves in black, lace veils before their eyes. "I'm sorry, honey. God bless you."

Meredith refilled Caroline's water glass, though it was less than half empty. "He's a sweetheart, Gene," she said. "Some days he knows me, some days he don't."

Caroline stayed until almost closing time. Meredith brought her coffee she hadn't ordered, and she sipped it, spreading a book open on the table, observing Meredith between paragraphs wiping down tables. On her way from one table to another, she made a detour to the hostess's station and plucked a peppermint from a straw bowl, unwrapped it, and popped it into her mouth. So far from the emaciated, gray-faced, needy thing Caroline had anticipated—the junkie. Her cheeks were flushed pink, and she was solid, self-healing, arm muscles flexing from the motion of the rag. She made Caroline think of springtime; of that resilient patch of twinpod she and Daniel had come across on a steep, white outcrop one morning; of ring release, how a tree can defoliate early, sorry-looking and barren, leaving a growth ring almost too tiny to count at its perimeter, a record of a starved year, and still recover. Something happens—a neighboring tree falls, more sunlight or water becomes available, and a period of starvation ends. Years later, a scientist comes along and finds a large, healthy ring triumphant after so many small ones.

She composed her last letter to Meredith there at the table between refills, dumping sugar into her coffee.

Dear Meredith,

I'm moving. Don't be angry if you don't hear from me for a while. I guess the cancer scare has opened my eyes—I have a life to live. I have traveling to do, then the wedding (which will go on—we went through a bit of a rough patch, you know, but in the end, I think it will only bring us closer together), and then the move... I'm excited for it all, for my new home, and especially for your six months of sobriety (congratulations!). Your friendship has been like medicine to me. There are many things to be happy for. The happiest thing, for me, is knowing I won't ever be alone.

Below her signature, she wrote, *P.S. I'm thinking of keeping our name.*

Some of it was true. Some of it wasn't but might be. And it could be that the whole letter was free of lies, because Caroline had no idea, as she signed it, where all she might still go.

She picked up the bill, Meredith's name scribbled at the bottom alongside a smiley face. Caroline paid and signed her name at the bottom of the slip. Then she plucked the last remaining sugar packet from its holder, opened it, and poured a bit of sugar into her mouth, tasted its sweetness on her tongue.

She considered leaving Meredith's letter on the table, but thought better of it and took it with her. Maybe Meredith would recognize her handwriting at the bottom of the bill, the penmanship ringing some remote tinny bell inside her brain. Maybe she had caught a glimpse of the letter as Caroline wrote it—a corner of a page, a few lines of script. Maybe when she opened it and registered the words on the page, she would sense their vague familiarity half-consciously, a feeling like déjà vu: *I have been here before*. A feeling that passes with time.

The Problem with You Is That

SAM

Sam sits on a seesaw on her old elementary school playground, human boulder on the down end of a sun-bleached plank. On the up end, wearing a tiny T-shirt—size kids' large—that doesn't quite cover her slim midsection, Maddy says, "I love him so much it makes my toes hurt. It makes my *eyes* hurt. It makes my *teeth vibrate*."

Sam considers letting the plank slam to the ground, sending Maddy flying like a character in a Saturday morning cartoon. "Your *teeth*?" she asks, and rises a bit, props one leg on the wood in front of her while the other stays planted on the ground, springing half-heartedly. If Maddy were her student, Sam would say something wise here, play the mentor. But Maddy is not her student; she's her sister, and she's an iconoclast—

first she'd look right through Sam's wisdom as if it were a stained-glass window, and then, unimpressed, she would smash it.

In the sunlight, Maddy's pupils are two tiny holes worn in the blue fabric of her irises. She says, "Doesn't it bother you being so much heavier than me? I don't know how you can stand sitting there like that, with your end weighed down. I'd kill myself."

Sam lets the seesaw hit the ground hard beneath her and watches Maddy bump on the other side, twelve years younger and lighter, buoyed by an adolescent sense of invincibility. She is searching for an identity, Sam knows, and lately, she's been trying on cruelty for size. There it is again: *size*. Sam has put on ten pounds since Evan left, since moving back into her parents' house. Back in with Maddy. The creep of her past back into her present, into her body: it's something she lets in slowly, like a swig of whiskey; she feels it in her stomach, icy and hot. Old fears, old memories, and silly schoolyard preoccupations resurface: that if you stepped on a sidewalk crack you'd cripple your mother, that if you swallowed watermelon seeds, melons would grow inside your body, green vines crawling, threaded through your ivory ribs. Hard to believe there had been a time when disasters like these had been the greatest ones Sam could imagine—a watermelon gut.

She puts her hands up to her face. She finds, there, the blood smell the seesaw's iron handlebar has left on her palms.

Home: the great cherry-bump. She'd thought she was on her way up, and then—slam! Sam allows herself, for a moment, to think of her wedding to the man who has now left her—that day when she'd believed she was leaving her old self, her childhood self, behind. This was six years ago. She'd worn a tea-length dress without sequins or beads. Maddy had been cute, just ten, carrying a bouquet of purple hyacinths, though beforehand, she'd had an episode, the first of many, and had wandered around pale-faced and faint.

"My heart," she'd said, all clammy. "It feels like butterflies."

They had passed her around, Sam and her mother and her aunts, poking, searching.

"She doesn't have a pulse," Sam said. "I can't find it anywhere." She knelt and put her head to Maddy's chest, where her heart beat much faster than usual. Then she pressed two fingers to Maddy's wrist, her neck. Nothing.

Their mother, the nurse, said, "Impossible." She prodded Maddy until they were both on the verge of tears. Maddy lay in the grass white and motionless until her blood pressure and heartbeat returned to normal, then went through the ceremony without issue. It still happens sometimes; Maddy will feel light-headed, and it will seem to disappear again, that most essential rhythm. Within a few minutes the spell is over and her blood back to normal, pushing just hard enough. It is their mother's white whale, her daughter's seemingly bloodless body. Oh, for crying out loud, she'll say, frustrated with Maddy and her unsolvable mysteries. Frustrated with Sam for—what? She'd said the same thing on the phone when Sam had called and delivered the news about Evan. Sam had mouthed the words right along with her: *Oh, for crying out loud.*

Her mother likes to brag that she's a master of knowing precisely where to place the needle in a patient's arm, better than all the other nurses in the ER. *I can find a vein like nobody's business*, she says, another of her signature phrases. It's a bad play, living at home with her, every line predictable. It might be true, usually, her miner's claim to gifted vein-finding, but not when it comes to Maddy. And no wonder, Sam thinks now, as Maddy chatters on about the numbness in her legs every time what's-his-name comes around, lacing her monologue with pointed references to her lightness, Sam's weight. Slight and toned as Maddy is, it would take a mine shaft for anyone but what's-his-name to find her heart—somewhere in there, surely.

Over her shoulder the sun hangs low, too heavy for the sky. Just a few more minutes and they can go home. By then, the motorcycle will be in its place in the driveway, dropped off by the dealer with a silver bow tied on the handlebars, and the storm of their mother's wrath will have blown over. Sam has arranged for the motorcycle to be delivered shortly before her father comes home from work while her mother is preparing dinner. He'll find it waiting at the edge of the driveway, a brand new Harley 883 Sportster, shimmering. He'll think, at first, it's a mirage. Rub his eyes. Her mother will come out of the house with a kitchen towel on her arm. She'll blame him at first, but her anger will subside when she realizes he's as surprised as she is. They will stand staring at the motorcycle until the sun slips below the horizon. Then Sam's mother will go back into the kitchen and pluck a bubbling casserole from the oven.

It is a gift for her father, a way of saying thank you. He was the one who'd told her she could come back home without shame, commute from home to the town where she and Evan had lived and where she still taught American history at a private high school. Though she would never say so, Sam's mother seems to think that Sam has failed in some way in losing Evan—she'd always liked him—and Maddy has looked with undisguised contempt at her ever since she moved back into the house. Her sister and mother seem to be united against her. She'd been saving to buy Evan a boat but, now that he was gone, couldn't bring herself to spend the money on herself. Couldn't think of anything she wanted. This gift will infuriate her mother, but so be it. Sam isn't afraid. She has nothing to lose.

Sam bends her knees and springs upward, Maddy's end of the seesaw plummeting, her own ascending, her body, if only for a second, soaring. What a strange concoction, this family, any family. She wouldn't have picked or designed it, no, but where else is she to go?

STEPHEN

He thinks, at first, it's a mirage.

A brand new 883 Sportster, shimmering. A silver bow tied on the handlebars. Stephen looks around. He can hear the faint noise of Robin banging around in the kitchen, pans clanging. An ordinary evening. His birthday is two days away, but he already knows what Robin bought him: a lavender shirt that she wrapped right in front of him a few nights ago, a package of socks, a new garden hose.

He's been taking—and passing—the same motorcycle class once a year for five years. He owns a helmet but (until now) no bike to go with it. Robin, a nurse, has forbidden it. She has seen too much head trauma. Brains turned to mush, skulls crushed. Blood. Robin says, *I know what those things can do*. She says, *It's only because I love you*. Stephen accepts the verdict. He takes the class again and again, low-speed and supervised. He rides in circles in the high school parking lot Saturday mornings. The instructor doesn't bother watching him anymore, just lets him have his fun.

Stephen parks his car and kills the engine. He approaches the motorcycle as one might approach an animal escaped from the zoo, tentative yet intent on capture. There is a tag on the handlebar next to the bow, his name printed in unfamiliar handwriting. On the reverse, the Harley logo, the address of the local dealer.

Sam? It could only have been her. But how? She must have saved money living at home these past few months, but surely not enough for this. *He* doesn't have enough for this.

Stephen is a client service associate at a financial services company. Clients call with questions about their retirement plans, and Stephen answers them. He has a second job driving Amish people around in his car. They call him from group telephones in wooden shacks, having no phones in their homes, and they wait for him by the side of the road. It's easy money and surprisingly enjoyable. They always say thank you.

He drives them through a landscape studded with anachronisms, this small town and its surrounding hills. Farmhouses, barns, buggies, they make him feel weirdly safe, though they are not his own, and beyond pulling over in front of them to offer rides to their owners, he is not welcome to them—he's not welcome back in time. There's no swimming against some currents. Watching the Amish live a life of the past, Stephen is like a scientist, they like a species whose habits he chronicles in charts and graphs. His hair is going gray.

Speaking of blood: last night he picked up an Amish woman who needed a lift to the hospital fifteen miles away. Her forearm had been sliced open by a kitchen knife and the cut packed with flour to stop the bleeding. She met him by the road with a pie and a pair of creased bills and the flour-caked arm bound in a sling made of a white bed sheet spotted red. The pie was neatly wrapped and on top was a sticker on which she'd written in a tidy script, Blueberry Pie Jesus Died For You. She had a child with her that didn't yet speak English, or was afraid to, and a second bonneted woman she introduced as her sister. The women were quiet, smoothing their aprons over their knees, their hair coiled on the backs of their heads and veiled under gauzy white caps.

Sometimes Robin is working when he brings them to the hospital, and he finds her at work in her scrubs, sees her as strangers see her, scurrying about in bright white Keds. She's often so busy that she doesn't get to eat a whole meal during her shift. So Stephen keeps a stash of Mr. Goodbars in his glove compartment, her favorite, and brings her one as a snack each time he enters the emergency room.

She says she wants to travel to Jamaica. Last year, it was Aruba, though Stephen isn't sure what the difference would be. He wonders if she's just making her way through that Beach Boys song. She says she wants to lie on a beach with a few good books and a steady stream of piña coladas and not move for a whole week. She could never do it, though she seems not to realize it; she'd be on her feet after a few minutes, needing a project: something to make, something to do, something to worry about. She would wear that swimsuit with the skirt, the one that balloons out parachute-like in the water.

His own dream has always been a month-long motorcycle ride across the country, alone.

When he tells his fantasy to Robin, he inserts her onto the imaginary bike for the sake of the story. He puts her there in leather, arms around his midsection, a helmet smashing the gelled spikes of her hair. You'd be so sexy, he says. Even though she protests, laughing—*There's no way you'll ever get me on one of those things*—and even though privately, shamefully, he wishes her away, he keeps her there in the fiction that he shares with her. You can do that when you know the thing you're talking about is never going to happen, anyway. Only now—now what? After a while you get used to wanting things. You do it recreationally, complacently. What do you do when those things become possible? How do you react? How do you act?

Maybe this is part of why he enjoys driving the Amish: they seem almost superhumanly impervious to desire. They never cry, not even a whimper, even the children, no matter how intense the pain or how deep the cut. Stephen likes imagining them at home, churning butter, pitting cherries, raising barns. It's like an Amen—all of it, that woman's blessed blueberry pie, her hair balled underneath her gossamer bonnet looking edible. At home, maybe, she threads a needle, stuffs a quilt, careful not to prick her finger. Her husband drags a saw across a hickory plank that will become the headboard of someone's bed, and sawdust flakes the barn floor. They give thanks for every meal, seated at a table he sanded himself. Stephen thinks of them occasionally in his day-to-day routine, half wishfully. Wishing he could be so grateful.

Maddy says he's stuck in the past, himself, and maybe she's right. A dinosaur with a pocket protector (which went missing, strangely, a few days ago). But in many ways, the past seems so obviously preferable to the present—in Maddy's case, for instance. What he would give to go back to holding her balanced on one arm, stretching out her tiny hands to touch him: the accidental child, the mistake that, in those moments, he considered himself so lucky to have made. Now, at sixteen, she practically spits venom.

And now, a motorcycle in his driveway and his name on it. Stephen squares his shoulders and steps toward the house.

ROBIN

The motorcycle sits in the driveway for five days. On the sixth day, Robin comes home from a half shift at the hospital while Stephen is still at work and finds the side of the bike streaked with bird shit. She's had a long day: a man who'd shot himself with a nail gun, two inches of steel protruding from his neck. And one of their regulars, the one who swallows razor blades.

Why? Robin wants to ask the razor blade man. She's been thinking about it all day but hardly understands what she means by the question, what it is she really wants to ask him. Why do you keep trying? Or the opposite: Why do you keep failing? This was the third time. His method and the results were always the same, and Robin isn't sure what makes her sadder: the many attempts or the many failures.

Meanwhile, this shit-streaked motorcycle. Robin sets her canvas work bag on the front stoop. She takes out a bucket and rag and fetches Stephen's birthday garden hose from the garage, carefully removes the still-attached but weathered bow and tag from the bike, and sprays it down. She scrubs at the white marks until they're gone, then dries the bike with an old towel and replaces the tag and bow. There. No one will know.

She knows Sam bought the motorcycle. She knows from the way Sam sat quietly at the dinner table the night of the bike's arrival. They were always in cahoots, Sam and Stephen. And they will make Robin be the villain again. Like when she refused to buy Sam a trampoline when she was in middle school—out of the question. Robin has seen too much head trauma. Skulls crushed. Blood. Why can't they see it's only because she loves them?

She always figured Stephen's motorcycle dreams would pass. That the classes would end up being some kind of midlife crisis and that he'd thank her someday for her pragmatism. But back and back he goes, silver-flamed helmet tucked absurdly under his arm. He's so constant, loyal. The problem with Stephen is that he's just too nice. Someone has to lay down the law. Robin thinks of Stephen, his Amish errands, his candy bar deliveries, with a mix of pity and admiration. She wishes he'd stop bringing the chocolate but doesn't have the heart to tell him—she's watching her weight. She wants to go to Bermuda, spend a week on the beach not moving. Wearing something new, something sexy.

But she couldn't go now anyway. She couldn't stand to bring Maddy, and she couldn't stand to leave her behind, either, to do God knows what. These days, Maddy slinks around the house, bitter about everything—the creaking floor, the density of air, the presence of other bodies on the planet. She rarely appears happy, except when she's talking about what's-his-name, whose eyes Robin has still never seen; his hair hangs over them in a way she finds distinctly equine. In Robin's nightmares, Maddy ends up pregnant, has a horsey little baby that she—Robin—cares for, feeds mashed peas, carries on her hip while Maddy finishes school. A few weeks ago, she took Maddy to the doctor and had her put on birth control. Maddy protested she didn't need it, embarrassed, but Robin insisted—it would help her complexion, regardless—and Maddy relented more readily than usual. Stephen doesn't know; he'd freak. Robin doesn't know if it was necessary, doesn't *want* to know, but what she does know for certain is that you can't be too careful. She'd hoped Sam would have children; they all had. But Maddy? God help them.

Robin tiptoes into Maddy's bedroom each morning before sunrise just to get a look at her sleeping, to fuel up on love for her while she's unconscious, under control. Lately, things keep disappearing, and Robin suspects Maddy is responsible, what with her rummaging through boxes and drawers and the corners of closets for reasons she won't disclose. Robin doesn't know what Maddy does with the disappearing objects. All she knows is that sometimes in the morning, she'll reach for a pair of earrings or a certain ceramic mug for her morning cup of Nescafé and find it suddenly, decisively gone. Sold, perhaps. It should make Robin furious that Maddy is selling her things, if indeed it's true. But a little part of her is pleased that there are people out there who would buy her scraps.

Robin puts away the hose, goes inside. She's got three free hours to work on her dollhouse.

She hates the word "dollhouse" for what she's creating, but she's not sure what else to call it. There are no dolls involved. Robin wants a house empty of people. She's been assembling it piece by piece for over a month.

You can buy anything in miniature. On her way home from work, Robin routinely stops at the miniatures store on Third to buy new furniture for the tiny house. She wanders through aisles of petite beds and armchairs, of penny-sized plates, bowls, and bread baskets barely large enough to rest on the tip of a thumb arranged on tabletops smaller than credit cards. She touches tiny rolling pins, milk bottles with illegibly small labels, sticks of plastic butter that settle in the crease of her palm.

It's a perfect, static world in that wooden dollhouse, with window boxes full of flowers that bloom all year. Everything is in place, right down to the tiny glass bottle of aspirin standing beside the bathroom sink, its tablets like crumbs. Sometimes Robin reaches into the house's rooms with a pair of tweezers and rocks the little rocking chair that sits by the fake fireplace, moves an ear of plastic corn or a medallion of synthetic steak from one miniature plate to another, or situates a toilet brush too small to hold in place at the base of the bowl.

"Those are for *kids*," Maddy says whenever she catches Robin working on the house. "Jesus, Mom."

Building the house started out as a form of escape; it was to be entirely different, better, than the real house they lived in. The problem is that the more she works on it, the more it begins to resemble that real house. She noticed this progression toward semblance only after Stephen paused one day in front of the house, gave a grunt of unsolicited approval, and said, "I like it. It's us." And she realized that it was.

Are our destinies so fixed? Robin wonders. Was it inevitable she'd reconstruct in miniature a world she'd wished to leave behind? Was it childish, as Maddy insisted, to imagine herself away, temporarily, from the real world? From her family?

She should let Stephen keep the bike. She should give him her blessing. Robin feels this knowledge fluttering in her chest, a trapped moth. Everything's a weapon: nail guns, razor blades, kitchen knives—one's no worse than another, necessarily, in the grand scheme of things. Even one's own voice: you can wear out your own lungs shouting. Maddy's proof of this, always screaming, and Robin lets her. Lets her let it out. Why not let Stephen ride?

With a drop of wood glue the size of a pinhead perched on the end of a toothpick, Robin sticks a mirror to the little house's bathroom wall. It hangs there for a few seconds, then slips onto the floor of the tiny room.

"Oh, for crying out loud," Robin says.

MADDY

She's done it at last: she's saved her one-thousandth dollar. She's saved a thousand dollars so that she can run away. Her mother's trinkets, her father's forgotten ties and outmoded sport jackets from the back of the closet: these are the fuel that will carry Maddy away from here, from her family, and they don't suspect a thing.

They were always in cahoots, the three of them, leaving Maddy out. She's an accident, so much younger than Sam, and her accidentness trumpets itself wherever the four of them go; she's the spare tire on this family car. She can practically hear her father's words when they found out about her conception, when she was just a goopy speck inside her mother's womb: his usual calm "We'll make it work."

They make her prop the bedroom door open with a shoe when her boyfriend comes over. They make her be home by eleven. They don't accommodate her dietary preferences—she's going vegetarian. Like right now, at the dinner table:

"This has *beef* in it," Maddy says, picking chunks out of her stroganoff. "Goddamn it!"

Her mother says, "It's grassfed."

Her father says, "Don't swear. It's unbecoming."

"*Unbecoming?*" Maddy cries. "What year is this?"

And so tonight's screaming match begins over beef and noodles. It escalates. Her father is the worst—too mild-mannered, old-fashioned. A dinosaur with a pocket protector (which Maddy sold last week on eBay for $4.99). And her mother—the problem with her is that she operates as if by buttons and switches: press here for anger, here for passive aggression, here for sorrow. And as her mother likes to remind her, Maddy still hasn't learned which button is which.

She throws a fork. It whizzes past Sam's head.

"Jesus," Sam says. "Thank God I didn't have kids. Thank *God*."

Maddy storms out of the dining room. An ordinary evening.

Meanwhile the motorcycle sits in the driveway, untouched for over a week. The keys arrived the day after the bike itself, in a small box addressed to her father, no return address. Maddy's mother waits to bring down her iron fist. Her father waits for permission. Her sister—moping around over her loser husband—Maddy wishes her sister would get onto that bike she has so obviously bought and take off. But it's Maddy who will leave, who is leaving at last. She grabs a gym bag and gathers her clothes.

She's spent the last few days watching YouTube videos: How to Ride a Motorcycle. She's spotted her window of opportunity and is ready to dash through it; she and her boyfriend are running away. They met at one of the Amish parties, held in a dark field. She had not tried any drugs and neither had he, though the Amish boys had passed them around with ease, and Maddy wants to tell her parents this each time they look at her boyfriend with furrowed brows—they'd barely drank, and he'd given her a safe ride home, along with an Amish girl who'd asked him to pull over halfway to her house so that she could lift her skirts and pee right there on the highway. The girl had been pregnant and, back in the car, after peeing, had wept silently next to Maddy, her face turned to the window, her thin shoulders trembling. But Maddy knows that in her parents' eyes, none of this would count for anything—not the way she and her boyfriend had turned away as the Amish girl hiked her dress around her waist, not the way Maddy had reached out and held her hand as she cried. No, however laudably she behaved, her goodness would be eclipsed by her guilt for having been at the party at all. And her boyfriend? They'd cut him no slack. Hell, they hadn't even bothered to learn his name.

He's the lead screamer in a metal band, and he's teaching her how to scream. There's a right way to do it. Too loud, too hard and you'll hurt yourself. In her bedroom after school with the door cracked, he trains her to breathe from her stomach, through her diaphragm, not her chest, while warming up with vowel sounds: *Yaaaahhhh, Yeeeeeee,* on a scale. She flexes her abs as if anticipating a punch, and he puts his hand below her belly button and pushes to force the sound from her stomach. Push down, he says, like a poop, haha. It's harder than you'd think, and she's pretty sure she's still doing it wrong, because it hurts sometimes, and after a screaming session she often can't talk for hours. By the time she's finished screaming, she feels spent, and for a time, she can't remember what she had to scream about in the first place—what aspect of her accidental life flared up and flew out through her throat like moths—but she knows that it will return, sooner or later, the unnamable frustration that only he understands. On these days, when she has pushed her lungs to the brink, her mother serves her hot water with honey to soothe her damaged vocal chords. She presses a palm to Maddy's forehead, though they both know she does not have a fever.

"Mama," Maddy says weakly in such moments, her voice hoarse, feeling like a hurricane has blown through her body. "It hurts." The honey coats her throat. She has more to tell her mother but can't quite figure out what, and besides, it would hurt too much to say more.

"It's okay," her mother says. "It's okay, baby."

Maddy fills her gym bag to bursting and zips it closed. She puts on her sneakers, tucks the laces in like she saw in the video. Low speed, back brake. Let the clutch out slowly.

Who will boil the water when she has run away? Who will pour the honey?

I'll do it myself, she decides. She picks up her phone and waits to hear his voice.

SAM

She married a somnambulist. Even in his sleep he was always ready to run. Generally, he did harmless things in his sleep; she'd find him scrubbing half-heartedly the bottom of the tub, a soapless sponge in hand. One night, he sent a surprisingly readable unconscious text message to a friend inviting him for drinks the following afternoon, and they'd been confused when the friend showed up on their front stoop the next day bearing a bottle of cheap pinot and wondering why they seemed surprised to see him. But once Sam woke to the sound of the fire alarm and found a pair of her sandals smoking in the oven, Evan standing there spectral. Each time she would guide him back to their bed and beg him to stay there, then remember he couldn't hear her.

They'd married hastily, too young. Eventually, they'd bought a three-bedroom, two-story house but, due to his sleepwalking, slept like guests in the small spare room on the ground floor so he wouldn't tumble down the stairs at night. They kept the windows locked, covered the glass with heavy drapes, stashed sharp objects out of easy reach, a lot like childproofing. He tried medication but said it gave him nightmares. After a while, Sam couldn't sleep, either.

Of course, it wasn't his sleepwalking that ended it. But when she found out there was someone else, she half expected him to explain it all away by saying he'd been asleep the whole time, dialing her number from the fog of a slow NREM sleep stage. As he told her he was in love, and not with her, he must have read the question on her face.

In fact, I feel awake for the very first time, he said. I think I've never been so alive.

It was worse than the cheesiest movie, worse than the lamest sad song, and yet it stung. Maddy had asked her, when she'd told the story to her mother in tears: "What'd you do to chase him away?"

Maddy. It's funny how much you can love someone and still dislike them. Sam is annoyed at having to keep her valuables under lock and key in her own home lest they be sold online. She still wears her wedding ring, not out of attachment to Evan but out of resolve that she should be the one to sell it, soon. Someday. Living with a teenage Maddy is a lot like what Sam imagines it would be like to live under an oppressive regime, paranoia and dear things disappearing in the night, strange screaming. But she doesn't give Maddy away, even as their mother begins to question her sanity. Sam tries to treat Maddy like one of her students, with a friendly formality.

The problem with Maddy is that she doesn't know how to pick her battles. Just launches herself headlong into all of them, utterly undiscriminating and shouting all the time. *She's going to end up pregnant*, Sam said to their mother one day shortly after moving in. *God help us all.*

Sam lost the first baby in a blot of blood early in her pregnancy. The second: bad news during an ultrasound. No heartbeat. Everyone moved on so quickly. Sam tells herself she has too. But she mourns the babies every day, the family that never was, her lost history.

In college, Sam knew a girl who drowned in the Pacific Ocean, and for some reason, she has thought of her often since the miscarriages, even more since moving back in with her family. Sandra was her name. Studying abroad in Southeast Asia, turquoise water and palm fronds hushing in a breeze like conspirators. A weak swimmer and traveling alone, sucked out by the undertow. Taken in and gulped down. A turn of the tide, the tug of the moon. She would like to think that distress cries need no translation, but then she imagines Sandra calling out, magneted to the horizon and no one strong swimming to save her, and she isn't sure. The memory stays with her now, not so much because she misses the girl or even pities her but because of its suggestion that there is no universal language, none at all, that even the language of desperation is particular and private.

Sam lies awake in bed. She hasn't yet adjusted to life without a sleepwalker. Because of this, she knows things her family doesn't know she knows: about the morning rounds her mother makes, for instance, peeping in on sleeping Maddy and sometimes on Sam as well. These moments, Sam keeps her eyes pressed shut, fakes the steady breathing of the unconscious. Feels safe. And because of this, too, she hears the quiet click of Maddy's door when it opens then shuts sometime around 4 a.m. Hears an engine start up below.

Sam tiptoes to Maddy's door and pushes it open. She gets there just in time to see, through the window, Maddy wobble down the street below, grasping at the motorcycle's handlebars, feet dangling.

For a while Sam just waits, sitting on the edge of Maddy's bed. She could let Maddy get as far as she could before their parents chased her down. If Sam foils her now, she'll just try again later. The first and best-known rule of history: it repeats itself. Sam considers this.

Then she gets up, tiptoes downstairs, and pulls on the first pair of shoes she finds by the door, a pair of her mother's work Keds. It's still dark, and it's raining a little, and the roads are slick and hiss under the tires. She drives by what's-his-name's house but finds no sign of the motorcycle or Maddy, so she drives on. After a while she notices that it's stopped raining but that her windshield wipers are still swiping at the dry glass, squealing, and she wonders how long it's been that way, how long she's been oblivious.

She finds the motorcycle parked crookedly in the lot of a park five blocks from what's-his-name's house on the far end of town. It's barely sunrise, but though the rain has let up, the clouds have held, and there's still no color in the world. Sam finds Maddy lying on a rain-spattered bench, hands crossed at her chest, pale, like a cadaver. It's her heart again. Sam sits down on the bench and presses two fingers to Maddy's wrist. Nothing.

"I'm fine," Maddy says, her voice thin. "Go away. He'll be here any minute."

"And where are you going?"

"Somewhere better."

"What will you do when you get there?"

"I'll be happy. He'll start a new band. They'll get famous; it's only a matter of time. I'll be a barista. I'll get a tattoo." Maddy keeps her eyes closed while she speaks. "What time is it?"

"Almost five."

"Goddamn it," Maddy says. "He should've been here fifteen minutes ago."

"Honey, I don't think—"

"He is," Maddy says. "He's going to come. What do you know?"

"Oh, Maddy," Sam says, smoothing her sister's hair, disheveled by wind and water. "The problem with you is that you take things too far. You think you can get away from everything, and that you should." You don't realize, Sam thinks, how even when you move out, marry, leave, you feel this tug like the undertow that carried Sandra out to sea. You wear it like another kind of band around your finger.

"Oh, for crying out loud," Maddy says. "Save your lectures for the classroom." But she lets Sam leave her hand on her forehead, though they both know she does not have a fever.

Sam herds Maddy into her car—*There's no way you're getting back on that thing*—and for once, Maddy doesn't argue, even though it means their parents will find out. They leave the motorcycle in the parking lot. They'll be back within the hour, just in time for their mother's phantom wanderings, in time to hear their father's alarm clock ring. He will drive the bike home without ever having had to drive it away first.

And this will be Sam's gift to her mother: one crisis averted, and Maddy—the smallest, the least of them—safe back at home in her almost-still-warm bed.

For now, they remain on the bench until the color returns to Maddy's face and her heartbeat slows. Sam takes hold of her sister's wrist again and squeezes. There it is: their blood.

Burden

FOR LAURA, Little Bean would have been a burden too heavy to bear. If she had been allowed to grow, she (because Bean would've been a she, Laura was sure) would not have stayed a bean forever. She would have blown Laura up like a balloon and weighed her down. She would have kept Laura off the stage, possibly forever. She would have tied Laura down—Laura who, since first leaving her home in Maine, had lived in three cities and danced with three companies and who meant to go on floating.

People did it, of course. It being babies. But Laura was not people; Laura was Laura, alone, no spouse, no family, no interest in shuffling down the diaper aisle, flip-flopped and leaking—no. The decision was painful but quick, a reflex: spare herself a burden, spare the bean a body and a name. Laura's own body existed continually under so much stress that it was eleven weeks before she realized Bean was part of it at all, twelve before she had her syringed away. The choice left Laura's body rigid with sadness and certainty. For a while, once she made it, she could not move. But the body would bend. It always did.

What was a body, anyway? Little Bean would have grown tall and lanky, like Laura, tripping over her own feet. It would have taken years of cursing her gangly form and training it—begging it—to morph from clumsy to beautiful for her to finally grow out of her long-limbed awkwardness. If she were lucky, diligent, disciplined, she would have learned, like Laura, how to move her body thoughtfully and deliberately, as if she were writing poems in air. Only with luck and diligence and discipline would she have learned, eventually, where to be stiff and where to be loose, when to harden, when to soften. It would have taken practice and pain, a bit of instinct coupled with a stroke of good fortune, for her to have mastered the movement of her limbs, right down to her pointed toes, all the way through to the tips of her fingers.

Laura knew that the odds were against such mastery. Such luck, such restraint, such unlikely triumph over the slop of everyday life. Everyone was hurt, everyone was fat, everyone was crippled, heavy, unbalanced. Even Laura was too often overstretched and sore to see her body as much more than an encumbrance. The price of elegance was high; Laura's skin was callused and her toes were infected, bloody sometimes after dancing, their nails ingrown. Her back was sore—interspinous sprain, lower lumbar vertebrae. Pain when overarching. Sometimes it was shin splints, a snapping hip. And sometimes, Laura was just plain tired.

Of course, the audiences who admired her knew none of this. Instead, at the end of a performance, their willing disbelief in the reality of her body extended into the encore and beyond. They did not distinguish Laura the dancer with a lonely sixth-story studio apartment and a one-eyed cat and back problems from Odette the swan-maiden, or Giselle gone back to the grave. They weren't supposed to. Because the audience didn't want to know about the bunions on the dancer called Laura's feet or the way that her toes, permanently distorted, curled in odd directions, nails discolored, skin raw and hard. They wanted to believe in magic. In their minds, they made her superhuman.

But Laura knew about the cramps and the stress fractures, about the hard and unacknowledged work of perfection, even if the audience didn't, and she couldn't pretend that one day all too soon she wouldn't age, slouch, fail. Costumed and made up, yet still conscious of this inevitable fact, Laura occasionally felt a twinge of panic under the hot lights while the audience admired her arms and her legs that were chiseled and defined like Michelangelo marble. It seemed, sometimes, as if she were telling a lie. While they gaped at her gracefulness and shoved roses into the angles of her arms she would often think with embarrassment and some distaste how, for all her performing, she was just like them. Aside from strict physical discipline and an unfaltering commitment to beauty, not much distinguished her from the people who crammed into theaters in their finest evening clothes to let themselves believe, for a little while at least, in fantasy. In reality, Laura was breakable, just like them. It was a secret she kept well; it was part of why she loved to dance. It was exhilarating, telling that lie.

It was the same cruel fate that curved spines and pulled muscles that had planted the bean in Laura's body. It was just a little bean in there, she told herself. A problem that could go away. It was completely logical to take the simple step that would rid her of the bean, rid the bean of the curse of flawed, fleeting corporeality, and preserve her own beauty and agility just a little, little longer.

She had done her research and yet could not be satisfactorily sure, beyond any doubt, that Bean would not feel pain. It wasn't like anyone could ask. And even if they could, Bean, whose vocal cords, at week twelve, were just beginning to form, would not have answered. One week earlier, Laura read, Little Bean's toes had separated and the webbing between her fingers had vanished, fingerprint swirls like Van Gogh stars already evident on their tips.

Laura dialed the clinic's number. On the phone, she said, "I don't want it to hurt. I mean, I don't want to hurt it."

When Laura bought a new pair of pointe shoes, she broke them in the old-fashioned way. She grabbed them by their shiny satin heels and slammed their tips, hard masses of layered glue and burlap, against cement sidewalks and the brick walls of the studio. She wet the boxes in the tips of the toes with hot paper towels to weaken them, to soften their hardness; she danced in them to mold them to her form and then shellacked the boxes to keep them dry and tailored to her feet like fossils. Sometimes she bent them on door frames. If she was angry, she would occasionally shut them in the closet door with more force than was perhaps necessary, because whether they were new or old, their damage could only help her dance with less pain.

When it hurt—or when she was unable to forget that it hurt—she would line the tips of the shoes with lambs' wool or gel or plastic bags or wadded-up old pairs of tights to pad her muddled toes. She'd tried painkillers, but her body became too smart for them. She jumped from brand to brand for a while until she grew used to each and immune to its effects. After a while, she gave them up. She took pride in the knowledge that she iced her own sore muscles, dealt with her wounds on her own.

A few days after Laura's appointment at the clinic, she wore new shoes to the studio and began the ritual breaking-in. She would autograph the old ones and toss them into a basket at a kiosk in the theater lobby, where they would be sold to young aspiring dancers at intermission. She went to the barre and stretched and pointed, flexed. She danced for a long time, then took off the shoes and sat down on the hardwood floor beneath the barre, facing the mirror. She continued to bend their stiff fabric, pointing and flexing the shoes long after her feet had been released from their insides, which remained firm and oppressive.

Little Bean had been removed. Physically, Laura was just plain Laura again.

She tried not to think about the clinic and its pastel-papered walls, or about Bean and the way she would be sent to a lab for pathology, then "properly disposed of," as Laura had been told when she'd asked the doctor exactly where Bean would go. Sitting alone in the studio, though, Laura was surprised at how hard she had to fight not to think and not to cry, overcome with relief and grief, those close cousins. As she pressed her eyes shut and breathed deep breaths, she thought about how strange it was that she should try so hard to keep some things, like tears, inside and yet send other things so decisively out and away.

Laura went home to her apartment and her one-eyed cat. She reclined on the couch under a blanket and switched on the TV. She tried not to think.

But thinking was as natural and automatic as breathing—more natural and more automatic than dancing, even for Laura. And somehow Bean made it out of the lab for pathology and away from her proper disposal and out into the city and in through Laura's slightly open window on the back of a fly that flew in and around the house, buzzing. She had acquired the ability to move on her own three weeks ago, during week nine: tiny joints capable of bending.

Inside the house Bean played among the skin cells that made up Laura's household dust. Bean never had skin, only a transparent film through which her veins and insides would have been visible, like leaves and blossoms under greenhouse glass.

Laura sat up and watched her twirling and somersaulting in the dust.

"Go away, Bean-ghost," she said. She kept her voice low. "Go away, spirit." She lay back down, pulled the blanket tight around her and turned away. In time, Bean floated over to Laura's body and in through a hole in the old fleece blanket in which it was wrapped. She nestled into the arch of a foot. Laura pointed, then flexed her away.

"Go *away*, figment. Figment of my imagination."

She thought about calling Liz, her sister, but Liz never picked up the phone. Ever since their father's funeral, Liz and their mother had been more distant from Laura than ever. Laura had been her father's girl. In the end, it wasn't because he never failed to bring her roses after every childhood recital that she loved him the most. It was because he let her go.

In middle school, when Laura was teased for her height, he bought her a punching bag. He drove her, at age seventeen, from Maine to New York to audition for the Ailey School. And when she was accepted and announced, five days before her senior year would have begun, that she wouldn't be going back to her old high school, he'd kissed her forehead, helped her pack her things, and set her up with a New York roommate through an old high-school friend. He didn't make a fuss about her refusal to "just be normal," as her mother and Liz, then a sophomore at the local community college, had.

Laura's absence at her father's funeral solidified her mother's and Liz's disapproval of her. Her father's parents had been Russian immigrants, but, born on American soil, he had never seen the country. The day he died, Laura bought a plane ticket to Moscow. She took herself to the Bolshoi Theatre, where *Swan Lake* had first premiered in 1877, and let herself heal in her own way. Alone in her father's land, she returned his favor to her; she let him go.

Now, with Little Bean still floating in the room, disobedient, Laura picked up the phone and held it in her hand, listened to the dial tone for a while, and then hung up. She breathed in deep and blew onto the dust on her end table, blew her ghost away. She slumped back onto the cushions, curled up, pulled the blanket over her head.

Oh, you little bean, she thought. If you could only have stayed forever small, a secret in a hidden place inside my body, we could have been something, you and me.

Laura had not mentioned the whole Bean affair to Gary. She never would.

When he woke in the mornings, Gary looked at himself in the mirror, flexed his biceps, and smiled a superstar smile. He examined his features and his grin from a variety of angles. He always flossed three times a day. He performed these rituals with the bathroom door open just a crack, thinking Laura couldn't see.

When Laura first met him, he had just completed his Accelerated Freefall training and earned his skydiving instructor certification. They'd both been standing in a long line at Starbucks; she wore a loose T-shirt, its collar torn off so that the cotton fabric draped over the edges of her shoulders and left her neck and the top of her back exposed. She'd just come from the studio, had been sweating, and a few strands of hair, come loose from her bun, clung to the side of her neck. Gary had made his move without even seeing her face.

He leaned forward and muttered into her neck, "Ever done flips in the air at twelve thousand feet?"

Laura turned around. "No," she said.

He was overconfident in a way that provoked her, and so she went on. "I like to do mine at about two feet. A lot less room for error."

Gary laughed. Laura didn't. A few minutes later, she was setting her hazelnut latte down on the sidewalk and tucking in her shirt. She turned a front aerial, picked up the latte, said, "You have a great afternoon," and turned to walk home. Gary followed.

He'd always seemed like the type who would cheat. Laura had thought so right from the moment she met him. Now, when she thought about her past with him, she figured this was a large part of the reason why she let him stick around: he didn't need her. He kept her company without requiring her to make promises or sign contracts. She always imagined herself knocking on his door some afternoon and finding it answered by some woman who'd never met anybody who did flips in the air at twelve thousand feet before. But Gary stuck around.

She guessed she should have been happy he wanted to be with her. But she found his fidelity oppressive, his presence tiring. At first, his attention to her body had been flattering, and even his preoccupation with his own had been endearing in its own way. It just got to be too much.

Months after the Starbucks meeting, it was Laura who broke it off. It made no sense to go on with a reckless man-child who threw himself out of airplanes and coaxed others to do the same for what he called a living. She had enough to worry about. Besides, the last thing she wanted, at the end of a long day, was to come home from the studio or the stage only to be asked to dance some more, this time for an audience of one. Meanwhile, her back was sore, her feet were tired, and her bed seemed far too small with Gary in it next to her, going on about body awareness and altitude awareness and how everyone started out jumping tandem, hooked up to an instructor (like him), and then eventually—if they persevered—ended up falling alone. Free, he said. Free-*fallin'*. He sang Tom Petty, propped against a pink pillow.

Laura cut him off. "Do you think," she asked, "you could leave?"

So Gary left.

What a family they'd have made, Laura thought. Always in the air, always tumbling.

The company was performing *Swan Lake*, Laura's favorite. There had always been something about that ballet that had spoken to her. It would be her second time dancing the part of Odette—half human, half bird. Under the spell of a sorcerer, she lives a swan by day and a woman by night in a forest by a lake formed out of the tears of her grief-stricken parents, from whom she was stolen. The spell isn't broken in the end; she and her lover both drown.

Laura called Liz and was not surprised to find that she'd been right: Liz didn't answer. Laura left a voicemail. "Hi," she said. "It's . . . your sister, wondering if maybe you'd like to take a break for the weekend and come see the opening of *Swan Lake*? It would be nice. To have you."

As soon as she said it, she realized how true it was, and she dusted her apartment that night, in anticipation of a guest.

In addition to performing, Laura taught beginner ballet twice a week to girls whose parents could afford to send them to classes with members of the company. Her students would perform with the company in the winter, as the children at the Stahlbaums' party and under Mother Ginger's giant skirt in *The Nutcracker*. Last week, right after finding out about the bean, Laura had been distracted. She'd ended her instruction early and told the girls to play dance freeze tag for the second half of class. Megan and Jill took turns pushing each other across the floor, each counting the number of shoves it took to force the other from one wall to the opposite. Julie stood on her head. Anya and Eva played wheelbarrow. Molly hung from the barre, which was not allowed. Martina tickled Julie, who still stood on her head. Julie squealed. Jessi, fat Jessi, piggy legs poking from under the absurd pink tutu she insisted on wearing each week and that only accentuated her squat form, said, "Miss Laura, I have to pee. Miss Laura, I have to pee."

When Laura, in her distraction, didn't hear her, she made a run for the door. Through it all, Laura stood by the stereo, switching the music on and off, muttering "Freeze" at intervals. "Freeze," she said, and paused Tchaikovsky. The room erupted in giggles, and Jessi, mid-dash to the bathroom, froze, obedient, and cringed.

"Miss Laura!" The insides of Jessi's light pink tights darkened. She started to cry. Laura called the janitor, dismissed the girls, and zombie-walked all the way home.

This week, Laura told herself as she entered the studio, would be different.

She sat on the floor and stretched, facing the mirror, and watched twelve small bodies follow hers. The front and one of the side walls of the studio were completely lined with mirrors so that the girls' movements were reflected both from the front and from the side. When Laura turned at a slight angle, she could see the girls multiply around her: their actual, tangible bodies (twelve), the bodies with faces in the front mirror (twenty-four), and their profiles, with their ponytails swinging, in the side mirror (thirty-six). Thirty-six daughters. Other people's daughters—the daughters of mothers with stretch marks and dyed hair. Laura tightened her abs, centered herself, arched her back, observed the girls reflected around her. The thin ones, the strong, serious ones who might actually have a shot. The chubby ones, lumpen and languid. The girls chattered as they stretched, soprano voices ricocheting off the glass.

To keep her students from being sloppy, Laura taught them to envision pearls rolling from their shoulders, down their arms, accelerating around the curves of their elbows, slipping off their fingertips like tiny ski jumpers. The technique did not always work. Her students were always dropping imaginary pearls, swearing they heard them hitting the floor like hailstones.

Bean, too, had she had the chance, would one day have moved as if she were balancing invisible pearls on her contours. She would have been one of the girls who now moved from one corner of the room to the opposite, leaping and turning across the floor in pairs. Instead, Bean was in the pearls. She was balled inside them as they dropped from clumsy arms and bounced against the wood and rolled under the stereo where they caught in cobwebs and gathered in piles. Laura could feel her in the room and struggled to ignore her. She could sense her in the girls, all thirty-six of them with their healthy bodies and bottomless reserves of energy. She was curled up round and shiny, glowing in the pupils of their eyes. She tumbled in the dust that the girls kicked up with their chaîné turns and grand jetés, the dust that clumped in corners along with gold hairs and black hairs and dirt to be swept away later.

Liz didn't come to see *Swan Lake*. She left a voicemail on Laura's phone saying she was sorry, she was busy.

Liz with her love handles, Liz with her split ends. It wasn't just that she didn't respect Laura, her ways. No, what bothered Laura most was that Liz didn't respect herself—her body, all that it could have been. Just let herself go. It was sad, a waste, when there was surely something special in their shared genes, something sturdy in their makeup, the capacity for art.

"You're so *full* of yourself," Liz used to tell Laura, but she didn't understand. People without confidence are often offended when they see it in others. And confidence was necessary in dance—as necessary as talent, as necessary as hard work. Liz was wrong, Laura insisted, to take her sister's confidence personally. It was not about Liz, it was not about comparison or contrast; it was about the long hours Laura spent with her own reflection, studying herself in the mirror, creating herself, her masterpiece.

When Laura crawled under the covers the night before opening night, in the bed where she slept alone, Bean sat sentinel on the windowsill, looking out over the lights of the city. Laura watched her rocking there, slow and sad, back and forth.

"You hate me, don't you," she said. She paused. "Do you hate me?"

Of course, there was no answer. Laura closed her eyes.

On the opening night of *Swan Lake*, every seat was full. The audience draped themselves in diamonds, buttoned themselves into suits, and left small children at home with sitters who let them watch forbidden television shows. They laid aside their worries for the evening, left their loads at the theater door. To them, Laura was far more swan than woman.

But Bean remembered the thump of her heartbeat, knew the warm walls of her insides.

Bean watched the dance from a post on the tarnished gold of a chandelier. Laura sensed her there. Was the audience aware of her sacrifice perched above their heads? Laura thought of the lie she was telling in her sequins and feathers. She was not a swan. But they believed in her, those faces, watching. She was giving them something they wouldn't—couldn't—find anywhere else. She was giving them perfection. And Bean—surely Bean was proud of this: Laura's body, her talent and her discipline, the rarity of these things. The beauty.

Under the lights, Laura wondered how many women had danced the part of Odette before her, from unknown sisters in other companies to the great Pierina Legnani and other masters long dead. How many would dance it after she was gone. How long it would be before she was thrown out, driven off the stage and out of the spotlight and replaced by someone younger, stronger. She would not be allowed to go on there forever. Yet when she was gone, her role filled, her body replaced with another, the choreography would change little, the music not at all, and the dance would go on, on, without her. She had given herself completely to dance, but she had not been the first to do so, and she would not be the last. She had given herself exclusively, and it would never—could never—return her commitment, but that was not the point. No, she had always been glad to let it break her.

This room is full of ghosts, Laura thought. They were rustling in velvet curtains, they were sliding down banisters, they were spinning in dust, all day, all night, forever. She thought, *When I am a ghost, I'll live here too.* There would be no one for her to follow. She would live a swan and fool the world for as long as her body allowed it, until the end of the day, when night fell and she was just a woman, worn out.

There had almost been a person who would have loved her then, too, but Laura had sent her away. And even in her costume, then, even midair, she hurt for the both of them, a hurt she couldn't ignore—like an incessant ringing in the ears, an unquenchable thirst; the hurt was a sound, a nagging thought, a mourning garment. It was a vision of herself and Little Bean, two ghosts veiled in the unseen corners and the shadows of a dim theater, watching the dance of the centuries, watching each other in silence from opposite ends of a room crowded with bodies, and never, ever touching.

But perhaps it was possible to mark the world without leaving anything physical behind in it. Perhaps the kindest thing she could do for this hulking, heartbroken planet was to offer it a little bit of beauty and, when she could offer it no longer, leave it quietly and completely.

She took her bow. Oh, it never got old, this moment, this *You're welcome.* The applause rose to the chandeliered ceiling, where Bean sat perched alone, small spirit curled close to a light bulb, soaking up its heat in a place only Laura could see. She might wish to clap with her gummy palms, to make a noise like the rest of the crowd for her almost-mother; she might try to feel the sting of flesh against flesh but fail. She might kick her nonfeet against the chandelier's gold in frustration. But she would make no noise for Laura. The stuff only of dreams, now, there was no sound she could produce, no word she could say to alleviate either of their burdens.

Happy Like This

HOPE MISSES the city, and I miss Hope. So every other weekend, I buy a bottle of wine and drive up the valley to see her and Little Girl in their new suburban home, where they live with Hope's boyfriend, a pilot. The pilot is away for three or four days at a time each week, and Hope is often alone and always lonely. The drive takes an hour and a half, and I sing off-key with the radio even when I don't know the words. I like to think that I know my limitations and that I accept them.

Like me, this valley accepts its flaws. During air inversions, it embraces its pollution as if it is precious, the mountains hugging a bluish haze, the air a finely spun net. To live here is to be ever reminded of the messes we make of our lives: smokestacks at the copper mine, distant forest fires caused by carelessness, burning juniper, refineries, wood stoves, aerosol sprays, and me. You see, I'm part of the problem: my clunker barely passes emissions, and I don't carpool. I'm a party of one.

At Hope's, I never have to ring the bell. Possibly it's because she's waiting like a child by the window, anxious for any company, not necessarily mine, but let's take a sweeter view. Say she feels me coming from a mile away because we're cut from the same cloth, tuned to the same wavelength, formed from the same exploded star. Call us celestial sisters. Say she senses my arrival the way one in sync with the elements senses a subtle change of season or climate in the marrow of the bone. Whatever it is, she greets me on the porch before I've put the car in park. She calls, loudly so the neighbors will hear: "Jesus Christ, where the fuck have you been?"

All the neighbors are Mormon, and the streets are numbered outward from a temple whose god we don't recognize. This is no place for an atheist, let alone two and a very vocal baby born out of wedlock. From Hope's yard, you can practically hear the drone of the neighbors' whispered prayers for our lost souls.

I arrive with presents for Little Girl—a new dress, an elastic headband she'll pull off and fling away—and the wine. Say its label reads Primal Roots, its sinful red hue tinted blackish through the green glass of its bottle. Hope and I are linguists—students of linguistics, anyway—masters but not quite doctors of our philosophy. Our studies brought us westward, Hope from Georgia, me from Ohio. We choose wine based on name, not palate.

It's no particular day I'm telling about. It's a pattern, a cycle. There is the time we lock ourselves out of the house, the time I lock my keys in the car. There is the time we attend a bridal shower for one of Hope's neighbors, who are friendly in a sales-pitch sort of way, and sit smashed together on a couch, Little Girl screaming in Hope's lap as the bride to be unwraps our gift: the Eternity Gravy Ladle, $14.99, from the registry. "Oh, Charles *loves* gravy," the bride says earnestly, and Hope chokes, "Oh, *God*," and we leave the party early.

"What would you like to do today?" one of us asks.

"Everything," says the other.

Most nights, we say we'll feast but end up preparing boxed macaroni and cheese or eating oatmeal while taking turns feeding Little Girl pear-spinach mash from a squeezable tube. After dinner, we look around, waiting for life to happen. We fall asleep in our clothes, my feet propped on an overflowing laundry hamper, Hope's on an unpacked cardboard box.

You'll notice I'm calling her Little Girl—not because she doesn't have a name but because she could be anybody, any girl; she could be you, she could be me, once upon a time.

What a commitment, to name something. We laughed off the task in the months before Little Girl came, so that when she got here, she ended up spending several days nameless. Hope and the pilot could never agree, so we hid from their disagreement behind a screen of humor. Areola, we said, once we knew she'd be a girl. Giardia. Nicotine—she's mischievous, spunky, a tomboy called "Nick" for short. Asthma, Ebola. All lovely, don't you think? Now and then signifiers sing in a different key from the things they signify.

My own name? Not relevant here. What you need to know about me is I'm an orphan and I'm single. Nobody's wife, nobody's girlfriend, nobody's partner, daughter, sister. Nobody special. When I was a child, I had a bunny, and you know what its name was? Bunny.

I wish I could tell you a better story: one in which things happen, one with a climax and a resolution. This isn't any of that. What happens in this story is that Hope and I survive.

It isn't as easy as you might think. Hope's parents, southern evangelists, haven't forgiven her for the surprise pregnancy, for not marrying the pilot, for not baptizing the baby. Her housewife neighbors bring her brownies laced with prayer, smug little cupcakes sprinkled with the Spirit. They treat her with a special syrupy kind of kindness reserved for nonbelievers. Their children are many and always clean. They are blissful in their domesticity, while Hope is blue.

The pilot's father owns the house, which is why he and Hope went to live there, left the city. They pay next to nothing. The pilot's name is Glenn, and I never know when he's joking. "I do like to bust out one or two of those mini vodkas every once in a while," he said, for instance, when I asked him what secret things go on in the cockpit—such a seedy-sounding place. "Just kidding." But something about his voice makes it impossible to say for sure.

Between my comings and goings and the goings and comings of the pilot, Hope is worried that Little Girl's first word might be goodbye, or some infant-mauled variant thereof.

"What a place to begin," she says.

Meanwhile, her dissertation sits abandoned. On the phone, while I sit pretend-writing, drinking alone, she cries, "I wasn't supposed to live this 1950s life."

I tell her this is the Problem That Has No Name. Except that now it has a name: the Problem That Has No Name. Oh, what would Betty do? Besides write a treatise and start a revolution? Is this a treatise? Where is our revolution?

Little Girl loves sand, and so on clear days we take her to Antelope Island, to the lake, that freak of nature whose image—turquoise blue and pristine—clashes with its smell, a potpourri of hydrogen sulfide, salt, decaying brine shrimp, and algae. Bison pace the parking lot. The baby is buoyant and salty as cured meat. Some days we don't bother with the lake, just take Little Girl, who pulls off her socks and stuffs them into her mouth, to the high school track at the end of Hope's block and plop her into the long jump pit. We say this is a valuable lesson in the use of imagination, a lesson it's never too soon to learn. "Resourcefulness," we say.

Hope jams a pacifier into Little Girl's mouth to stop her from eating sand. She draws fistfuls of it; it lodges in her fat rolls. Later, I wheel Little Girl around the track in her stroller while Hope runs. She's getting her body back; I'm letting mine go. On the clock face of the track, I'm hours, she's minutes, running laps around me.

Afterward, we bust out our Primal Urges and drink straight from the bottle, which we stash between sips beneath Little Girl's stroller.

A is for apple and B is for boy, and all the rest. We recite these facts to Little Girl because science says her brain is a sponge ready to soak up everything it's fed. Survival tips and language, things that will make it so that she can make it one day. It's packing an overnight bag for someone about to embark on a journey, one on which the weather will be unpredictable and the temperatures potentially extreme. She is a traveler who will need a Swiss Army knife, a down coat, sunscreen, a plastic safety whistle on a key chain, C is for cat, D is for dog.

We could wreck this kid. So small and helpless she could drown in the puff of her own pillow. Suppose we muddle signifier and signified, teach her that forward is backward and up is down, train her to wear her socks on her hands, as in fact she is doing right now. Would we be ruining her or liberating her?

To live outside language—outside of *E is for, F is for*—is that a kind of prison or a kind of freedom? An impossible question, a paradox, as it requires language both to ask and to answer. Little Girl grabs a stick from the ground and draws it to her mouth. I toss it away and take her on my lap.

Welcome to life, Little Girl, where you spend as many years as you've got touching all the things you're not supposed to. This filthy stick. Matches. Breakable objects on boutique shelves, wealthier people's trinkets, some lover who's all wrong for you as anyone can see.

L is for life and H is for home, but what are these things? What makes a home? Wood and plaster, knives and spoons, frosted panes and fireplaces, appliances, white noise, a dash of love, a teaspoon or two of desperation? What makes a homemaker? I have no idea.

• • •

I am generally lost, but people always ask me for directions. The secret is to look like you know where you're going and are in a hurry to get there so that you might do something very important. I walk with a purpose, heels tapping, eyes set straight ahead, and people are always saying, "Excuse me, do you know ______?"

I don't.

Beholden to no commandment, answering to no god, I sometimes lie. For instance, on the phone I tell Hope I've gone out when I haven't. I tell her I've been dating, dancing. I tell her these stories because she needs them, needs to live vicariously through me, or through her idea of me, which is much like her idea of who she used to be. The Book of Hope is clear: be selfish while you can, go out while you can, dance, never skip a pill. I've become a symbol of something. Freedom. Independence. Blah, blah, blah.

"Do this in memory of me," Hope quotes.

In fact I am largely sedentary, largely alone. My dissertation moves slowly; the prospect of a job search upon completion scares me. I tumbled here and I'll tumble on, who knows where, to what, to whom. The people I see most, besides Hope and Little Girl, are my students. They are nineteen and starry-eyed and compose essays that begin, "In the world today. . ." My house is a mess, though I have no excuse. I use my futon as a table and my bed as a desk. I'm like my own burdensome pet, something that has to be fed and watered and that keeps me from going on vacation for long periods of time. I'm like my own baby.

Hope consumes my dating stories hungrily. I'm pretty sure she's on to me, but she at least pretends to believe.

"Turns out," I say, "he was a polygamist."

Hope shovels formula into a bottle, fills it up, and shakes. "Believe me," she says, "there could be worse things than a sister wife."

Sometimes Hope is chipper when I arrive, like on the day she tells me about inviting the missionaries in for coffee.

"They didn't drink it, did they?"

"Not a drop," she says. "They stayed two hours. You wouldn't believe how much fits inside those backpacks."

She shows me a pamphlet the missionaries left: "Women in the Church: Women Are a Necessary Part of the Plan of Happiness." She hands me another booklet: "I Walked to Zion: Women's Voices from the Mormon Trail."

"Imagine giving birth in the back of a covered wagon, or under the night sky on a prairie. They did it, pioneer women. They did it in rainstorms with their sisters holding up pots and pans to catch the rain that would have fallen on the mother and child."

She tells me about a woman with frostbite, feet amputated, who walked on her knees for the rest of her life, went on to have six children, and thanked God every wobble-step of the way. Hope shakes her head. "Anyway," she says, "how are you? How's the diss?"

"Do I have to have balls to say it has me by the balls?"

"Yes," says Hope, "you do."

We sip Forbidden Urges. Little Girl looks up with animal eyes from her padded pen, mesh prints on tiny palms. Hope hands her one of the booklets, and she presses her mouth to the face of a saint. *Women participate in the work of salvation*. Little Girl releases a stream of drool.

My last lover believed my apartment was full of spirits, so he smudged the place with sandalwood oil and sage. His thumbs left smears above doorways and mirrors. Afterward, he pinned the half-blackened bundle of sage above the door. For protection, he said. Hope said it looked like a witch's tampon.

"Tell me you love me," my lover said, sprig of sage in hand. "Just say it."

I couldn't. Looking into the phrase was like looking into a lake dark with depth, no sign of the bottom. He was patient, said he'd wait. I was the one who ended it.

The one before him moved here with me from Ohio but fled shortly after. "This place is too weird," he said when we first arrived.

I had been about to say the place was perfect. Perfectly weird, perfectly wonderful. But head over heels at the time, I'd been desperate to please, had wanted him to stay. I said, "You took the words right out of my mouth."

After the first snow, I resurrect an old artificial tree from the back of my closet. I load it into the car for my drive to Hope's—clear air today, the world festive and full of possibility.

"What's the plan?" one of us says when I arrive.

"We'll bake cookies."

"We'll decorate the house."

"We'll make holiday cards. Nice, secular ones."

"We'll take Little Girl sledding."

"We'll cook a ham dinner."

The tree's lights are prestrung, and when we plug them in, only half of them work. I locate a baggie of spare bulbs and testers and try each light, one by one, searching for the problem bulb.

I don't find it. Little Girl eats synthetic pine needles. We order takeout from the Hu-Dat Noodle House. Short a sled, we load Little Girl into the cats' spare litter box and push her around the yard in pajamas and parkas.

Dear Little Girl, someday I'll tell you about the night I first learned you'd be coming into the world, about the red light I ran driving home after hearing the news, not registering symbols, and about the turn I missed, too preoccupied trying to imagine your face to find my way home. I know what it is to come newly into a strange land—one whose codes you don't recognize, one in which colors are just colors, not commands, and all the streets look the same and none of them look like home. Is this how it feels to be you, baby, everything so fresh and frightening and meaningless? If so, we're not so different.

We're never braver pioneers, perhaps, than we are in our first moments. Too bad we forget them, or maybe not. Maybe we couldn't live like that, remembering how boldly we forced ourselves into the world, realizing we reached the pinnacle of our courage before we knew our names.

What I'm saying is, I admire you, Little Girl, so tiny yet so indomitable, with your skin that's like silk stuffed with a fluff of cotton—how you changed our world, a small god, and never thought twice about it. It will always seem natural to you that you should be here, that you should be Hope's. You'll be the center of your universe, but once upon a time, Little Girl, you weren't the center of ours: we were. Now our love for you, Hope's love for you, is bigger than mountains and more frightening, as much a part of us as the bad air we breathe in, breathe out.

My mother's hair was long. Long enough that when I was a child, I would hold a fistful of her hair, not her hands, when we crossed streets or traversed busy sidewalks.

My mother sewed on buttons and patched holes. I used to believe she'd sewn the house itself from scraps she'd gathered, bits of wood, brick, and stone, and that she had a hand even in natural creations, like birds' nests. I remember peering into a nest built from coils of our own hair, which my mother had harvested from our hairbrushes and strewn on the porch, birdseed scattered among strands, an offering.

My mother believed in a god whose great man-voice booms like thunder, who tells us what love is, how to do it, where to find it: in washed feet, in nails through the wrist, in solemn marriage beds, in sacrifice, in song. I remember going to Mass before she died when I was eighteen. A statue of the Virgin, crown of sharp-pointed silver stars above her head, a rose without thorns in her hand. Faint blue at the base of the candle flames. For years, I saw her in my dreams, but I haven't lately, and I wonder if my ex-lover smudged her away.

I don't remember my first word.

It's not that Hope and I were ever that wild, that spontaneous or adventurous, before Little Girl. We met when we both rolled our eyes at the same thing, at the same time, during a lecture by a Very Prestigious Scholar. From across the room, our eyes found each other, and we knew. I loved her for her hard outer shell, which matched my own. Before Little Girl, we studied, we spoke about speaking, we exchanged words about words, we threw parties to which few people came. Other people had priorities; we had each other. Since Little Girl, those days have taken on a kind of glow, especially for Hope, changing diapers and scrubbing up spit-up. This is how gospels are written: after the fact, so that their words take on the luster of retrospect, so that their scenes shine with nostalgia.

Do I miss the days before Little Girl? Sure. But no more than I miss *these* days, right now, still happening. I hold this child in my arms, and I miss her, this version of her that is already fast vanishing, like something spoken. I miss Hope, preemptively, because we won't both stay in this valley forever. We'll leave, grow, grow apart, I'm afraid. I miss my mother. I even miss religion now and then, that purple cloth and incense, that blind, stubborn certainty. I miss the mountains on the other side of the dirty air that hangs in the valley like a veil.

"Do you think she has cancer already? Or asthma?" Hope asks, Little Girl grabbing at the Dr. Seuss book she holds before her: Today you are you, that is truer than true. There is no one alive that is you-er than you.

"Definitely not."

"Such a lovely valley, such dirty habits."

"We live filthy lives."

"We live in a filthy age."

Little Girl grabs the book from Hope's hands and turns it upside down.

One of us says, "It's a shame you can't choose your decade."

"Which decade would you choose? Which century?"

"I don't know." We pour a second glass of Forbidden Pleasures. "But I would have a clawfoot tub. And a carriage house."

"And I would have a carriage."

"Little Girl would have a wet nurse."

"I would have a dumbwaiter."

"And I *am* a dumbwaiter."

Yes, we know the grass is always greener. We know that in another era, our shoes would have been too narrow, our feet squeezed like bananas in peels, our midsections laced in whalebone corsets—oppressions we'll never have to know, living in the world today. Still we imagine, indulge, idealize. In our other decade, bustled or beehived, we would drink tea from mismatched cups and saucers, not cheap wine from chipped mugs. We would not forget to turn off the oven or spray down the stainless steel pan. We would speak in antiquated terms, swapping sibilants for thorns, as in, *giveth*, as in, *taketh away*.

It's hard sometimes to imagine the pioneers in their westbound wagon trains drawing to a halt here to settle in what they thought was the promised land. "This is the place," they said, as if it had always been waiting for them.

I don't want to settle, but I don't want not to. I've always loved the tautological ring of that famous Mormon declaration: "This is the place," that's that, home is home, you know it when you find it.

And it's true—we might clog the air with waste and pump shit into rivers, but let me tell you this: when the air is clear, after a storm or a strong wind, there's no more beautiful place than this valley with the walls of mountains rising on either side, like you're rolling down the lifeline of a great, rocky cupped palm that wants nothing but to hold you.

Yes, you.

As it happens, Little Girl's first word is not "goodbye." As it happens, it is "bird poop." We catch her eating it, and Hope says, "Ugh, no, *no*! That's *bird poop*!" and Little Girl says, "Birpoo."

Picture us knocking back the last of our bottle of Ephemeral Pleasures. The walls absorb the neighbors' prayers, our lullabies. We're no easier to put to sleep at night than the baby—our thoughts race, a plane flies overhead, the world bears down. From Hope's arms, Little Girl whimpers, dreaming.

"What's she have to dream about?" I ask.

"Nipples, most likely," says Hope. "A baby is much like a man."

We contemplate this for a while, listing other similarities between the two supposedly opposite populations. Then Hope looks down at Little Girl with a kind of Renaissance-painting placidity I haven't seen before.

"She's not so bad, you know?" she says, and although I *do* know, although Little Girl's goodness was never in question, I feel a new loneliness spreading inside me. I see myself for the first time not as an essential member of this domestic scene but as a gawker standing outside a frame, one in which mother and child are contained like a work of art I can see but cannot enter.

"I used to wonder how they did it," she says after a while.

"How who did what?"

"The pioneers," she says, "the women. Jolting around in wagons, fleeing wolves. On their knees in the desert, babies in their arms, dust in their eyes, no running water, and who knows what they used for tampons. I used to wonder how they did it."

"With the help of their men?"

Hope laughs.

"Out of love for their children?"

"There was that," she said. "But you're still wrong. All that's just rhetoric, stuff for missionary pamphlets."

I know what she's getting at. But I can't say it any more than she can. We might be linguists, but we speak our love in waves and glances, energies and insinuations, never in words.

I make another guess. "By the grace of God?"

She shakes her head. "Wrong again."

What's the name for this part of our lives, this circling? A holding pattern, the pilot might say, but what for? When and where will we land, on whose orders, and will we still be holding on to each other when we touch down?

"What do you want to do?" Hope asks. "You're the guest here. What should we do?" Say our half-lit Christmas tree glows proudly and preposterously in the window. Say we burn a cake that doesn't rise but eat it anyway, all of it. Say the wine runs out while the night is young. Say a fuse blows and we lose power, the whole house in darkness, the dishes unwashed, and we find ourselves without candles, open the blinds and let in the finite light of evening. Say *love, love*. Love: two frightened women and a sleeping child who somehow, splendidly, have gotten one another through another smoggy day.

"Nothing," I tell her. "I'm happy like this."

Hope snorts. "Please."

But she has become my phantom limb, a part of me I sense though it's separate. She rolls her eyes, pretending cynicism, but I feel her assent like a wave of heat across a cold room. When she says she doesn't believe me, I don't believe her.

ACKNOWLEDGMENTS

MY DEEPEST gratitude goes to Carmen Maria Machado for selecting this book for publication. I am truly humbled—and a big fan. My most sincere thanks, also, to Jim McCoy and the University of Iowa Press for publishing it and making my dream come true.

I owe so much to my teachers, especially Gregory Spatz, who made me a writer and who told me and my classmates to "spend everything" in our work. I did not understand what you meant at the time, but I think I do now. Thank you, Kerry Neville, for showing me what I wanted to be when I grew up. Thank you Antonya Nelson, Robert Boswell, Chitra Divakaruni, and the whole of the University of Houston Creative Writing Program; I did not truly take myself seriously as a writer until you did. Thank you, Ann Christensen, for making me a better, wiser feminist, and for taking care of me.

I am indebted to my friends and classmates at Eastern Washington University and the University of Houston—particularly those in Toni Nelson's master workshop who read and critiqued an early draft of this manuscript: Aja Gabel, Dana Kroos, Dickson Lam, Austin Tremblay, and Michelle Mariano—for the feedback that helped bring many of these stories into being. Thank you, Jaime Wood, Dylan Smith, Brent Schaeffer, Kennan Knudson, and Scott Michel for being my people in Spokane and supporting me personally and creatively.

Thank you, Ryan.

As Virginia tells us, a woman must have money and a room of her own if she is to write fiction. For generous financial support of my work, and for the vote of confidence such support entails, I am deeply grateful to Inprint Houston and its Alexander Prize in Fiction; the University of Houston Women's, Gender, and Sexuality Studies Program and its Blanche Espy Chenoweth Fellowship; j. Kastely and the University of Houston Creative Writing Program; and the University of Montevallo.

For rooms of my own away from home, I thank the Vermont Studio Center and, especially, the I-Park International Artists-in-Residence Program, which offered me the time, space, validation, and inspiration to finish this book. Special thanks to my fellow I-Park residents for the good company and conversation they provided at a time when I desperately needed it.

For expertise and insight into worlds and fields I knew nothing about, I thank my father, Howard Wurzbacher (motorcycles and Biltmore sticks and deer guts); my sister, Sarah Wurzbacher (tree rings and research labs); my mother, Cindy Wurzbacher (nursing); Emma Atwood (mermaiding and diving); Beau Smith (prison beagles); Michael Del Monte (bodybuilding); and Marcela Acosta (professional dance).

Versions of the stories in this collection have appeared in the following publications: "Happy Like This" in *Michigan Quarterly Review*; "Fake Mermaid" in the *Kenyon Review Online*; "The Problem with You Is That" in the *Florida Review*; "Ripped" in *Colorado Review*; "Make Yourself at Home" in the *Gettysburg Review*; "Sickness and Health" in the *Cincinnati Review*; "What It's Like to Be Us" in *Prairie Schooner*; "Burden" in the *Iowa Review*; and "American Moon" in *Barnstorm* as "Foreign Girl." To the editorial staffs of these magazines, thank you for believing in my work.

Thank you, Montevallo friends and colleagues, for helping me find happiness in Alabama—especially Alex Beringer, Andrea Eckelman, Melissa Shepherd, Rob Atwood, and Emma Atwood, mermaid extraordinaire. Thank you, Vinnie.

Thank you to my students, for teaching me so much.

Thank you to the fierce and brilliant women whose solidarity and love guided me through the doctoral program and my years in Houston as I worked on this book: Kay Cosgrove, Sarah McClung, Jameelah Lang, Allison Sawyer, Isbah Raja, and my sister goddess, Allie Rowbottom.

Thank you to all the women writers before me who so bravely blazed this trail.

Finally, I thank my family, whose support and love make everything possible, especially my grandmothers, who are the most fabulous women I know; Karen Griffith, who is the best storyteller; Sarah, Eric, and Sandy, my best friends; and most of all, my parents, who offered me a Wurzbacher Fellowship and a residency at the Pleasantville Studio Center (up to fifty-two weeks a year in a small, not-so-diverse creative community on a not-so-historical campus nestled amongst the wild woods of Pleasantville, Pennsylvania!) when no one else would have me, and who told me I could be whatever I wanted to be. I want to be more like you.

THE IOWA SHORT FICTION AWARD AND THE JOHN SIMMONS SHORT FICTION AWARD WINNERS, 1970–2019

Donald Anderson
Fire Road

Dianne Benedict
Shiny Objects

Marie-Helene Bertino
Safe as Houses

Will Boast
Power Ballads

David Borofka
Hints of His Mortality

Robert Boswell
Dancing in the Movies

Mark Brazaitis
The River of Lost Voices: Stories from Guatemala

Jack Cady
The Burning and Other Stories

Pat Carr
The Women in the Mirror

Kathryn Chetkovich
Friendly Fire

Cyrus Colter
The Beach Umbrella

Marian Crotty
What Counts as Love

Jennine Capó Crucet
How to Leave Hialeah

Jennifer S. Davis
Her Kind of Want

Janet Desaulniers
What You've Been Missing

Sharon Dilworth
The Long White

Susan M. Dodd
Old Wives' Tales

Merrill Feitell
Here Beneath Low-Flying Planes

Christian Felt
The Lightning Jar

James Fetler
Impossible Appetites

Starkey Flythe, Jr.
Lent: The Slow Fast
Kathleen Founds
When Mystical Creatures Attack!
Sohrab Homi Fracis
Ticket to Minto: Stories of India and America
H. E. Francis
The Itinerary of Beggars
Abby Frucht
Fruit of the Month
Tereze Glück
May You Live in Interesting Times
Ivy Goodman
Heart Failure
Barbara Hamby
Lester Higata's 20th Century
Edward Hamlin
Night in Erg Chebbi and Other Stories
Ann Harleman
Happiness
Elizabeth Harris
The Ant Generator
Ryan Harty
Bring Me Your Saddest Arizona
Charles Haverty
Excommunicados
Mary Hedin
Fly Away Home
Beth Helms
American Wives
Jim Henry
Thank You for Being Concerned and Sensitive
Allegra Hyde
Of This New World
Matthew Lansburgh
Outside Is the Ocean
Lisa Lenzo
Within the Lighted City
Kathryn Ma
All That Work and Still No Boys
Renée Manfredi
Where Love Leaves Us
Susan Onthank Mates
The Good Doctor
John McNally
Troublemakers
Molly McNett
One Dog Happy
Tessa Mellas
Lungs Full of Noise
Kate Milliken
If I'd Known You Were Coming
Kevin Moffett
Permanent Visitors
Lee B. Montgomery
Whose World Is This?
Rod Val Moore
Igloo among Palms

Lucia Nevai
Star Game
Thisbe Nissen
Out of the Girls' Room and into the Night
Dan O'Brien
Eminent Domain
Philip F. O'Connor
Old Morals, Small Continents, Darker Times
Robert Oldshue
November Storm
Sondra Spatt Olsen
Traps
Elizabeth Oness
Articles of Faith
Lon Otto
A Nest of Hooks
Natalie Petesch
After the First Death There Is No Other
Marilène Phipps-Kettlewell
The Company of Heaven: Stories from Haiti
Glen Pourciau
Invite
C. E. Poverman
The Black Velvet Girl
Michael Pritchett
The Venus Tree
Nancy Reisman
House Fires
Josh Rolnick
Pulp and Paper
Elizabeth Searle
My Body to You
Enid Shomer
Imaginary Men
Chad Simpson
Tell Everyone I Said Hi
Heather A. Slomski
The Lovers Set Down Their Spoons
Marly Swick
A Hole in the Language
Barry Targan
Harry Belten and the Mendelssohn Violin Concerto
Annabel Thomas
The Phototropic Woman
Jim Tomlinson
Things Kept, Things Left Behind
Doug Trevor
The Thin Tear in the Fabric of Space
Laura Valeri
The Kind of Things Saints Do
Anthony Varallo
This Day in History
Ruvanee Pietersz Vilhauer
The Water Diviner and Other Stories
Don Waters
Desert Gothic

Lex Williford
Macauley's Thumb
Miles Wilson
Line of Fall
Russell Working
Resurrectionists
Emily Wortman-Wunder
Not a Thing to Comfort You
Ashley Wurzbacher
Happy Like This
Charles Wyatt
Listening to Mozart
Don Zancanella
Western Electric